future PERFECT

future

PE

RFECT

JEN LARSEN

HARPER TEEN
An Imprint of HarperCollinsPublishers

HarperTeen is an imprint of HarperCollins Publishers.

Future Perfect
Copyright © 2015 by Jen Larsen

Library of Congress Cataloging-in-Publication Data
Larsen, Jen, 1973–
    Future perfect / Jen Larsen. — First edition.
        pages   cm
    Summary: "Ashley is offered the chance to have weight-loss surgery by her exacting
grandmother, who promises to provide tuition to her dream college in return" — Provided by
publisher.
    ISBN 978-0-06-232123-7 (hardback)
    [1. Self-esteem—Fiction.   2. Overweight persons—Fiction.   3. Grandmothers—Fiction.   4.
Single-parent families—Fiction.   5. Weight loss—Fiction.] I. Title.
PZ7.1.L36Fut   2015   2015006004
[Fic]—dc23   CIP
                                                            AC

Typography by Ellice M. Lee
15 16 17 18 19   CG/RRDH   10 9 8 7 6 5 4 3 2 1
❖
First Edition

FOR MONIQUE VAN DEN BERG,
THE ROBERT PENN WARREN OF GRATENESS

CHAPTER 1

Every year on my birthday, my grandmother, my father's mother, the woman we owe our whole lives to, reminds me that I am risking everything. That I am making a gigantic mistake. That big dreams like mine—Harvard; changing the world, medicine, social justice for all (and for all a good night)—rely on being flawless and unassailable.

She tells me that refusing to budge on the issue just means I am as stubborn and obstinate and fool-headed as my mother was. *Just tell her to stuff it,* my mother whispers in my head, and I shake that thought out.

The issue, my grandmother will be quick to tell you, is that I am fat.

I am also valedictorian, class president, former volleyball team captain, and was voted both Most Likely to Succeed and Best Personality two years in a row in our school's yearbook, which is really more of a pamphlet. I scored the winning point during the state volleyball finals last year. Unfortunately it was because I spiked the ball into the face of our rival captain, but still. I have a Platinum Star (which is an A plus at normal, less weird schools) in AP Organic Chemistry, and I earned that star despite being distracted by the presence of my best friend Laura's twin brother, who always seems to sit directly in front of me.

I have been described as ambitious, smart, outgoing, driven, stubborn, and sometimes bossy by people who love me, though that last one is not true. I've also been described as fat by my grandmother and select others, which *is* true.

But my grandmother thinks that *not being fat* is the part of me I should focus on. That being a size 18 (or sometimes 20) will ruin my life. She says, "You do not deserve to be automatically dismissed for utterly arbitrary aesthetic reasons that have nothing to do with your worth as a human being."

People in my life have a tendency toward pronouncements, which I respect.

I say, "That is unimportant. If they don't know the whole story they are not important and I do not care."

I don't have the gift of pronouncement. Maybe that's why I admire it.

"Oh my beautiful darling," my grandmother says. She is tall and elegant and blue-eyed and silver-haired and gorgeous. I look just like my mother—brown skin and brown eyes and waves of brown hair. Curves, rolls, softness. Boys have told me

I am beautiful, but I look nothing like my hard and glimmering diamond grandmother, who says, "I admire your bravado. Truly I do. But *they* care. And *you* can't escape it." She looks at my thighs and the width of my hips and my solid arms, and my cleavage, of which I admittedly have a lot, and sees bravado instead of just my body. She says, "The deck is already stacked against you."

"No," I say. "That shouldn't be true." I flush and I shift and I hate the feeling this fills me with. Like she's digging hard in the sand at the bottom of my mind and stirring it all up into a cloud that obscures everything, tiny particles floating in front of all the things I could say or should say or need to say.

"That's the only argument you have for me?" my grandmother says when she sees me fidget. When I can't look at her directly. "You argue passionately about everything else in the world, Ashley, but you cannot argue with me here."

This is my grandmother: When she was thirteen she was saving lives. When she was exactly that age she leaped into the water, right off the pier in town and into the Pacific Ocean, and towed back a boy who was drowning. And she's never stopped rescuing the world. She saved her mother, who was drowning in her second marriage, by reporting her stepfather for securities fraud; her sister, who lost her child—the money they won from the settlement didn't fix her sister's heart, but it gave her room to breathe. Of course my grandmother saved countless others in her career as a surgeon. And, finally, most salient to me, she saved my mother—pregnant with twins and in love with my father, who couldn't support a family as an artist and couldn't support my mother in college. She took them into her old and crumbling house; she found my father a job.

My grandmother's rescues are concrete and impregnable. Her advice to me is this: You are fat. Do not give them that foothold.

She's not wrong. There really are people in the world who have ready a list of adjectives about a fat person—including *lazy*, *stupid*, *messy*, *incompetent*—that they are certain describes her before she ever opens her mouth. And that is unimportant, because I won't let it be important.

But my grandmother insists on this because she loves me. She says this because she is never wrong. She says knowing how to succeed means knowing how the world works and playing the game.

I say, *what about the element of surprise?* She shakes her head at me.

Every year on my birthday she reminds me that she knows how my future will turn out. She'll hand me an envelope just a couple of days from now, as she does every year. She handed me the first one on my thirteenth birthday.

"Ashley," she said, with the small white card in her small white hand. "I want you to consider this very carefully."

"What is it?" I asked.

"Open it," she said. She never got irritated at my questions. I tore it open.

"A fair bargain," my grandmother said, tilting her chin at the slip of heavy paper in my hand. And it took me a minute to figure out what she was talking about. Her writing again, slightly neater:

Ashley Maria Perkins.
Good for one shopping trip every ten pounds.

My heart lurched. Across from me, my grandmother with her head tilted to the side. She looked like a bird, watching me.

"I want you to be happy," she said.

"Okay," I said. "I want that too."

"You're never going to be happy if you're . . . of size."

"*Of size,*" I said. "What is that supposed to mean?" I am *a* size, I thought, but so is everyone else. My older brothers are taller than I am but narrow, taking after my father. He got too skinny sometimes, when he forgot to eat. My mother, I didn't remember, but everyone said I looked like her.

"You are gaining quite a lot of weight, Ashley," she said.

"No," I said. "I don't think so." I knew the width of my own hips: I fit precisely between the two coast live oaks on the path behind my father's studio—the one that winds down to the beach. My hips brushed each side as I walked between them. I knew I was as tall as the curio cabinet in the kitchen, where all my mother's dishes were. My feet fit in my mother's old shoes. My head fit in my grandmother's elaborate hats. These were all the sizes I had in my head.

"You're getting big," she said.

"Well, I just turned thirteen," I said. My friends' parents always said things like that, *how big you've gotten, oh you're growing up so fast*—but this felt different, and my grandmother was shaking her head. I had never thought about size, that it had any meaning beyond measurement.

"I mean *fat*, darling," she said. "You're getting somewhat fat." She continued, "That's what you get from your mother's side of the family. . . ."

But I wasn't listening anymore, because that's when the word *fat* became something real. Something that would follow along behind me and settle in dark corners and slither around the back corridors of my mind. Whether or not I acknowledged it, the idea was inside me.

For my birthday that year, my grandmother gave me my body. Or her idea of it. I learned what it meant when my uncle Gomer called me *gordita* that single visit we took to San Diego before my mother left. My grandmother never liked my mother's family.

The coupons have become a never-changing ceremony. My grandmother hands me the envelope and I try to give it back to her. She clasps her hands at her waist. She waits for me to open it. My hands shake and I hate every tremor. She wants the whole world for me, and this is the only thing I have to give her in return. She tells me this without actually saying the words. This is the only change I have to make.

The sensible, incisive voice inside my head, the one I rely on, goes incoherent and says, *I don't want to do it. I don't want to. I don't want to.* I hold on to everything I know about myself. The fact that I should not have to do this, should not.

The first time I just said "No," and she didn't argue with me. She took the card and she looked at it. She folded it neatly in half and slipped it into her pocket. She said, "I taught you to trust your instincts, Ashley." Her face was very serious but I couldn't help but find signs of disappointment all over it. Disappointed eyebrows and a disappointed mouth. We never talked about it again.

Instead, the cards kept appearing every birthday, because I did gain weight. Puberty changed the shape of my body and I got tall and broad and rounded and I saw that the definition of the word *fat* fit me, its length and width and breadth, but I refused to acknowledge its depth.

Ashley Maria Perkins.
50 pounds for a trip to Disneyland.

I said, "I don't want it." She wouldn't take it back that time, and it sat in my desk until I threw it out.

Ashley Maria Perkins.
75 pounds for a shopping trip in Paris.

I said, "I don't care about Paris." My grandmother said, "Don't be a barbarian." That one I crumpled into a ball and threw in the garbage disposal. I turned the water on and let the motor run for a long time.

And then last year. The look of pleasure on her face like she had finally found the button to push, the vulnerable spot to prod.

Ashley Maria Perkins. 80 pounds for a new car.

I said, "You've got to be kidding me."

She said, "You know I never *kid*. Any car is better than that rusted-out thing you're always running off in."

The ancient wreck of a Volvo is my father's car but I'm the only one who can drive it. I drive down the coast with my foot on the floor. I have to, to get away from a sagging house and incomplete college applications, and panic about getting the scholarship that is my only chance, and the noise in my head that sounds a lot like my grandmother but is starting to sound too much like it belongs to me.

My grandmother, attempting to bribe me with a car like she's Oprah. "How can you possibly afford that?" I said, throwing it across the room. It didn't go very far; it kind of fluttered down and landed face-up.

New car. My father and brothers and I have no money. No

cash. I have no idea what Grandmother has, or doesn't. She thinks talking about money is uncouth, but here she was, waving her hand in the air and saying, "I can move around some investments. I can sell some things. I can unbind your trust. You don't have to wait until I'm dead."

"No," I said. "I don't want it." I picked the card up and tore it in half, right between "for" and "a new car."

I don't want it was the extent of the argument I was able to muster up, and still is. That is the best I can do and the only thing I can use to defend myself.

I try, "Why do you keep giving me these cards?"

She says, "I hope you'll change your mind, of course. I hope you'll understand what I'm trying to tell you."

"I don't want to hear it anymore," I tell her.

My grandmother thinks this is resignation. That even perfect things should never stop being perfected.

I will never admit this: The part of me that wonders how I fit in this family of tall and slender people, the part that trusts my grandmother unconditionally, the weak little part that forgets who I am, that quakes every birthday when she gives me another coupon—is *tempted*.

So tempted.

And there's this feeling I have: This year, she'll make the stakes higher. This year she will offer me something I truly can't refuse and every time I think about it I feel like I am full of ants.

But I can't think about that. I am swimming hard for the shore, paddling madly, towing everything I have to do behind me—an AP calculus quiz two days from now and a layout proposal for our laughably short yearbook and a list of potential charity trips to present at the student government meeting and the double shift I have to work at my job after school to cover Amy and sometimes it feels like maybe this is the time I won't make it—I'll drop something, forget something, screw up, and it will sink me.

But I will never screw up. The idea of it is enough to keep my eyes on the shore, keep breathing even when the air feels like acid in my lungs and the water below me is dark, and cold, and deep.

I will never screw up.

Because that would mean that my grandmother is right.

CHAPTER 2

'm awake at two a.m., waiting for the storm. The air's getting thick with the smell of ozone washing in from over the ocean and swallowing us all whole. Everything is holding its breath, waiting for the sky to crack open. Especially me. I am sixteen years old and thunder still makes me jump. Lightning makes me wince.

Because this is centralish California and it is the law, we got 340 days of sunshine last year. There are days when everything and everyone looks bright and flawless and washed clean by sunshine. The sun makes it easy to forget that it won't always be there. Sitting on the boardwalk, stretching out on the sand, strolling down the whole two blocks of Main Street—everyone talks about the genuinely miraculous healing power of the sun's invisible gamma rays. This is my oddball little town, a place full of people too weird for San Francisco.

On the sunniest days I've found myself leaning against the railing overlooking the beach, where the water always seems like rolling glass and the sky is an impossible, pure blue. When I tilt my head back and close my eyes against the light and heat, I find myself believing, just a little bit, in the magic of those invisible gamma rays.

It's easy then to forget that rain is eventually going to pour down the roof of my grandmother's ancient house, sweeping away more shingles and splashing through the holes in the gutters and sheeting down the windows and gushing through the cracks and the seams and making puddles all over the house. The attic will flood. My father will sit up on the couch and put his romance novel down and complain about the damp. I'll go get armfuls of towels and put out pots all over to catch the leaks before they warp the floors even more. Every time a board creaks under my feet I cringe. I hear my mother's voice in my head, the voice I've made up, since I don't remember her real one. She's arguing with my father: *Why doesn't your mother fix the damn roof? Does she leave it to spite me?* while my father murmurs something soothing and pointless.

The storm is coming, and the faraway rumbling underscores the drumbeat of two-a.m. thoughts pounding through my head— all the things I have to do, all the things I haven't done.

The house is sighing at me as the wind skims over the surface of the ocean and tumbles onto shore, crashing into us.

The worst of it is my college-application essay. The essay that has to get me into school. Win me a scholarship or I can't go, even if I get in. Establish world peace and cure cancer.

It sits undone, the impossible thing I don't want to do for no real reason that I can figure out, because my only other choice is to stare at the ceiling and feel the essay deadline ticking like a countdown to failure.

Sotomayor flops over and lets out her long, satisfied, rumbling grunt. I lean down and press my face to the side of her thick neck. She smells like a dog and that is the most comforting smell in the world, ahead of the smell of wood fires and Ivory soap and that fresh-ink, new textbook smell. Toby, our latest foster dog, is lying on his back with all four paws in the air. She's a quarter of Soto's size, a squirrely little dachshund to a big muscular pit bull, but she takes over most of the bed. When Soto snorts and rolls half on top of Toby, I wish I could roll over too and turn off the light and we could all just sleep. Or I could shake them awake and creep down the back stairs and out to the driveway and be gone, Soto hanging out the window with her tongue flapping like a flag and Toby spinning in circles in the backseat and the wind in my hair and everything left behind.

But you've always got to come back. My father could need something in the middle of the night—he sleeps worse than I do. My grandmother could check on me. She never sleeps, period. She doesn't make a disappointed face, she doesn't sigh or scold me, but when I do escape down the coast for brief, glorious moments, no matter what time I get back she is sitting in the drawing room right off the foyer, in her dressing gown, sipping tea. I know she can hear the creak of the hinges but she doesn't call out. And I can never stop myself from peering around the door to see if maybe this is the time she won't be there waiting for me. She looks up at me and says, "Good night," and I know I am dismissed back to my room to work or study or write an essay or try to sleep until I can't stand it again and have to just go.

Sometimes the thought of her waiting when I come back means I never leave.

I can't leave now. The important things, they have a gravity that's impossible to escape. This essay is the most important thing.

I've had the actual application finished for ages, except for this part, and the deadline is only weeks away. First the storm and then my birthday and then time running out. So many worrisome things all in a row.

When I was eight, at dinner my father said, "What do you want to be when you grow up, Ashley?" This would be before my mother had left, because he was still talking to us. He had stopped for a while after, as if he knew he'd have to confess that her disappearance was his fault.

My mother said, "A veterinarian, I bet." But I remember that I stopped sculpting my mashed potatoes into a perfect cube and I said, "Grandmother. I want to be Grandmother," and my mother pushed back her chair and went into the kitchen. She didn't come back out.

What I meant was that I wanted to be someone who knows everything.

It was an endless frustration to me that not everything made perfect sense. I needed a way to straighten it all out, once and for all. My grandmother always seemed to know *everything*. With extreme certainty.

"Go ask your grandmother," my father always said, and I asked her all the questions I had.

The idea of Harvard? Maybe I got that from my mother. There's a picture of her on the lawn in front of the law school, hugely pregnant with my brothers, leaning back on her hands with her face turned to the sky. I don't remember ever seeing her that happy in real life.

But she dropped out. She gave up. I'm not the kind of person who does that, and I never will be. My grandmother would rather I go to Stanford. But it has to be Harvard. It must be. Because it's the best school in the country. Because it would give me irrefutable prestige, the kind of credentials no one can ever argue with. Even if . . . well, even if my grandmother were right about other things.

And I'm the kind of person who goes to Harvard. People say, "Harvard? Well of course." I think that's a compliment, most of the time.

That night long ago, at the dinner table, my mom knocked her chair back and disappeared into the kitchen, but Dad laughed and my older brothers snorted. My grandmother said, "You mean a doctor, darling? Like me?" and I nodded and she actually smiled. She said, "You will be."

My grandmother explained how things would work out from then on and I believed her, because my grandmother knows everything. After dinner I locked the door to my bedroom and thought about how *I* would graduate Harvard, and then I would know everything one day. The noise and the confusion of the world would settle into something I could hold in my hand and take apart and put back together and finally, *finally* understand.

From my grandmother: anatomy books and medical dictionaries and histories of science. Models and chemistry sets and microscopes. A gold pendant shaped like a strand of DNA that I won't ever take off. Subscriptions to science magazines, the popular and the professional kind. I put each one in a binder to save.

She said: A broad background that you'll narrow down into your scope and focus.

Scope and focus have always been my gift.

It is a feeling of gratitude sometimes when someone cares that much about you. It is hard not to want to live up to those expectations.

My future was set like an atomic clock that night. My grandmother's expectations are not hopes, they're certainty.

I could write an essay about *that*, I think. Instead I shut the laptop and put my face in a pillow until Soto finds me and shoves her big snouty face in mine to lick everything she can reach.

I could flee, just for an hour, just down the coast. But everything is always waiting for me. Everything is always about to happen.

I can feel the laptop hot and whirring against my shoulder. You get five hundred words for your personal statement, which is about a page if you double-space and a page and a half if you single-space. I checked. I don't know what to tell Harvard that they can't just figure out from my transcripts, from my application, my writing supplement, my SATs, my school report, my teacher reports, my midyear school report, my final school report, the article clippings from all my volleyball wins, the feature in the *Chronicle* about leading a Habitat for Humanity project.

There I am, on paper. All the important parts. Everything I've done and had to do for them. Do they seriously need me to spend a page explaining it all to them?

None of my personal essay attempts have been anything but approximations of me. They have felt empty and strange. Like lies.

My father said, "Personnel essay? Why do they want you to write an essay about staff members?" and laughed at his own joke, as he does. He is not helpful.

My grandmother bought me a book called *50 Successful Harvard Applications* and left it on my bed.

My boyfriend, Hector, says, "If you can't write it, maybe that is a sign that it wasn't meant to be." And he doesn't mean to be, I know he doesn't—but Hector is sometimes irritating in his sense that the world is something you just sit back and let happen to you. He noodles on his guitar and never remembers the lyrics he forgets to write down and shrugs when I ask him why he doesn't just carry a pen and notebook already. All of his songs are beautiful, and then they're gone forever and he doesn't seem to care.

I have time before I have to start to worry. I will come up with something soon. I always do. But the wind and the noise of the storm outside are not helping me concentrate.

A thought, vivid and pleasant: Maybe this is the year the house will soak up all the rain and start to collapse like cardboard, in slow motion, and be carried away on the river that Highway 1 becomes, all the way down to San Ysidro.

Then my grandmother will forget that it's my birthday.

She'll be so busy being ruthlessly competent—salvaging the rattling old furniture and the antique rugs and establishing a new residence and replenishing our personal items and calling insurance companies to speak to them in icy tones—that she won't remember it's time to draw me aside and hand me the little envelope and watch me while I debate whether this year I tear it in half or crumple it into a ball or scream or cry or whatever. All while she looks at me as though I have disappointed her. As though she has done everything in the world for me, and I can't do this one thing for her.

When the knock at the door comes I jump like I've been shot out of a cannon. "What the hell?" I say, probably too loudly. My father squeaks open the door.

"You're still up," he says. His hair is a rat's nest on top of his head, a halo of frizzy dishwater blond curls. He squints at me in the low light of my bedroom because he can never find his glasses when he gets up at night. He's been restless since my mother left eight years ago. That's a long time to be restless. "Are you supposed to be up this late? What time is it even?"

"You should be asleep," I say. "You have meetings tomorrow. You need to be awake for them."

He crunches up his forehead and scratches his neck, and then his face clears. "Oh that's right. The boathouse thing." He leans against the jamb of my door with his arms crossed. He's wearing my mother's awful, hole-filled "100% Latina Bonita" T-shirt that I have begged him to burn and plaid pajama pants that have almost faded to just gray.

"The boathouse thing," I agree. "I put together the sales folders for you. Don't forget them." Soto chuffs like she's agreeing. Toby never stops snoring.

"You know how these people are, kiddo. If they're going to buy they've already made up their minds." He sounds less hopeless and more resigned. He is not so much cut out to be a real estate agent, and he knows it. He is not cut out to do much, which he knows, too. My father's boss, Gloria, is the only person in their three-person office who ever sells anything not just by accident. Her properties are the ones that keep the business afloat. She is one of my grandmother's oldest friends and the person who hired my father in the first place.

"You can still convince them," I say. "Grandmother says that confidence—"

"I know," he breaks in. He pushes away from the doorjamb and shuffles over to me. He pats the top of my head.

"I'm just saying—" I can hear my voice getting impatient, but he never seems to mind.

"Good night, sleep tight, don't let the bed bugs bite." He smiles at me.

I sigh. "If they do, I will bite them back."

"That's my girl," he says. He pats my head again and turns to shuffle back out of the room, yawning hugely.

"I have to finish my essay first," I say, opening my laptop.

He turns back around, and his face is a frown. "You work too hard, honey."

I shrug. "Not really."

"Your mother liked to keep busy, too."

I'm not sure how to answer that.

He shakes his head and waves his hand in the air. "You do what you need to, honey. You always do." He's halfway out the door now. Toby's head pops up next to me and his little tail starts thumping against the pillow.

"Don't forget your lunch," I call. "It's in the cooler in the fridge."

He gives me a thumbs-up and another yawn, and disappears into the dark hallway. Toby leaps over me and then down to the floor to trot after my dad. The light bulbs in the hall must have burned out again. The fixtures are too old and unreliable to ever stay lit long. The floorboards creak with every thud of my father's heels. You can map the movements of anyone in this house, where they are and what they're doing. He stops before he reaches his room, in front of the stairs up to my grandmother's room. I hear voices and tense up, but he's talking to Toby. The foster dogs all get attached to him, trail him like the tail of a comet, but he never seems to notice where they came from, or when they go.

His door squeaks, then shuts, and it's quiet now. Everything is quiet. Soto is curled warm and asleep in the crook of my legs. My laptop is open but my screen is blank. The window is open too and I smell the brine and before-storm air. But unless I concentrate I can't even hear the waves down through the backyard and past the trees, dragging the little sandbar back under the water.

I listen again. That slow, quiet, endless roar finds my ears.

It has always been there and always will be.

It's all I hear.

CHAPTER 3

"If you touch my latte one more time," I tell Hector, "I will end you."

He lifts the cup to his lips and makes slurping noises while he sips. Laura is rolling her eyes but she doesn't lift her head from her sketchbook.

"Goddammit, Hector," I say, reaching for the cup. But he's got the longest arms and even though I'm tall, I don't have monkey reach. He is smiling in his sweet and silly way, and I settle back in my chair. I refuse to sulk. I am stronger than caffeine.

"I won't actually end you," I say comfortingly, if a little grudgingly. His dimples deepen.

"I don't know. You could probably take me," he says.

I ignore that, and ignore my impulse to glance around and see if anyone heard him. I pick up the printed-out pages I brought to class and then toss them back on the table. I'm scooted back with my calculus book open on my knees because linear approximations are still pissing me off and now my midterm is tomorrow instead of two days away and I don't want to think about personal essays anymore.

"She was up all night, Hector," Jolene says, looking up from her own printout.

The rest of us are slouching at the big round table, but Jolene sits as if she's been carefully, gracefully arranged into place. Her hands never stop moving, creasing the corners of her pages. Her small face is serious, but it almost always is.

Hector glances at her, and then back at me, still smiling. He has a gift, and all of it is centered in that dimple on his cheek.

"What were you doing?" he says. Hector's problem is that he smiles a lot. The word *sunny* was invented for him. The word *cheerful* is inscribed across his heart. I feel guilty when he irritates me, as if he is a sweet puppy who should only be loved.

"The essay," I say. I am speaking so carefully and deliberately. "The assignment that I am very annoyed you forgot about." I can hear how rough-edged my voice is. It could leave behind abrasions. I close my mouth in case I'm just baring my teeth instead of making an actual smile. He wouldn't notice, though. Or if he did, it wouldn't bother him. I am grateful for that, even when it irritates me.

He reaches out and tucks a curl behind my ear. "You work too hard," he says. "You don't have to kill yourself all the time, you know. It makes you cranky."

"Yes, Hector, I am extremely cranky," I say.

"See, I do learn," he says. He makes a check mark in the air with his finger. "Gold star for Hector! But you shouldn't have stayed up all night."

Laura glances up from her sketchbook and squints at him. She says, "Hector. Honey." He cocks his head at her. "You remember Harvard, I assume, and I have to assume because otherwise I am worried about your brain capacity and your ability to retain and retrieve essential, life-saving information."

"Well yeah," he says. He slips his arm around my back. He is so easy and thoughtless in his gestures and I don't understand how that works. I wonder how it would be to not have everything feel like a chess game, planning three moves in advance. Especially when, like me, you are terrible at chess.

"I'm just saying. She doesn't have to work so hard. She's in. She's got this. She's on it. Early admission and a free ride." He leans over like he's going to kiss the side of my neck.

"Quit," I say, ducking, but I can't quite keep myself from smiling at him. He grins and kisses my temple instead. He flips his pen a few times, tapping it on the pad of paper in front of him, but stops when Jolene frowns at him.

Everyone is writing again, and the whole guidance class is a low-pitched buzz of typing and pen scratching and whispering. Today we're supposed to be "pausing for a breath." Writing down all our best qualities, the things that make us unique and interesting and stand head and shoulders above all the other candidates and other handy guidance-counselor phrases. It's supposed to help us take a fresh look at the draft of the personal essay we've already finished. That I haven't finished. It will help us revise it with clear eyes, Dr. Ellman says.

I am not interested in my best qualities. I am interested in not messing up my calc grade. I look at the textbook in my lap, the wandering numbers across my notebook, and realize I have screwed up this function. I flip to the back of the book because sometimes that's where the answers are.

Hector goes back to drawing interlocking squares all over his paper. Some people have their heads down and are scribbling away furiously, others finished twenty minutes ago and are now comparing their long lists of best qualities with each other. So many of us have nannies and tutors imported from San Francisco or San Diego, who have spent most of their careers telling us that we are unique in hundreds of ways that the world will appreciate and celebrate, so everyone's got plenty to scribble down.

Not me. As I sit here in the hyacinth-colored room in the northwest corner of George Love Academy, I can hear the buzz of the hive. Everyone here is busy, achieving, overachieving. I am not a special snowflake. I know that anyone could overtake me at any moment.

Our school was founded by a disillusioned millionaire oil executive (named George Love, of course) who wanted to drop out and tune in to intellectual rigor and spiritual growth. There are only 150 of us in this place, but we are all moonflower spirits whose great and beautiful gifts are being massaged here under the hot lights of our high-school incubator into greatness that will transform the world for the goodness of all mankind—or at least that's what the plaque above the door says.

I like to think Mr. George is off in whatever afterlife he imagined, feeling good about his time on earth. But this school is only *partly* what he imagined.

Rich people move to Santa Ansia just to enroll their kids here—that's how my best friend, Laura, ended up here. Her dad is a mergers, acquisitions, and divestitures lawyer; her mom is a charity-gala hostess/bon vivant/drinker of coconut drinks in a wide variety of tropical locations. Super important. Super busy. Easier to toss their kid into a fancy school than to pay attention to her, Laura says. Her parents are pretty standard-issue, for this town.

Our teachers, on the other hand, believe very, very hard in their mission. Our Principle (who would be called *principal* in a normal school) actually says things like, "It's so essentially vital to me to be a Sherpa to my students. To hoist you and convey you onward into your destiny when you can't go on your own— to use the popularized Christian vernacular in which so many take true and welcoming comfort. Such a lyrical metaphor. Such magnanimity." She really says that. All the time.

Principle Simons has been here from the start. She's the one who wrote the *Humanism Handbook* that is required reading every year—how to respect your body and your spirit, and the bodies and spirits of those around you. She's not wrong, obviously, clearly. But all that sincerity gets overwhelming.

Somehow, simultaneous to all this conveyance and respecting and Sherpa-ing, we get written up in national newspapers for our outstanding innovation in educational theories and practice—our alternative physical education program, a fully equipped physics lab, a vegetarian cafeteria, stringent rhetoric and debate and Latin requirements, and a bank of three personal days.

Which means those parent types come in droves, so that George Love Academy becomes this spicy organic vegetable soup of intense competition, and yoga instead of gym, and discussion of chakras, and a question, at the start of each school year, about what your preferred gender pronoun is.

My mother refused to let my brothers go to GLA when she was still around. I wonder how she feels about me being valedictorian of the place. If she knows. Wherever she is.

I picture my mother back home in San Diego. Or maybe she fled all the way to Bogotá to live with the rest of the extended family we never got to meet. Wherever she is, I picture her relieved to be gone.

Anyway. The thing about going to school with the same people for your entire life is that we all know what everyone else is writing. Emily, the new head of the volleyball team, is writing down "upper-body strength" and "winner." Jared, the school treasurer, wrote "go-getter attitude" and "chocolate-chip cookies." Morgan, the salutatorian to my valedictorian—and oh, does she hate that—is writing down adjectives as if she's been waiting her whole life for this opportunity. Brandon, Laura's twin, should still be writing because he has a ridiculous number of positive qualities, though many of them are external.

Laura and Brandon look so much alike. But where Laura is a bright and bobbing balloon on a windy day, he is currently lounging in his chair like he has all the time in the world, his hand threaded into Morgan's blunt bob and his eyes half closed in a sleepy, sexy way.

Ace, my boyfriend back in seventh grade, is filling his entire page with the word *butts*. Hector isn't writing anything because he's going to Europe or South America or somewhere instead of college, because his parents think he needs time to experience the world before he finds his place in it or something like that. He hasn't decided where he wants to travel yet, but they'll send him anywhere he wants. He is going to write an album about seeing the world, he says. If he remembers his pen.

I know Jolene has written "prevailing" somewhere on her list and she has leaned forward over her paper, a wing of her blond hair curving along her cheek. She's chewing on her lip and tapping on the table and making faces at the paper and shaking her head at herself because she can never quite be still. Laura has written "arty" and then filled the rest of the page with tiny, intricate sketches that bleed into each other and make the page look like it is a thousand miles deep. She's going to set the Rhode Island School of Design on fire—and then the rest of the world. Right now she's just sitting with her heels up on the chair and her sketchbook propped on her knees and her afro of rough-velvet curls framing her face.

Jolene and Laura—I could take both their lists and add a thousand more entries for them.

As discussed, I haven't written anything.

I write out the next calc equation and frown at it. I dislike approximations. Math should have solid answers with no wiggle room.

Laura looks up from her sketchbook with big eyes. "Ooh!" she says, waving her pencil. "An idea, I have an idea. Okay, what if everyone brought their own food?"

"For what?" I say.

"Your birthday party," she says.

"A party? I don't have time for that," I say.

"Liar," she says. "You've been devising intricate plans and writing lists for three months. I know it because I know you and I have seen how you write endless lists when you're planning and I don't even understand how they don't give you panic attacks."

"I like to be organized," I say.

"So, my idea," she says.

"So what you're saying is everyone brings their own food to eat?" I ask. Jolene laughs.

"*Well*, that would be an incredible cost savings and possibly also net you some easy clean-up with a tradeoff for the environmental damage factor with all the disposable plates and things. But no!" She slaps her sketchbook down on the desk. "We assign everyone a country and they bring a food from it."

"We're inviting the entire class," I say. "Are there that many countries?"

Laura rolls her eyes at me.

"And are we that organized?" I say.

"I know you are," Laura says.

"The real question is, do I want to be?" I counter.

Jolene says to Laura, "I would rather not organize a global buffet." She glances up as Dr. Ellman strolls by. "Organizing buffets is not my strongest skill," Jolene says innocently.

Dr. Ellman stops at my chair. "Psst," she says, leaning over my shoulder. "One of your best qualities is *conviction*." She winks at me and then strolls away with her hands behind her back. Her oxfords are very shiny.

"I don't even know what that means," I say. "Why is she telling me this?" I throw my pen down and it bounces across the table and then slides onto the floor.

"I think your best quality is self-assuredness," Jolene says.

"I think it's your eyebrows," Laura says.

"I think it's your chili," Hector says. He is not wrong.

"Also," Laura says, "feather boas and tiaras! And beads and scarves and masks and dancing."

I blink. "What?" Those don't sound like qualities.

"For the party?" she says. Sometimes it is hard to follow in her wake. Everything looks easy and effortless for her and Brandon. And they both seem to understand how the world works. They know how to survive outside of this little hothouse of a town. I suspect the rest of us are going to find out the hard way.

"Yes of course for the party," she says.

"Will there *really* be tiaras?" I say suspiciously.

"You do love tiaras," Jolene says to me. She's smiling. Her eyes are the frostiest blue and her skin is pale and freckled, so she always looks like she is dappled with sunlight. Her bob is a bright knife-edge along the line of her jaw. Laura always says someday she'll be someone's yuppie dream mom, in tailored shirts and cuffed shorts and perfect, unscuffed flats.

"I don't mind tiaras," I say. "They're kind of whimsical." I pause. "My best quality is whimsy."

Hector raises his eyebrows at me. "I don't think you should write that one down."

"What do you mean? I am filled with humor and light!" I argue.

Jolene is laughing because she knows when I'm joking. Laura

frowns at me because she worries when I joke.

"What about pizza?" Hector says.

"No," I say.

"You never listen to me," he says.

"So why start now?" Laura asks.

"Hector has a point. Everyone likes pizza," Jolene points out. She picks up the pen and writes "PIZZA" all in caps.

"Yes, but it's *my* birthday. I care about what *I'd* like," I say.

Jolene crosses it out again.

Dr. Ellman is suddenly at her side. "Your best quality is pizza?" she says. She cocks her head.

"No," Jolene says. "I just had another idea."

Dr. Ellman leans in. She looks thoughtful and serious and compassionate. She taps a short, ragged fingernail against her narrow lips. Jolene shoots us a wide-eyed, panicked look. She knows what happens when teachers put on that face.

"Have you considered the power of your story, Jolene?" Dr. Ellman says. Her voice is pitched low and intimate.

Jolene is the third person in our school to come out as transgender, so no one really blinked when she did it in the fourth grade. But teachers like to remind her that they're open-minded and accepting, and that she is special. This backfires. All they really remind her of is that they have no idea what they're talking about.

"Yes," Jolene says. She flips her paper over.

We initiate Distraction Technique C—the Everyone's Got Their Something maneuver.

"Dr. Ellman, is it too much of a downer to discuss my abandonment as a child in my personal essay?" I ask. At the same time Laura says, "Dr. Ellman, would the admissions board be rocked by the power of my quest to become a female designer or maybe an artist in a male-dominated world?"

Hector is glancing back and forth between us and Jolene just sighs, but Dr. Ellman's mouth is opening and closing like an aquarium fish. There's too much to *affirm*. Too much to *validate*. Dr. Ellman is immobilized. A moment later she is distracted by an argument in the corner about what constitutes a "quality" as opposed to an "ingrained behavior" and squeaks off in her oxfords.

I have wondered myself what Jolene's essay will be. She does not often talk about her parents, their anger at her, her conviction that has had to turn into bravery too often. She wore a dress to the first day of fourth grade—a dress my grandmother bought Jolene because her parents wouldn't listen to her, refused to listen to her, slammed doors on her for a year. Jolene asked everyone politely that they call her Jolene please and not everyone has been polite all the time, not always, despite the *Humanism Handbook*, and the other kids who came before her. People get curious. They ask her prying, detailed questions about her body. Jolene does not like it when I'm angry for her.

There's a moment of silence after Dr. Ellman's retreat. Then

Jolene calmly says, "Not pizza then."

"Grandmother hates pizza," I say. "If she even tries to eat it she just tears off all the cheese and toppings and then has a couple of bites of the bread and then she dabs at her lips with a napkin and throws it all away."

"That's terrible," Hector says.

Jolene says, "Maybe she just thinks it's too greasy."

Laura thumps her feet down on the floor and leans forward, pushing her sketchbook across the table. The page of heavy, curving interlinking lines is geometrically beautiful and a little dizzying. "I don't understand your grandmother," she says, and I look up from the sketchbook. "She's so strange about that stuff."

"What stuff?" Hector says, but Laura's not stopping.

"And I don't get the whole birthday bribe every year because what is she trying to say exactly and why doesn't she realize that she's just out of her mind?"

"She's not out of her mind," I say.

"She's kind of out of her mind!" Laura throws her hands in the air and her pencil goes flying. "It's not her business. Your body isn't her business."

Laura lives in a world where she doesn't have to answer to anyone, especially not her dad and stepmom. She can disappear into San Francisco for a weekend without a word. My father says, Jesus, don't they ever keep an eye on those kids? but then he goes back to his romance novels and eating entire bags of home-baked granola, totally ruining his dinner.

"Laura," I say. "She wants to help."

"The weight-loss coupons," Hector says, a furrow between his eyes.

I shake my head at him, trying to signal *please stop talking*, but he says, "How are they helpful? I think they'd probably make someone feel bad about themselves."

"I don't feel bad about myself," I snap.

"You shouldn't," he says, surprised.

"Well I don't," I say, and slap my calculus book shut with a bang that makes Laura jump and frown at me.

Jolene says, "I think she doesn't know any other way to help you with your future. It's logical to her."

"I don't want to talk about this anymore," I say. I flip open the book on my lap again, hard.

"Hey, you could write about that for your essay," Laura says. "Unique and powerful topic that reveals a facet of your personality, check. I bet 'my grandmother is wildly bribing me to diet' is not in your transcript."

"No." I can hear the anger in my voice and I flinch at it.

Laura just looks at me. "But she's trying to help," she says mildly, and I hate it when she's smug.

"That's a pretty good idea," Hector says.

"Hector—" I start, and I'm not sure what I'm about to say and I am guessing I'll regret it but I can't seem to stop and so I guess I should be grateful when a knee knocks into my temple.

"Goddammit, Ace," I say, grabbing at my forehead. "That hurt!"

"Sorry! Sorry!" he chirps, looking down at me. He's climbed up on his chair, holding a piece of notebook paper over his head and away from Morgan. He is probably the only person in school who would need to stand on a chair to be taller than Morgan. Dr. Ellman turns to see what's going on.

Morgan has her field-hockey face on, the one that makes opponents terrified of her as she lunges after them. She is many things: current class president, having beaten me this year for the first time, the most popular girl in school by many metrics (though the *Humanism Handbook* rejects notions of social peer ranking). Morgan thinks gossip is the smallest unit of personal connection and "essential for the social lubrication of groups of every size," which I know because she did a paper on the topic in the Communications and Linguistics class we had, but also because she just wants to know all the worst things about everyone.

We don't dislike each other. Not liking someone at all is very different from disliking someone. I did not like her long before she started dating Brandon. I did not like her from the day in second grade when she told me I would splash too hard and empty the pool if I tried to jump in. And then I pushed her in.

I felt bad after, because that's no way to deal with someone who sucks. But to this day, every time Morgan makes a snide remark I remember that moment and her big eyes as she fell backward and it is *still* satisfying.

Jolene says Morgan is like a shark. She's more scared of you than you are of her. Jolene watches a lot of *Animal Planet*. I say she's exactly like a shark and every time I see her teeth I know something bad is going to happen. Jolene says I don't understand sharks. I do understand Morgan, though.

She is small and awful and right now she's getting louder as Ace dances away from her.

"Help, Dr. Ellman," Ace says. "She's going to kill me." He's jumped off the chair and is backing away around the table with that notebook paper in his hand, and Morgan is stalking after him.

"Morgan is going to have an aneurism!" I say. I can hear the delight in my voice.

"This is the best," Laura says.

"He is going to hurt himself," Jolene says, as Ace backs into Emily's chair.

"Give it to me right now," Morgan says.

"But I'm not finished reading it!" Ace says, still backing away. "'Dear diary,'" he reads, squinting at the paper he's holding out and away from Morgan's grasping hands.

"Ace Valentino Farber," Morgan growls.

Dr. Ellman seems to be trying to speak in measured tones, which no one can hear. Brandon is poking at his phone. Morgan rushes at Ace and there's a horrible tearing noise. Ace says, "I'm sorry, Morgan. I'm really sorry, Dr. Ellman." He's holding up a crumpled, shredded piece of paper. Morgan has the other half. His expression is contrite.

"He's not sorry," Morgan says with her teeth gritted. You can only do that when you're really mad; otherwise you sound like you're trying to talk with your mouth full. She waves her half of the paper at him. "I was *working* on that."

"I'm really sorry," Ace says.

"You will be," I say quietly, and Jolene laughs.

"Everyone sit down," Dr. Ellman says. "That's enough adrenaline. It's time to breathe. You," she says to Ace. "You sit down here." She taps our table.

"Oh come on," I say. I know what's coming.

"Ashley," Dr. Ellman says, "You sit at Ace's table." She surveys Morgan and me. "Valedictorian and salutatorian. There we go. Nice and peaceful."

Laura makes an attempt at a save. "But, Dr. Ellman, I was just about to ask Ashley's advice about my essay. Because we are both persons of color I think it's important to address our intersectionality."

But I think Dr. Ellman's reached her limit for the day. "Just. Write," she says.

Morgan smiles sweetly up at me as I pull out my chair and drop my notebook on the table. Brandon winks at me, which is awful because it is so very cheesy, and because he looks far too cute when he does that.

"Oh god, Brandon, don't wink," I say.

"I had something in my eye," he says, and then he winks again.

"Please stop that," I say, but I'm smiling at him.

Jessica Loh, sitting next to him, has turned pink and started giggling into her notebook as if he were talking to her. She has always seemed to get contact highs from boys.

"So!" Morgan says. "What *were* we talking about over there?" She leans forward and looks at my notebook. "Oh honey," she says. "Pizza? You've really written down *pizza*. Well, I suppose there are clichés for a reason."

"Morgan, was that supposed to be a fat joke?"

"I don't know," she says. "Do you *feel* fat?"

"I *feel* like your material needs some work," I say. I slap my notebook shut and smile at her big. "Speaking of! How's your essay going?" I nod at the wadded ball of paper in front of her.

"Just fine," she says. "I've already applied for early admittance to NYU. I'm not worried." Of course she has. Of course she isn't.

"That will give you plenty of time to finish your other application to clown school," I say. *Makes devastating comebacks* is not on my transcripts either.

Jessica is yearning at Brandon. She looks like she is made of cotton candy, swathed in acres of fluffy sweater and fluffy skirt and heart shapes instead of pupils. He's ignoring all of us, still staring at his phone.

"Don't worry. I won't get my acceptance in time for your birthday party," Morgan says. "That'll be my gift to you." She shows me her shark teeth.

"That would be hard to wrap," I say.

"But what about your *other* gifts?" she continues. "I heard your grandmother's getting you something special this year." She widens her eyes and leans forward when she sees me stiffen. "She was at the dealership a couple of days ago. Talking to my father. You know, as they do. Just talking . . . about *everything*."

"I'm sure," I say. My grandmother is good at small talk. I am picturing the Volvo showroom three towns away, my grandmother glancing around at the dumpy little cars and frowning because she has never understood why I liked them. Thinking about the coupon she's probably already written out. That is sitting on the writing desk in her office.

"She didn't tell me she was going to the dealer," I say before I can stop myself.

"Well, it's a surprise, isn't it?" Morgan says. "She tries to get you something surprising every year. Doesn't she?"

I stare at Morgan, her sharp little nose and her wide-set eyes and the smirk on her face, and glance over at Brandon and Jessica. What does Morgan know exactly?

"That's how birthdays work," I say slowly.

Morgan glances away when Dr. Ellman claps her hands, and I breathe for the first time in what seems like minutes.

Behind us Ace is arguing that *butts* could be an abstract quality instead of a concrete noun.

"Okay, people," Dr. Ellman says. "We're just about done here. We're going to stop, and we're going to breathe through the chime, which is—" She pauses for a moment, then glances at her watch. "Well, almost now. In just a second. There it is," she says as it chimes over her voice.

Brandon stretches when he stands, and his shirt lifts, showing an expanse of his smooth skin. I'm not staring. Or I shouldn't be, anyway.

"No more winks," he says to me. He slides his arm around Morgan while she's shuffling her papers into her bag and she is distracted by the way he looks down at her. They're out the door ahead of me and Ace is at my elbow.

"Did you enjoy chatting about your future with Morgan?" I ask.

"Did you know that Morgan thinks she has no 'best' qualities because all of her qualities are equally superior?" he says.

"You're joking," I say.

"You're exaggerating," Jolene says, slightly scolding.

I'm annoyed that something Morgan said actually amuses me.

"If only I were. But alas, Morgan keeps living up to our expectations." He sweeps away ahead of us.

Laura says, "Why is she so awful? I don't understand why anyone would be so awful for no good reason. It's like she takes awful pills and washes them down with awful juice and then rolls around in awfulness."

"She doesn't mean to be," Jolene says. "She just is."

"She was trying to scare me, I think," I say. And I realize that's exactly it, this feeling like gravity has stopped working inside me—fear. And a tiny flare of dread that I have worked hard to stomp out. That no one else is ever supposed to see.

"Scare you?" Jolene says. "With what?"

I don't answer.

"There's nothing she can scare you with," Laura says. "She's being ridiculous. She's being—"

"Awful," Jolene says.

"Right," I say.

CHAPTER 4

When I break my third glass I wish it were magically time to go home, but I'm only thirty minutes into my shift. Usually I am not ready to go home until at least an hour's worth of Early Bird Special customers have asked me for another basket of sourdough bread and then want to know how school is and tell me how big I'm getting and how they remember when I was just this tall and to say hello to my father and grandmother.

Cap'n Bill's is busy after school because our town is full of retired people who enjoy a deal on clam chowder, which I started to loathe after a month of working here and have hated every day for the entire year following.

I am kneeling in the pass-through, picking up big chunks of glass when Laura bumps up against me with a dustpan.

"Thank you," I say, taking it from her. She doesn't need to work, but she likes it. Her father had the idea initially. Gain a sense of responsibility and structure, he said. Get a feel for the real world outside her head and her grand schemes and something else about her ability to develop practical skills that would stand her in good stead, and maybe also a distraction from the divorce and the fact that he and her stepmom are never home. She claims she doesn't understand why her father wasn't happy when she decided to come keep me company instead of taking an internship with his law firm.

Nancy, the owner for twenty years, decorated this restaurant in "nautical," which somehow translates to heavy wood tables and wood paneling and anchors draped with nets on the wall and a giant mounted swordfish that looks worried about the state of the world and bumps softly against the wall as the breeze rattles through. I love this place because none of the kids in town, or their parents, ever show up here. Though they would tip better than the regulars we do get. Laura loves this place because she admires a commitment to a theme and our customers' dedication to routine.

She is frowning at me and she shakes her head. "Okay. So. What is with you?" she says. "What's going on? Are you okay? You're all—" She waves her hands around her like she's going to catch the words buzzing by her head. She sits down next to me on the rubber mat. "Seriously," she says.

"You're sitting in a puddle," I point out. "And you're going to cut your butt on glass. And you're going to piss Nancy off if she catches you."

She waves that away. "Nancy is worried about many things and I can't do anything about any of them because I am not responsible for her well-being."

"You're responsible for the sourdough," I say.

She sighs. "I *am* responsible for the sourdough."

"With great sourdough comes great responsibility," I say.

"Don't make jokes. You make me nervous when you make jokes."

"It wasn't funny?" I say. "I thought it was funny."

"You make jokes when you're upset," she says. "You try to distract me." She peers at my face, and I look away, finish sweeping up the wet glass, and drop it into the bin. She's still sitting on the floor, looking up at me, and I can't help sitting back down next to her. She smiles at me.

"I am tired of bringing more sourdough bread to the Monroes," she says. "They don't even wait until they've finished the last basket. It's like they're afraid someone else will order it first and then they'll be shit out of luck and their entire day will be ruined because a day without sourdough is a day without sunshine."

I snort, and she laughs. She reaches out and pats my head, tucks the piece of hair that always flies out of my ponytail back behind my ear. She is always grooming me like she is a mama cat, and I find it strangely soothing. "You sure you're okay? Everything is well and good and right?"

I nod. "Do you want me to take the bread to the Monroes?" I haul myself back up and wipe my hands down on my apron. "How does this place get so filthy?" I wash my hands at the bar sink, squirt soap onto Laura's hands when she holds them out for me.

"What are you doing after work?" she says. She sniffs her hands and makes a *blargh* face. "I hate this stuff. It smells like a hospital died."

"Food to dad. Dogs. Homework. Another midterm tomorrow and then the party."

"Oh yeah, I should study for my history test," she says. "I haven't really felt like studying lately." She digs her hands into her hair and pulls it back from her face. It springs back briskly.

I open my mouth and she puts her finger on my lips.

"Yes, I've been going to class," she says.

"You have to keep your grades up for RISD—"

"Sure," she says.

"I'm glad," I say.

"I know." She leans against the wall and we sigh in tandem. The sounds of the restaurant swell up, all murmurs and chewing and knives on plates, the same it would be anywhere. The floor-to-ceiling windows have been thrown open and they rock in the breeze off the ocean. Gulls are screaming about gull things outside on the deck railings. I have never seen one fly inside, but Nancy has a lot of stories about torn-off hairpieces and knocked-over tables.

"Mrs. Tam probably needs more bread," I say finally.

"The Monroes definitely need more bread," she says. "It isn't even worth checking first. I should never walk by their table if I am not ready to produce another basket."

We both push off the wall together. She picks up two baskets of bread and I pick up one of the water pitchers that Clarence, Nancy's nephew and wage-free busboy, fills up with enthusiasm. We don't go through pitchers as fast as he fills them for us, but he is glad to have a job to do.

"Omar wants me to come up to the studio tonight so he can work on his portfolio," Laura says as we slip through the tables.

"He wants you to drive three hours up to San Francisco tonight so *you* can work on his portfolio," I say flatly.

"Well, he was all, *I've got this idea for a series of nature portraits except nature is ugly and cruel.*" She frowns. "I'm sure it'll turn out better than it sounds. He's basically interested in the intersection between our constructs of beauty and the beauty that doesn't conform to that ideal but is, nonetheless, beautiful. Like we talked about in Art and Aesthetics. I'll have to write his artist's statement for this one."

"You do every time anyway," I say. Laura has been collecting art theory books since she graduated from Crayola crayons, and the things she knows are sometimes breathtaking. I'm smiling at her until she says, "So are you going to come?"

"Can I get more bread?" Mrs. Tam says, glancing between

us. I'm refilling her glass carefully, because she does not like excessive ice.

"Sure," I say. "No," I say to Laura.

"Just one more basket," Mrs. Tam says. "I have a lot of soup left."

"Of course," I say to her. "Just as soon as you finish that last piece I'll have it right out."

"Oh I didn't even notice that there!" she says, blinking like she's just emerged from a terrible dream.

"I have to bring dinner home," I say to Laura, turning to the next table.

"Just drop by for a minute and then come with me," Laura says, gathering up empty plates and smiling distractedly at the Smiths as she passes their table. The Smiths are nudists but only on their own property since most business owners on the pier started banning them for hygiene reasons. "Bread? You got it!" Laura says, and gives them a thumbs-up.

"Laura, that is nuts and I have had a crap day." I wave my pitcher around and it sloshes. "Shit! I'm sorry, Mrs. Tam." I lower my voice as Laura passes me, and follow her toward the back. "Morgan was—I am so tired of that class. It's so pointless. The early deadline is in three weeks and this endless busywork is not helping. *I* should ditch that class."

"You wouldn't ever possibly even begin to consider potentially even thinking about ditching," Laura says, dumping her armful of empties into a bus bin. "You couldn't. You are physically, emotionally, and spiritually incapable of it."

She's right. The idea is hilarious. Just the idea of skipping makes me physically uncomfortable, twitchy, unsettled.

"The East Coast sounds so far away, doesn't it?" I say. "Jolene gets into Sarah Lawrence, and you'll be, like, an hour away. I'll be at Harvard, and everyone else will be three thousand miles away."

"Three thousand miles isn't that far. I can still come visit," she says. "Here." She hands me a stack of fresh baskets, and I start draping them with napkins. She picks up hunks of sourdough and starts tossing them in.

"Unsanitary," I say.

She rolls her eyes at me and stabs the tongs into the platter full of bread and thrusts it at me. "Could you bring this to them?"

I take it from her, but I don't move, because "visit"?

"What?" she says.

"You're going to RISD, right?" I ask.

"Rhode Island," she says. "Can you imagine spending four years in *Rhode Island*?" She grabs the basket back out of my hand and kisses my shoulder as she passes by.

"You're going to get your MFA," I say. "You have that whole college fund thing!" I ignore that twist of envy in my stomach that happens every single time I think about how easy it'll be for her to afford college. She won't need to default to community college if she doesn't get a scholarship because her parents have all the dollars. I'm following her back out onto the floor like a baby duck, and I watch her smile at the Smiths, who beam up at her like she's just produced their first grandchild for them.

"It's really not a college fund," Laura says over her shoulder.

"Ashley," Mrs. Tam calls. She holds up her empty basket. She sounds hurt and betrayed. I have always suspected she just dumps the bread in her purse but now I know it.

"We're baking fresh right now," Laura says to her, and Mr. Monroe grunts and shoves his basket back across the table.

"This isn't fresh," he says.

"You haven't tried it yet," Laura says sweetly. "It just came out a second ago."

"It's not hot," he says.

"It's plenty hot," Mrs. Monroe says. "Look at how soft this butter is." Mr. Monroe is poking at the loaf and grumbling while Laura makes soothing noises and Mrs. Tam leans over to tell them to be grateful they have any bread at all.

I try to settle them down and smooth everything over, but I'm doing it even less diplomatically than usual. When I'm back from changing out their bread, I see Laura tucked at the end of the room with her arms crossed, leaning against the giant fiberglass swordfish that takes up most of the wall.

I lean against the wall next to her, wiping my hands on my apron.

"San Francisco," she says quietly, not looking at me.

"Instead of college," I say.

Omar has been telling Laura to come live in San Francisco since they met. *It's where art lives,* he says. *Unchained,* he says. Laura doesn't even seem to mind when he starts talking like that.

"Anything instead of college," she says. "Instead of knocking myself out. Instead of staying up all night and worrying."

"You're just going to work for a few months then? Hang out in the city for a while and then go to RISD after a semester or something?"

She shakes her head. "I turned them down," she says. She's not looking at me. She's watching everyone eat their bread like she's going to spring into action the moment a basket is empty. "I don't know if you're supposed to do something like that, call them up and say, Oh hey, yeah, thank you and everything but unfortunately your goals and mine do not currently coincide in any meaningful way, but thank you for your attention and support."

I stand up straight. "Laura," I say. She's still studying the tables, still not meeting my eyes.

"You didn't even tell me you had gotten in," I say.

She glances at me for the tiniest second and looks away. "I didn't want to—I wasn't sure. And you and Jolene are so anxious and I didn't want to come sugarplum-dancing out the door and rain on your worry parade, you know?"

"Sugarplum—what?"

"I'm an artist," she says. She is the only person in the world who can say that without sounding pretentious. She shrugs. "Why do I need to spend four years being told that I'm not an artist yet but I could be if I listen to *them* when I can already listen to myself because I know who I am and what I can do, you know?"

I'm quiet for a moment. We're both watching Mrs. Tam butter every slice of her loaf slowly and methodically, and then line them up along the edge of the table.

"Say something," Laura says in a voice that's too casual. "You always have something to say."

"Okay," I say. "So you're just going to drive to San Francisco and hope everything works out and you don't die starving and poor on the street?"

"Well, *that* was something to say."

"Am I wrong? Do you have a better plan?"

"Omar knows people," she says.

"Okay," I say. "So the plan is that you are going to move to San Francisco and hope that *knowing people* is going to work out while he takes blurry black-and-white photos and you"—I wave my hand around—"and you be an artist. Which is lucrative."

She stalks back toward the maze of tables.

"Laura," I say, trying to catch up to her.

She stops at the sagging palm tree festooned with nets and ropes and sad-looking plastic fish, and turns. Her eyes flicker over my face and she reaches out to squeeze my hand.

"It's just that it's not a good idea," I say.

She sighs, but she doesn't drop my hand. "It's okay," she says. "Do you not want to come up to Omar's then?"

"I just don't want you to do anything stupid," I say.

"I know," she says.

"Have you told Jolene?" I ask.

"I haven't told anyone," she says.

"So I don't count, ha ha?"

She grins at me quick, her lightning-flash smile that illuminates everything. "Maybe Omar can convince you that we've got the talent to make it in the big city on our wits, our convictions, and our old-fashioned work ethic." She bats one of the palm tree leaves out of her way.

"Maybe," I say, because anything can happen, and the crash of glass that just came from the kitchen wasn't my fault this time.

CHAPTER 5

The problem is that I name them, and once I name them I
never want to give them away.

But she just looks like an Annabelle Lee. She's the smallest
shih tzu I've ever seen, just a fluff of tangled fur on my knees and
little worried black eyes that don't look away from mine, even as I
feed her tiny bits of our dinner. She doesn't even startle when the
gulls squawk or flocks of tourists flap by to take pictures of the
flaking fiberglass lighthouse at the end of the dock.

This is my favorite part of the day, after my work shift and
before there is anything else to do right away. The sun is starting
to set red-gold and the ocean looks bright and strange in the light,
like an alien landscape. My father is late as always to come meet
me, but I never mind. My feet hurt and my back hurts but no one
is talking to me and I can *not think* for just a couple of minutes.

I had been considering breaking into the big bag of fried
things I'm bringing home for dinner and stealing a couple of

fries before they got cold and gross, and then the little dog came slinking close. She crouched down low to the planks of the dock and delicately, deliberately placed her tiny paws down one by one until she was a foot away, stretching out her nose and sniffing at the greasy paper. She stared wide-eyed and intense as I ripped the staple at the top of the bag off and dug around until I found the breaded codfish fillet.

And now she's slowly working her way through my meal, licking my fingertips carefully after each crumb. I jump when my father appears in front of me, his hands on his hips. He's got Toby bouncing around at the end of his leash, ricocheting off Soto's sides and my father's knees. Soto bumps her head into my arm and then sits politely. I kiss her face and the top of her big block head and rest my forehead on the side of her neck. Annabelle Lee licks my wrist and settles her chin on top of my hand.

"Doggone it," my father says, scooping up Toby under his armpits.

"Ha," I say.

"Why do we have so many dogs?" my father says. Toby is hanging from my father's arm, panting and smiling hugely.

"You tell me it's because you're a sucker with a heart of gold who lets your daughter collect them," I say.

"I'm something," he says.

"How was the open house?"

He's got paint in his hair and on his dress pants and undershirt.

He never remembers to change when he gets home, especially when things had gone poorly. He notices me looking at the stains and fingers the stiff splash of orange on the hem of his shirt. "It'll come out," he says. "You always get it out."

"I always end up buying you new pants," I say.

"They all look the same," he says, and shrugs in that easy, fluid way that my older brothers have inherited, with the rolling shoulders and head rocking to the side. Toby starts wiggling under his arm and Dad is trying to get a better grip. "I'm going to drop him," he says, and it sounds more like a threat than a statement.

"You could have left Toby at home," I point out, setting Annabelle Lee on the step beside me and standing up. She's investigating the big dinner bag, which is starting to turn dark brown with grease. "No more of that," I say to her, and pick her up.

"What is that?" my father says.

"Dinner," I say, tucking the bag under my arm. I'm already greasy from work.

"It doesn't have much meat on its bones," he says. Toby is hanging limp now from Dad's arm but has started to whine, high-pitched and utterly forlorn. "I feel the same way, buddy," my father says.

"I'll clean her up and bring her in to the shelter in San Luis Obispo tomorrow," I say as I settle Annabelle Lee against my shoulder.

My father drops Toby down and takes the bag of food from me.

"And then what?" he asks.

"And then I'll bring her back because they have no room," I say.

"Your grandmother isn't going to be happy." He frowns, but he drifts off. He's looking off at the water like he just caught a glimpse of something.

"She's never happy," I say, and set off down the marina with Soto at my heel and Annabelle Lee under my arm.

Toby shoots by, dragging my father behind. "That's not true!" my father says, out of breath. Toby jerks to a halt to examine a post and yanks my father to a stop. "Toby, why are you doing this to me? Why?" Toby lifts his leg. "I mean," my father says, "there must have been a couple of minutes in 1984 where she might have thought about smiling."

"History shows that she is unlikely to even notice another dog," I say.

"It's expensive," my father argues, nudging Toby away from a small mound of something that came out of a seagull. "Isn't it?" He's never bought dog food or cat food or any groceries. "They eat like animals," he says, and elbows me. *Ha, ha. Big joke. Get it?*

"It's fine," I say. "My paycheck covers it." Soto bumps her head against my knee and I start walking again, too fast. My father is hurrying behind me, and Toby is trying to keep up on stubby little legs as we turn off Main Street and down the side roads toward home.

"That's because they're animals," he says. "That they eat that way."

"Yes, I got it," I say.

He stops when Toby pulls to sniff at a lilac bush. My father stands there with his hands in his pockets, watching Toby demonstrate laser focus and slight bewilderment. The lights in the Victorian houses around us are starting to flicker on. Here they're all freshly painted in whites and grays and sands and pale blues like they're trying to remind you that the beach is never far away.

"You ever think about spending your money on something fun?" my father asks. "Buy a golf cart. Rent a bouncy house. Eat a lot of candy. So much candy. Be a little bit more laid-back, like your friend Laura."

"Yes, I could go live like a bum in San Francisco," I say.

"Why not," he says absently, rocking back on his heels.

"I can't do that," I say, but I know he's not really listening.

"Sure you can," he says. He's still wearing his dress shoes, and they're scuffed. "You can eat all the candy you want."

"Dad."

"Eat thine candy whilst thy may," he intones.

I sigh. "I don't like candy very much," I say.

"You never did," he says, tugging Toby back into motion. He watches me juggle Annabelle Lee into the crook of my other arm and try to untangle my necklace from my hair. "Those parties your mother used to throw." We both wait through his pregnant, before-the-joke pause. "She had a great arm."

"The Easter-egg hunt, you mean?"

"Your brothers got so mad every year."

"I was methodical!"

"Your mother would hide a metric ton of those plastic eggs all over the yard and the house and she'd have better places every year and kids from all over the neighborhood would go swarming but you'd find twenty of them in under twenty minutes."

"I had a plan," I say.

"Your brothers swore you were cheating."

"I would never cheat!" I can feel my face getting hot just like it did when I was barely nine years old and my heart swelled with the injustice of it when they insisted, their baskets empty and mine overflowing, that I was somehow stealing eggs from them.

"Oh, I know you wouldn't," he says, slipping his arm around me and tangling Toby in my legs. "I saw your campaign maps."

"I gave one to Mateo," I mutter, stepping over the leash. "He didn't even look at it."

"Your brothers aren't strategists, kid."

"Well, that's not my fault," I say. I shift Annabelle Lee back over to my other arm.

"Do you want me to put that thing in my pocket?" He gestures at Annabelle. "Or make Soto useful. Let's strap her on top."

"She's fine," I say. Then I realize she's snoring. She looks like a dishcloth and sounds like a blender.

"You didn't have to sell your extra candy back to them, though," my father says.

"I was saving up," I say. You'd think I'd have saved enough for college by now, but it's funny how much it costs to support my father, who refuses to ever ask Grandmother for cash.

He glances over at me. "You know, my place is hiring," he says.

I am startled. "What, the brokerage?" The real-estate company my father works for has only had three employees since the dawn of time. This is mostly because their clients are the kind who have a half-acre parcel of land they need to sell fast and cheap to buy a kidney, or cabins hours from the coast with no running water, which have to be sold as quickly as possible in order to cover legal fees for assorted issues that are never quite clarified. My father takes the clients with hard-luck stories, the hard-to-sell houses that none of the big companies would ever touch. Those guys are trading multimillion-dollar Victorians back and forth between their buyers and sellers—the houses we're strolling by now. The kind of house where the front landscaping looks as if a team of garden specialists descended with measuring tapes and calculators and geometry fetishes.

"Do they have enough business to actually hire someone?" I say, mostly because their business strategy never fails to fascinate me.

"Gloria is retiring," my father says. "I don't know when she got tired in the first place." Toby slows down to a crawl, his nose pushed to the ground and working overtime as we walk past the Alvarez house, where his boyfriend, the German shepherd, lives. The love is not mutual but that will never stop Toby. We stop and watch him inhale the essence of Duke.

People tell me all the time my dad doesn't look old enough to be a dad, and that's probably true. He doesn't have any gray, and when his face relaxes he looks so much like my brothers.

"It would make more sense to just split everything up between you and George," I tell him.

"Hmm?" he says. He looks over at me. "Don't you think they should paint this place purple?" He tilts his chin at Duke's house.

"Wouldn't that lower the resale value?" I say.

He shrugs. "Does it matter?"

"Dad, why are you even in the real-estate business?"

"It's a living," he says jovially.

No, not really. But instead I say, "Is she selling? Or is she just not working anymore?"

He shrugs. "Who knows. She does what she wants."

"Right, but do you even have a job?"

"Sure I do," he says. "She would have said something. It hasn't really come up."

"It 'hasn't really'?" My voice seems to bounce off the sky, and a group of birds flap off from the topmost branches of the oak a few yards down.

"You worry too much, honey. It's fine," he says comfortably, patting my shoulder. Toby sighs and snorts and starts waddling forward, ready for dinner. All the light has leaked out of the sky when we turn onto our gravel-scattered road.

"Right, but what happens when I graduate?"

"You could come work for us," he says. "Eh? Then it's all in the family."

"I would need—I'm not old enough. And I would need a license." I am talking like I'm taking his meandering seriously, and I hate when I do that.

"I think eighteen is plenty old enough," he says. "When is your birthday, is it Saturday? Is that tomorrow? This week went by fast." He's shaking his head.

"Seventeen," I say. "I'm going to be seventeen."

"Then you hang out for a year. Take a couple of classes at that two-year college in Santa Maria. That ought to be a walk in the cake for you. And wouldn't it be nice to take a year off? Your grandmother would be thrilled to have you stay around. She would be rattling around in that old house like a ball bearing if you went off somewhere for college."

I start with, "You'll still be living there" and "She's actually never home," but he's still talking.

"I bet you'll be a natural," he says. "You've got the Perkins charm. You've got your grandmother's drive and go-getterism, don't you think?"

"I'm getting my medical degree," I say slowly and carefully. I do not want my voice to shake in the wake of the whistling hollow in my chest.

"You're so much like your mom," he says, beaming at me. "But Santa Maria has a first-aid certificate!" my dad says. "A lot cheaper, I bet, than Princeton." His face is a pale blue-white blur in this light and my eyes hurt looking at him. Annabelle Lee huffs in the crook of my arm and I loosen my grip and I don't say anything, because my father is a rushing creek and anything you toss in there will be swept away, Ping-Ponging in the current and bobbing its way out to sea.

"Right, is that what you told Mom?" I find myself saying. I don't know, or even care, where that came from.

He frowns at me. "I couldn't tell your mother anything."

In the picture of her at Harvard, with her Harvard T-shirt stretched over her pregnant belly and barely covering it, she's grinning maybe because she will be back when things settle down, when life is smooth, when my father's landed a full-time job and the twins are old enough to make their own sandwiches or at least be cared for by someone else. And then I came along and it was too late.

I imagine that when she left us it was to go back to her real life. The one she should have had without my father.

"She never went back to school," I say.

"She didn't need to," my father says.

"Could she have?"

He laughs. "She could do anything."

"You know that's not what I meant."

I can suddenly picture my father with his arms around her and dream-light conviction and confidence in his voice telling her everything is just fine, just fine right here and now and always. My mother, swept downstream under a sunny sky, trying to make it back to shore.

He puts his arm around me and squeezes. "You're a good kid," he says to me. "You know that?" Annabelle Lee huffs again.

"Careful!" I snap, and shift her to my other arm, pulling away from him.

"Whoops!" he says cheerfully. "Did I flatten her? She'll spring right back. She's just a big fluff."

We stop in front of our house, the rattiest on the block. All the lights are on, in every room, bright enough that it looks like the sun has come back up. I will walk through the whole house and turn them all off, one by one. The overhead lights and the table lamps and the wall sconces and the standing lamps and the desk lamps and the task lights, all of them except the one on the end table next to the couch my father will stretch out on to supposedly go through new MLS listings but actually fall asleep.

"Everything will be okay," he says suddenly. He's looking at the blazing bright house instead of me. The refrain of my childhood and every year of my life and every bump and scrape and bruise inside and out. *Everything will be okay,* or could be. I knew it wasn't true. Not everything was okay. But for my father, it's still an unshakeable, unassailable fact about the world.

"Right, Toby?" he says. Toby barks and spins in circles.

I trust Soto's judgment more, and her face is as sad as ever.

"Toby knows what I'm talking about," my father says.

"Toby might be the only one," I say, and he elbows me.

"Chip off the old blockhead," he says, and takes the front steps up two at a time, the dogs bobbing along in his wake.

CHAPTER 6

On Saturday I wake up seventeen years old and the first thing I do is run to the bathroom and drop to my knees. It's the gift that keeps on giving—I'm sick for a long time, hanging on to the side of the bowl with my eyes closed and my heart jittering, holding my hair back with one hand. I can hear Soto snuffling at the bottom of the door, and then the jangling of her collar. The sound of tiny claws on the wood floor tell me Toby and Annabelle Lee have joined the party.

The doorknob rattles and then the knocking starts, louder than my heart.

"No," I say, hunched over the bowl and resting my forehead on my arm.

"What are you doing?" my brother says. His voice is muffled and loud, like he's smooshed his face against the door. Soto makes her tiny happy yelp. "Aw, hi, honey. Hallo. You are such a good girl. What is this thing? This is a dog?"

"Mateo?" I say. My brothers are supposed to be at college. My stomach lurches.

"Best surprise ever," Mateo says. "Are you throwing up?"

"Yes," I say.

"Do you have bulimia?" he asks.

"Shut up, Mateo," I say. Nausea is oozing through my body, up my throat, and I am trying not to let it out again. I swipe away the strands of hair that are sticking to my forehead.

"Aha, you *do* have bulimia!"

"I don't have bulimia, Mateo."

"Oh okay," he says. He sounds disappointed. "I've heard good things about it."

I grimace. "Why are you here?" I slump back against the wall and rub my eyes.

"It's your birthday," he says. "Surprise! Are you coming out of there? Clara wants you to come down for breakfast. Why are you throwing up again?"

I cover my face with my hands. Maybe if I am quiet and it's dark he'll go away. But he's like a tick, or my conscience. I scrub at my cheeks with the palms of my hands.

"Are you really sick?" he says, and he sounds concerned this time. "Did you eat bad clams?"

"I'll be out in a second," I say.

"Okay," he says. "Hurry up. Waffles!" He goes thumping down the hallway, Soto's toenails clacking along behind him, and

Toby and Annabelle Lee scurrying to keep up. I can hear him shouting at Lucas, the shaking of the house as they all thunder downstairs.

Both my brothers are here, then. Everyone is downstairs waiting for me. I drink a glass of water, tepid from the tap, and then refill it again and then one more time. I brush my teeth and wash my face and avoid looking in the mirror. Even through the bathroom door I can hear my brothers shouting over each other and pans clattering and chairs being dragged screaming across the old linoleum.

When I appear at the kitchen door, Soto makes a happy circle and Toby yaps and races around the kitchen island. Annabelle Lee yips from the crook of Mateo's arm. Lucas takes two long strides over from the center island and hauls me into a hug. "Ashley!" he says. He rocks back, lifting me just a tiny bit, and goes, "Oof!" and I push away. Soto circles around me and I scratch her head until she huffs and wanders off. Mateo's sitting at the island with a plate of bacon in front of him, feeding strips into his face like he's a wood chipper and ignoring Annabelle Lee's tiny bark, which is vibrating her entire body. My father's hair is sticking straight out from his head in all directions. He is practicing his pancake flips while my grandmother sips coffee out of a World's Best Grandma mug, which the twins bought her for her birthday last year because they thought it was hilarious. It suits her the way a propeller hat would suit a Tibetan monk. She uses it only when they visit, and that's because they take it out and put it in front of her. She is perfectly pulled together even though it's not even nine in the morning. The rest of us look like animals who just crawled out of hibernation.

"I thought we were having waffles," I say, tightening the belt of my big fuzzy pink robe.

"Happy birthday, kiddo!" my father says, glancing away from his pan. "Will you please shut that little thing up?" he says to Mateo.

"Dad thought waffles would be too messy," Mateo says, his mouth full of bacon. He hauls Annabelle Lee up against his chest and scratches the back of her neck while she squirms.

"I'm the one who washes the dishes," I say, pulling out the stool next to him and hopping up. I reach for a slice of bacon but Mateo slaps my hand away.

"It's my birthday!" I say.

"Matthew," my grandmother says. "You are not twelve years old."

"It's still my bacon," he says. Annabelle Lee sighs and collapses against his shoulder, quiet now.

"So share your bacon," I say.

Lucas grabs the plate from behind Mateo's other shoulder and walks around to the other side of the island.

"Dick!" Mateo says.

"I want bacon," I grumble. I can ignore my queasy stomach for bacon.

"Making more right this second," my father says. He steps back to peer into the oven window. "Almost ready. All of it yours."

"Is that my birthday gift?" I ask.

"I thought that was just a Tuesday," Mateo says, and nudges me in the side, his elbow sharp and pointy.

"No, on Tuesday I eat an entire cow," I say.

"Aw, don't look like that," he says. "You know I'm kidding."

My grandmother sets down her mug and pushes it toward Mateo. "Make yourself useful, Matthew," she says to my brother. He hops up and gives her a big smacking kiss on the cheek. He grabs her mug and wanders over to the coffee machine, Annabelle Lee still draped over his shoulder.

Lucas pushes the plate across the island to me. "Knock yourself out," he says.

"Thank you," I say, and take an extra-crispy piece.

"I'll just eat the fresh batch," he says.

"Why are you here?" I ask him. "Do you *have* to be here?"

"It's your last birthday at home," he says, with his hand in his chin. "How do you feel? Do you feel terrified about your future and all the stupid choices you've made and all the mistakes you're about to make?"

"I could come home for my birthday next year," I say. I take another piece of bacon.

"Once you leave you're not coming back," Mateo says,

hopping back on his stool and kicking mine in a steady beat.

"Why not? You come back all the time. It's like you've never left. It's like we're never going to get rid of you," I say.

"Yeah, but we're like ten minutes away." He leans over and drops Annabelle gently on the floor. She pads off around the island with Toby in fascinated pursuit. Soto is lying at my feet with her chin on her paws, looking off into the distance.

"Like five hours away," Lucas says.

"Fourteen hours and eight minutes," Grandmother says. "By car."

"Who's counting?" my father says. He was the one who drove on that trip and I think he has blocked it all out, the fights over the radio and my grandmother's giant paper map and her acid anger about speed limits and roadside diners and me lying in the backseat with my ear buds cranked up so loud even the open windows couldn't drown out the bass.

"Okay, an hour by plane, though," Mateo says.

"It's only eight hours for me," I say, as my father slides a pancake onto my plate. It is lumpy and pale on one side, black on the other.

"First one for the birthday girl," he says. "As is tradition."

"Thank you," I say. I pick it up and drop it on the floor, as is tradition. Soto snatches it before it lands. "Good girl," I say.

My father makes a *humph* noise at me and slides the next one onto my plate.

"Really?" I say. "Did you cook this?" I poke at it, and it oozes. "Are you eating these? You are going to make yourself sick."

"Really, Charles," my grandmother says. She slides gracefully off her stool and circles around to the stove. My father backs off as she lifts the handle of the pan and examines the pancake splatter that is currently bubbling. "This could be acceptable," she says. She sets the pan down and crosses her arms.

"It'll burn," my father says.

My grandmother doesn't answer. She arches her eyebrow at him in the way that I can too and he slinks away to peer into the fridge. Soto hauls herself up and pads over because my father with his head in the fridge is often an unexpected bounty of his impatience.

Mateo bounces up from his stool and heads for the foyer. The dogs all perk up and fling themselves away from the fridge and out of the room, barking. There are voices, and I think I recognize all of them. When Hector is at the kitchen door, still talking to Mateo about whatever, I am unsurprised. He looks around and finds me and his whole face lights up as he throws his arms out.

"Happy birthday!" he says. He's dragging me off my stool and he is squishing me. "Happy birthday, gorgeous girl!" He gives me a big smacking kiss on the side of my face, halfway between my mouth and my cheek and I can't help smiling. He drops me to shake hands with my dad. I stumble back and end up tipping my stool.

I catch it and settle it back into place while he's trading hellos and various physical greetings with all the people in my family. Fist bumps and cheek kisses and handshakes, and I sit myself back on my shaky stool and eat another piece of bacon and then another while Hector and my brothers talk about the various benefits of breakfast as the first meal of the day.

Soto has vacated, because she is nervous around Hector, and Annabelle Lee and Toby have come trampling through the kitchen and out the back patio door, off in the backyard to be small dumb dogs. I think it's for the best, because Hector has a swooping-and-overwhelming problem. He wants to gather up all the puppies into his arms at once and have quiet moments full of peace and unconditional love. I think sometimes that Hector does not actually understand how love works. There is a tiny piece of my heart that worries someday he might figure it out. And I'm not sure where that will leave me.

My grandmother slides two perfect pancakes onto my plate and smiles at me and my heart hurts.

"They are very beautiful," I say, because they are. They look like fashion-model pancakes and I suddenly feel hungry. I pull the syrup jar over and pour it in perfect, swooping gold loops across my perfect pancakes until Mateo smacks my hand and messes up the design.

"Don't hog it, hog," he says.

"Don't be an ass, ass," I say.

I drop the syrup on the table. He snatches it up and starts drowning his stack of pancakes, which are just as perfect as mine.

"Are you ready to go?" Hector is bouncing next to my stool. He looks on the outside the way I feel inside, full of itching powder. My mouth is full and I point at it. "Chew! Chew! Chew!" he says.

"All aboard!" my father says predictably.

I swallow. "Have a pancake," I say, pointing at the plate with my fork.

"I don't want a pancake," he says. "I want to go get your party stuff."

"Ashley will eat all the pancakes for you," Mateo says.

"She can eat them later," Hector says. He looks at me. "What if they're all sold out?"

"Of what?" I say with my mouth full again.

He shrugs. "I don't know. Napkins?"

"Unlikely," I say. I stab another bit of pancake and he watches me anxiously, like the dogs do sometimes. "Okay, fine," I say. "I'll go put pants on."

I pick up my plate and shuffle out of the room with it. I hear my grandmother say, "For god's sake, Hector, sit down."

I can feel myself dawdling. I run a brush through my hair and put it in a ponytail and take it back down and change T-shirts three times, even though each one is the same as the last, the

University of Seattle ones my brothers bring home to wash and then forget about. At the door, I pause and turn right toward my father's room instead. It's a mess, with piles of clothes and books and empty Fanta cans lining the windowsill. I dig through the clean laundry basket for my mother's Harvard T-shirt, run back to my room with it. It's tight at the boobs and it looks good on me. I'm the same size as she was, which I realize surprises me. But I'm smiling when I bounce back into the kitchen and sing, "Ready! Let's go! Let's go now!"

My grandmother smiles at me again and holds her arm out. She pats me on the shoulder when I lean over to kiss her soft cheek. "This will be a very good birthday, darling. I can promise you that."

"Oh," I say, and then Hector is pulling me by the elbow out the door.

I'm quiet in the car all the way to the next town over. Our town is too small to have its own party store. Hector's in the passenger seat, singing along to the terrible San Luis Obispo radio station we get, cranking it up another notch every time a new song comes on and shouting, "Oh man, I love this song!" He's out of the car and sprinting for the party store as soon as I hit the brakes.

"Why are you so excited?" I say as I catch up to him, and he throws an arm over my shoulder.

"I'm always excited," he says.

"But you're *extra* excited. Even for you," I say, shrugging out from under his arm and pushing through the jingling door. All the associates in the store look up.

"Hello there, can I help you with anything?" the cheerful-looking white man with the long gray braid says.

"No, thank you," I say as I follow Hector down the aisle, though it looks like he's disappeared. He'll be back soon; it is like he is attached to me by an elastic cord.

Hector sneaks back up behind me while I am considering Daisy Duck napkins, which are on sale. He slips a mask over my head. He laughs when I yelp. "You're Wonder Woman!" he says, spinning me around. I can't see much through the narrow, crooked eye holes.

I pull off the mask and look at Wonder Woman's empty eyes. I snap the elastic around my wrist because I don't want to leave her alone in the store. "Maybe," I say.

"You okay?" he says to me. He rests his forearms on my shoulder and peers into my face like he's going to find answers in my eyebrows.

"No," I say.

"Come on, it's your birthday," he says, rocking me side to side. "You love parties! You love cake!"

"Everyone loves cake."

"You love cake like a fat kid loves cake!" he says, grinning at me.

I yank myself away from him. "I love cake the way a fat kid loves *his friends and family*." I turn and stalk down the aisle away from him.

"Sure," he says, following after me. "But seriously, what's up?"

"I don't want a party."

"You don't have to have one," he says.

"My father wants me to have a party," I say.

My father throws these parties because that is how he shows he loves me. He understands love as noisy and demonstrative, messy and full of streamers. But he is fairly useless when it comes to practical issues. His eyes glaze over when I try to talk to him about fixing the irrigation system in the garden because it is, literally, a hundred years old, or suggest we find out what that knocking sound in the Volvo is. It is faster to do these things on my own, which is why I'm the one buying the napkins and the plates and the food and the cake and the soda. I do love parties. I still don't want this one.

"It won't be so bad," he says soothingly as he ambles next to me. He is almost as unhelpful as my father when it comes to shopping and making practical decisions, even about tiny things like how many packages of forks we need.

"I don't want Grandmother's coupon," I say. I told Hector about the coupons when we first started dating. He had looked puzzled by the idea. He looked at my body as if he was trying to understand the problem. The birthday bribes have always seemed like an abstract thing to him. This will be the first year he'll be around when I get one.

"The coupon," he says. "Oh. Well. Maybe you won't get one this year?"

He leans in to kiss me again. He knows I don't like it when he does it in public. I dodge him by leaning down to grab a package of Wonder Woman paper plates. Her head is still dangling from my wrist. On the plates she's punching the air. She looks determined, and she looks focused.

"Superhero theme," I say. I wave the plates at him and he is distracted.

"Really?" he says, delighted. "Everyone will wear masks!" I am pleased to have made him happy. "And have secret identities! What's your secret identity?" He pulls out the plain napkins I had given him and starts piling in the superhero-themed ones.

"I don't need a secret identity. Secret identities are for people with something to hide."

"You never hide anything," Hector says.

"Of course not," I say.

He kisses me on the forehead and brushes my hair back behind my ear. "Let's get masks anyway." He darts ahead of me and around the corner.

I pull Wonder Woman streamers off the rack and follow him to the masks. Superheroes and masks will be whimsical. My father is always telling me I need more whimsy in my life. Less taking things so literally and seriously.

Hector piles masks into my arms because there's no more room left in the basket he's got. He pulls my ponytail holder off and pushes a tiara into my mess of hair because my arms are full and I can't nudge him away. He snaps on his own squirrel mask like it's a hat. It mashes down his curls. I am looking for a cart, and then hear Hector talking to someone behind us.

"Does your sister need a basket?" the girl says. Our age. She doesn't go to our school, because I don't recognize her. She is white and pretty and pink-cheeked. She looks like the kind of girl who goes to all her school's games, both home and away, and has six football boyfriends.

I think that, but how do I know? I shake my head. I'm just as bad as anybody.

"No," Hector says to the girl. He smiles at her and turns away. He doesn't know what she was implying? I catch up to him. I am glad to resist the urge to glance back at her when he drapes his arm over my shoulder and rubs his thumb on my bare arm. He is just a little bit taller than me. When I look over at him he's smiling. Brown eyes almost gold. I press my cheek against his just briefly, a short hug, and he grins at me as if I have just thrown my arms around him and squeezed him until he was breathless.

The first time we had sex was on the beach behind my house, on a blanket from the trunk of the car, and I tried to cover myself because it was cold, because I couldn't imagine wanting to know what anyone else thought about my body. I just wanted him to touch me and he did, moving his hands across my body and down my sides and touching me everywhere, all of my skin, all of it bare and the moon up in the sky and his face close to mine and that smile on his face and his whisper that he loved me, he loved me, he loved me and I was so beautiful and he loved me, until I buried my face in his neck, not sure I could withstand the force of him anymore.

The force of him is sometimes too much to bear. Even at a party shop. This boy.

"Hector," I say, and stop. I'm not sure what I want to say to him. I can't stop myself from glancing behind us this time. The girl is still at the end of the aisle. Her white shorts are very short and her legs are very long. A girl who should run down the beach in slow motion with wind blowing through her hair.

I don't know what I want. To have the difference acknowledged. To have the difference dismissed. It's like he doesn't even know he has these options.

I say, "Thank you for helping me shop for my birthday party."

Hector smiles at me again. I wonder if he has ever had a moment of doubt.

He says, "It's your birthday!" He gives me a kiss on my temple with a smacking sound. "Everything is going to be awesome."

I know he genuinely does not notice those tiny kinds of

moments. Nobody seems to notice them as much as I do, I have realized. Hector is talking about superheroes, and the girl in the shorts is gone. I cannot decide if I am relieved or angry. Wonder Woman is dangling from my wrist and she is no help at all.

CHAPTER 7

"Ashley, is this a joke?" Jolene asks. I drape a feather boa around her neck and put a tiara on her head before I even let her off the veranda and through the front door. She pushes a paper streamer out of her face and it catches on her rhinestones. She is grinning though. The light is low in the foyer and her eyes are shining bright. She says, "Was this Hector's idea?"

I look at her and say, "Yes. And you are in a *dress*," because she is. She never dresses up. She wears tailored khaki shorts and button-down shirts. I can't remember if I've seen her in a dress since that day in fourth grade. This one is red gingham, with a small white collar and a row of shell buttons down the front. She dislikes what Laura calls "excessive displays of egregious status-quo feminine trappings," but she's dressing up for my birthday because she knows that symbols are important. She is smiling at me, and then she hugs me and I hug her back. She always seems so small. Sometimes I worry about overwhelming her and breaking her into bits.

I clear my throat when I step back. I never know when to stop hugging. She changes the subject. "Tiara!" she says. She's pointing at me.

I reach up and find one on top of my head. "I don't know where that came from," I say. I start to pull it off but it gets caught in my hair.

"You should wear it," Jolene says, reaching up to untangle the little sparkly crown. "It looks nice on you." She holds it out for me to take. "Here. It's your birthday."

Everyone keeps saying that. I find myself ducking my head and she is settling the tiara back into my curls.

She pats me on the shoulder. "There," she says. "That's perfect."

"Wait!" I say. I grab a cardboard box full of flimsy plastic Halloween masks from the mantel and shake them up. They're all twisted together. "It's whimsical," I say.

She raises her eyebrows at me. "Hector again."

"Who else?" I say.

She grins at me and takes the box, digging through it as we head down the hallway and into the kitchen. Paper streamers are everywhere. They brush across my face and hair. Her nose wrinkles. "Is that a Teenage Mutant Ninja Turtle?" She tilts the box to get a better look in the overhead light of the kitchen.

"I don't know," I say. "He is a turtle in a mask. He must be ashamed of being a mutant if that is what he is."

The kitchen is chaos. All the cupboard doors are open and coolers are stacked up by the door to the patio. Catering trays full of tamales and rice and beans and empanadas cover the entire kitchen island, and discarded wrappers from all the streamers and stars and napkins are a safety hazard all over the floor, and the dogs are circling around the island wondering when someone is going to pay attention to them, then stopping at the least convenient moment. I had wanted to cook all the food. Pinto beans bubbling all day, potatoes fried with onions, and warm, handmade tortillas. Soaking corn husks and kneading masa. My mother's recipe. She never taught me. I found it on an index card stuffed in one of my father's romance novels. But we did not have time for that. And it felt weirdly personal, too.

Mateo says, "If you knew anything about the Teenage Mutant Ninja Turtles you'd know that the masks are an essential part of their identities." He opens the fridge and takes out a can of Coke.

"I don't know what that means," I say. "Give me a Coke."

"You don't need one," he says. "It's all sugar and chemicals." He takes a long sip from his can. He doesn't burp, but that's just because Jolene is in the room. Sometimes he has dignity, though he never worries about what he says in front of her. He has known Jolene since her parents were still calling her David.

I say, "Shut up, Mateo," and he rolls his eyes and throws a can at me.

"Jolene?" he says, and hands her a soda very carefully.

"You suck," I say to him.

"You should open that before the fizz goes down and it doesn't explode all over you."

I set it down on the counter and take out a new one and smirk at him. "Check me out. I'm a criminal mastermind."

"I've licked the top of one of those cans and you'll never know which," he says. Jolene grimaces at her can. "Not yours," he assures her.

"I'm tired of you now," I say, hopping up onto one of the counter stools. "What are you doing? What have you been doing?"

"I napped," he said. "Now I'm going to go have a couple of beers and call my girlfriend."

"Grandmother wanted you to get chairs out of the studio."

He snorts and heads out the back door.

"Get chairs!" I yell after him. He yells back something I can't hear but I'm guessing isn't polite, because he always has to have the last word.

The party is just a few hours away but things are not ready yet. Laura arrived at noon. I have been cleaning floors and finding places to stuff away my father's romance novels and gathering up my mother's plates. She collected ceramic from everywhere. I don't know if she started before my grandmother let them move into the house or after. But her plates and cups are in every room.

They are under the end tables and stacked on bookcase shelves and behind the couch. There is a pile in my closet that I will never move.

Laura's been putting up the streamers, accompanied by the gentle jingling chime of her bracelets sliding up and down her arms. Streamers are hanging in the foyer and the hall and the dining room and kitchen. Now she's back in the dining room, standing on a chair and sticking up glow-in-the-dark stars in between each streamer.

"Laura!" I call. "Jolene is here."

"Jolene!" she yells. "Tell Ashley she's got to wear the sequined skirt."

Jolene frowns at me. "Do you want to wear the sequined skirt?" she asks me.

"No," I say.

Jolene leans through the door. "She'd prefer not to wear it," she says. "Why are you not using a stepladder?" Jolene looks at me. She is tapping on the doorframe in an anxious rhythm. "She's standing on a chair."

"I keep telling her she's going to fall."

"I'm not going to fall," Laura calls.

"You have the rug all bunched up under the chair legs," Jolene points out.

"Well, that isn't very safe," I say.

"Homeowner's insurance covers her, right?" my father says,

wandering into the room with a paperback in his hand.

"I'm not sure the policy extends to personal injury," I say. Jolene is still peering around the corner and worrying her hands.

"I do what I want!" Laura shouts. Her voice echoes. It's louder than the ice cubes crashing in the freezer.

"Here," I say to Jolene. "Will you help me wash my mom's plates?" I pat one of the piles.

Jolene is twisting her fingers together.

"Don't worry," I say.

She puts her hands behind her back as if she has seen me notice her twisting them. "I don't want to break one."

Lucas, hauling an armful of folding chairs through the door, snorts. "No one will notice. You know that."

My father says, "Don't break them, though." He reaches for the shook-up can of Coke Mateo had thrown at me.

"She will not break them," I say. "You won't break them," I tell Jolene. I take the can of Coke out of my father's hand and replace it with my unopened one. He shrugs and wanders off.

Jolene is looking at the stack I've made. We have no idea how many plates there are, or how many stacks we've missed. This is a very large house. I remember my mother saying they were important parts of history even though they came from mostly thrift stores. That's probably why she didn't take them with her.

My grandmother ignores them because my father wants to keep them. The house seems full of her, in every room.

I hand Jolene a stack and she looks alarmed but resolute. When she is given a task, she is very serious about it. Mateo shuffles back into the kitchen, talking on his phone, and Lucas throws himself at his back. They wrestle, and overturn the box of masks. My father wanders back into the kitchen with his Coke in one hand and a string cheese in the other.

Hector comes through the sliding doors from the back porch and hauls Toby up into his arms. Toby stares stoically off into the distance, all four of his paws sticking straight out as Hector bounces him gently, cheerfully singing the Toby song. "Toby! He's silly and he's cuddly! Toby! His belly's pretty fuzzy! Toby! Let's tell him that he's great! Good job, Toby!"

Toby doesn't seem impressed.

I find Laura in the study on her rickety chair. She has added dozens of pink bead strands around her neck. Her hair is a halo in the sun and she looks perfect. She always does and I am not sure how it is possible.

"I'm almost done!" she says when she sees me. She jumps off the chair. Her arms go around my neck and she squeezes. "I love you!" she says to me. "Happy birthday! Look how amazing this place looks, look at it!" The whole house is filled with stars and lights and streamers and it all comes together to make something beautiful. That's what Laura does.

She stops and looks at me and says, "Are you okay?"

I shake my head. "Noise," I say. "You know. They're so loud."

"I know," she says. She hands me a roll of streamers and gets up on a chair. "Hold this for me please? I have developed a system that has made it slightly more efficient to tape and hold and move and arrange but I am the first to admit that it's also very nice when you have someone come and be your backup tape-holding person." She grins at me and drags the chair over to the last corner, the throw rug still stuck on one of the back legs.

Laura is good at being silent, too, even when there are so many things we should be talking about. She tears off lengths of crepe paper and tapes them up. I steady the chair for her when she hops down and then I hold it when she hops back up. We fill the corner slowly. The noise in the kitchen gets louder but it seems far away, and it feels like we're leaving a comet tail of streamers behind us.

"There," Laura says. With a hand on my shoulder, she jumps down and says, "Okay?"

I say, "Thank you," and things are okay.

She kisses me on the cheek. In the kitchen Lucas is lugging in yet more chairs from the garage.

"Wait, do we need *even more* folding chairs?" I say.

Lucas shrugs. With one hand he pops open one of the catering trays and scoops a bunch of empanadas. He tosses an entire one into his mouth. "Where's Clara?" he asks me with his mouth full.

My grandmother is in her office at the top of the stairs because she will help fund a party but she will not help plan it or set it up.

The details are important but they're for someone else to worry about. Not her. My grandmother has very particular ideas about delegation and taking care of the work you're best suited for. She is not suited to getting her hands dirty, she says. Know where your skills lie and maximize your talent, she always says. She will come down for the party later, circulating through the crowd and remembering everyone's names, shimmering in something elegant.

"She is probably hiding from us," Jolene says.

"Hiding from your noise," Laura says. She is covered in star-adhesive backing.

"Mine?" Mateo says. "Ashley's a thundering herd of wildebeests." He pokes me in my knee and I kick him hard.

I have heard this enough. My brothers are the only ones who dare say a word to me and Laura is astonished and enraged every time. She is only sputtering now, but not for long. Before I have to listen to her lay into him, I gather up all the boxes and bags and trash, and their clatter drowns out her voice. I carry my mountain of refuse to the front door. I can't reach the handle, but I can't just drop everything. I am inching toward the floor to set the boxes down when the front door swings in toward me, knocking everything out of my hands and me almost onto my butt.

"Watch it," I say. I stagger to my feet and am looking at Laura's twin. Brandon. As stupidly gorgeous as ever. We haven't been alone since I asked him out last year, and my heart staggers to a halt.

Brandon takes my hand and says, "Are you okay?" He says it like he means it. He is narrow-shouldered and thin and not graceful. Though he looks like he should be graceful.

I like his mouth, I think. I shake that thought off and shake my hand out of his. "Yes!" I say. "Embarrassed about being clumsy mostly, I guess?"

He's got olive-colored eyes and he has cropped his afro short so it is dark against his scalp and I want to touch his face. "I'm early," he says, looking around. "I'm sorry. Are you still getting ready for the party?"

I look down at myself. "Is that a comment on my fancy formal wear?" I say. It's a joke because I'm still wearing ratty jeans and my T-shirt and I can feel my hair sticking to my neck.

"No, you look beautiful," he says. He says it emphatically and I'm sure he is sincere. I remember him saying, "You're beautiful" when I asked him out. It was something I know he wanted me to believe, because he had looked very steadily into my eyes. He said, "You're beautiful. You're just not my type. You understand that, right? It just happens sometimes." Then he smiled and said, "It's chemistry," and tapped the chemistry textbook he was holding under his arm, since it was directly after class.

"Sure right okay," I had said, because I am not one to mourn for lost causes and I didn't want to stand in the hallway for much longer. I didn't laugh at his joke, because it wasn't funny.

"Is that okay?" he had said. He looked so anxious.

"Yes of course it's okay," I said. And I meant it. Because there was no way I'd let him think any differently. I didn't want him to think I gave a damn that, whatever came out of his mouth, it was obvious that he thought—that he *thinks*—I'm too fat to date.

He smiles at me now in a way I recognize as hopeful. As if friendliness will erase his stupid words and everything that happened.

I want to tell him he doesn't need to erase anything, because *nothing* happened. I don't want someone who doesn't want me. I try to smile back and wonder what I look like in that moment, my mouth stretched over my teeth and everything about me feeling about three inches shifted to the left. I hate that my skin still prickles when he's near, a chemical reaction I have no control over, and it's even worse than the jittery uncomfortable feeling I have not been able to shake, the one that feels just a moment away from my stomach lurching again.

"Thank you," I say now. "You are very beautiful too!" He laughs, as he was meant to.

"Champagne," he says abruptly. "That's for you." He thrusts the paper bag he's been holding at me. "You have to chill it. It's from our stepmom."

"Oh," I say. "Does she know we're seventeen?"

He shrugs, and looks around at the mess. "Who cares? Here," he says, and turns and gathers up the boxes and trash in just a few sweeps. His shorts are worn and his T-shirt looks old and has a band on it that I don't care about. I stop thinking about what he is wearing before I get to his skinny ankles and his beat-up shoes because it is not important even though it is perfectly casual.

"Thank you," I say. I hold open the front door. "Could you toss them in recycling?" He smiles at me and I close the door behind him too quickly and then stop and crack it back open and flee through the streamers and down the hall. My brothers are sitting on the kitchen island, and Laura is making them laugh. My father is talking to Hector and Jolene, making big sweeping hand motions, which means he is telling a very bad and very long joke with a punchline like, "Do you have any grapes?"

Brandon comes in behind me, slips around me—making me shiver—to poke Laura in the side. She says something to him I can't hear over the noise of my brothers arguing. Brandon and Laura both look at me with their identical olive eyes. I shrug at them. My father says, "Brandon! Just the burly man I was looking for to do some weight lifting!" He claps Brandon on the back and points to the sliding door. They are going to go get *even more chairs* from the garage.

"What is it with the chairs?" I say to Laura, sliding the champagne into the freezer. I have no idea if it's okay there but it seems efficient.

"Are you mad I told Brandon to come?" she asks. Her mouth

is pinched up in a tiny grimace. Jolene jumps down next to us.

"What? No. I'm pretty sure everyone we have ever met is coming tonight," I said. "As per usual. It's fine."

"There will be so many people you will not even notice him," Jolene says. "He will be very busy also."

"There are no activities!" I say, freezing. "Oh god, do you think I should have planned activities? Is it too late to figure it out? Are birthday parties supposed to have activities?"

"You worry about this every year," Jolene says. "You don't need activities. Everyone will be just fine without party games." She pats my arm.

"I don't know," Lucas says. "I'd love to see Clara do a keg stand."

"No," I say.

"Beer pong."

"No!"

"Quarters."

"Maybe," I say. "I do have skills." But I am thinking longingly about how the noise and chaos could let me melt away into the crowd and not be found. At least for a little while. Though putting off the inevitable only makes the inevitable loom larger, more dangerous and terrible.

A stomach lurch. I slip out of the kitchen while Lucas is arguing with Laura about whether quarters should be an Olympic sport, and I run up the stairs to where everything is quiet for just a little while longer.

I know the party is starting because my bedroom window is at the side of the house, and I can hear the cars come down our quiet gravel road. They are pulling up in front of the house and lining the road on both sides. There's laughing and talking and then a loud, drawn-out honk.

Laura's on the bed with her feet tucked under her and the My Little Pony pillow on her lap, next to a pile of Soto and Toby. I think Annabelle Lee is in there somewhere; I can hear her noisy little snores. Laura is sipping champagne from a plastic cup, though it isn't quite cold yet. Jolene is combing out my hair and flat ironing the waves. She hasn't touched her glass. My tongue stings from the bubbles. My hair looks, I think, like someone spilled a puddle of chocolate sauce. This is incredibly poetic of me. I am trying to think about anything, everything else. Another test on Monday, all the studying I have to do, the essay I still haven't written, the reprimand from Dr. Ellman about how I'm putting my grades in jeopardy just because I'm being lazy about writing, the essay I may never write even though the early-acceptance deadline is two weeks away. November 1 and I'm done. I have until December 31 for the real deadline, but I cannot do that. I can't wait that long. I can't throw my application into a pile so large and broad and just hope.

"Oh my gosh, hold still!" Laura says from the bed. "You're bouncing around like you've got to pee and you're not going to like it when you end up knocking that flat iron out of her hand and into your lap. Or she's going to flat iron your ear."

"She's not going to flat iron my ear," I say. I take a slow breath in and hold it, trying to fill up the space in my gut with something besides these roller-coaster lurches.

"I am not going to burn her," Jolene says, pulling the comb down again expertly and sliding the iron smoothly. "You're okay," she says to me, patting my shoulder with her comb hand.

I know it is one of my brothers who puts his iPhone into the speakers above the fireplace in the parlor. The music is louder than the noise outside. In the mirror I see Soto's head pop up with a growl, and the little dogs start barking. Laura cuddles Annabelle Lee into her arms. Toby is bouncing on the bed, every bark taking him higher into the air.

"Hush, Toby." I sigh. "The neighbors are going to be so unhappy." Toby hops off the bed and trots to the window. He jumps up, putting his paws on the windowsill. "Toby!" I say. He jumps down and ducks his head. My heart twinges. "Aw, it's okay, buddy." I hold out my hand and he comes snuffling over and then presents his butt for scratching.

"Your dad said he talked to them. He invited them all, I think," Jolene said, waiting to continue her combing and flat ironing while I scratch my dog's bum.

"Of course he did," I say, sitting up and throwing my hair back. My dad buys the supermarket out of hot dogs every year on Memorial Day so he can invite everyone he has ever met to a barbecue and he knows none of them will turn him down. Toby whines and I glance down at him. "I know, buddy," I say.

"Poor baby is suffering," Laura says. "Come here, dopey," she says, patting the bedspread next to where she's sprawled out, and he bounces over to her and tries to kill her with kisses.

"I want tonight to be over with already," I blurt out.

Jolene meets my eyes in the mirror, and Laura sits up.

"It'll be okay," Jolene says. "You like parties." She pats me on the head.

"I know," I say. "I'm good at parties."

"You are popular," Jolene says. "Even though you hate it."

"I don't hate it," I say. I pause. "I just don't get it."

"You are nice," Jolene says, and I laugh. "You are helpful," she tries again.

"Please stop," I say.

Laura shrugs. "She ain't wrong."

"I don't like my birthday party," I say.

"Well, I don't blame you," Laura says. "I've been thinking about it all day and I don't know how you can even stand to wait through all this, I mean, even through the year. You could just tell her to back off." She means my grandmother.

"Or you could take the car," Jolene suggests. "It would be nice for you to drive a car that wasn't so old."

"No," I say. "I don't even know if she's offering me a car this year. I mean, who knows."

"Maybe it's a first-class trip around the world," Laura says. "I bet she thinks that's fair."

"Maybe she'll pay for Harvard," Jolene says and I am stunned by the flash of elation that lights up my insides, but I snuff it out.

"I don't want to diet," I say.

Jolene lifts another lock of hair and combs it smooth. "It's mean that she thinks you're fat."

"That's not what's mean," I say, jerking my head away and spinning in my seat. "You think that's what's mean? I'm upset that she's calling me fat? I'm fat."

"No you're not." She looks stubborn. She crosses her arms over her chest.

I stand up, towering over her. I hold my arms out to either side. "I am fat. I am a fat person. I have a fat body. I *like* my body how it is."

She's looking away from me. "That's not what I meant."

We've never had this conversation before. The coupons were intangible, undefined irritants; the whole idea of "dieting" a theoretical concept with no actual concrete outcome and basically ignored. The *idea* of the coupons was terrible, we all agreed, but we have not talked about what it really meant.

Laura says, "Your *body* isn't your *identity* and—"

"Stop!" I cut her off because she doesn't know what she's talking about. Jolene's head snaps up, and she looks like she wants to say something. Then she looks back down at the flat iron in her hand.

"I should get dressed," I say.

"Ashley," Jolene says. She's not looking at me. She is poking at the buttons on the iron. "I think—I think maybe your grandmother just wants you to be happy. She doesn't think you're happy with your body," Jolene says. She's still not looking at me. "Being fat." She curls up a little when she says it.

"Actually," I say. I hate people who use the word *actually* to start a sentence but there I am. "*Actually*, she says *other people* aren't happy with me being fat," I snap.

My stomach rolls over, and then again. I dislike that my stomach is connected so directly to my brain. That my body is connected to my brain, for that matter. That I am being selfish, thinking I am the only one whose body is focused on, dissected, public knowledge. But I don't know what to say to Jolene except, "Are we almost done?" I think my voice is steady. My hair is slick and glossy. It falls over my shoulders. I don't want to sit back down. She nods. "Thank you," I say, and move around her, toward the closet.

The music that fills up the room starts in on the thumping. I hate this song and need to change it. Immediately.

"So you're sure, really really totally sure, that you don't want to wear the very amazing sequined skirt that is more amazing than anything else in your wardrobe," Laura says. She clasps her hands at her chest. Her look is pleading. I like that she has a perfectly round face: round cheeks and round chin and curved mouth. She's the kind of beautiful that makes people say, "Do you have a boyfriend?" And the kind of fierce that makes them afraid when she snarls at them in answer.

"No," I snap. "I said no."

Laura says "Okay!" very cheerful. Very little gets Laura upset. There is always something else to be interested in. She heads for the closet. "I'll find—*this*. This is it. I mean, you would look amazing in this. What do you think?" She holds up the dress she's pulled out of the closet. Stretchy black and short and crisscrossed with zippers and cut low at the neck too.

"Yes," I say. My grandmother will hate it.

"Yes!" she says. She does a little hop in a circle and then hands me the dress with a flourish. I drop my jeans, pull off my T-shirt, and wiggle into it.

"That is a very good dress," Jolene says solemnly.

I open the closet door and shoes fall on my head. I pull down the robe and shirts and scarves that are draped over the mirror and try to angle the door so I can see myself full length.

My hair shiny and long. The dress tight and clingy. My legs are my best feature, I know, and the skirt is very short. My chest looks prominent. Prominent is definitely the word for it. My

DNA pendant is settled in my cleavage, glinting gold. I lift it, smooth it back down, pat it for luck.

"Are you happy?" Jolene says. "It's a very good dress."

"Gold mascara," Laura says and she leaps over to my dresser, where she's left her makeup bag. She's biting her lip while she applies it and I try not to blink. I do not like things near my eyes. It takes forever but finally she steps back. "There," she says. "You are perfect."

Before I can change my mind I say, "I'm going to go find Grandmother."

"To get it over with," Jolene says.

"To tell her that this is the last time, I hope," Laura says.

"I tell her that every time, Laura." I zip up my knee boots and stand in front of the mirror again.

"I hate that she doesn't listen to you," Laura says. She's got her arms folded and she's chewing her lip.

"She listens," Jolene says. My grandmother has been taking care of Jolene since we were kids, a calm, efficient barrier between her and the worst of her parents, and apparently listening too.

"She's trying to help," I say.

She *is* trying to help. And it is smart to get this, the conversation, over with now. It is smart to escape this room and this antsy, unhappy irritability that is spilling out around me like I've sprung a leak. To go find her and not spend the party worrying. But I am already running out of courage.

CHAPTER 8

At the top of the staircase, in the dark hallway, the roar and ebb of the party seems louder than the ocean. My entire school is here, even kids from the younger grades. They are filling up the hallways. They are bouncing against one another like superheated molecules. Up here nothing has changed yet, and nothing has to change. I can feel my hands just on the verge of trembling. I spread them out in front of me and look at my fingers. They're not shaking. Not yet.

I'm not afraid of my grandmother. How could I be?

I am not afraid of my grandmother. But here is a confession.

There is always a moment, a flash of time, when I think, *This might be the time I give in.* This might be the year that I give up trying to push back in this tiny, infinitesimal way. Something will overcome me—greed, or worry that she is right. I will lose my strength. I will forget all my ideas about myself.

That is what I fear.

In my head my imaginary mother, the one who stuck around, says, *You couldn't do that. You wouldn't.*

Standing at the top of the stairs, I can't hear myself breathing under the crash of the noise rising. Then for a second it pauses. A lull. The sound of someone calling my name makes me start downstairs almost automatically, since I've been summoned this way so many times before. I'm relieved to be in motion again. Moving forward. I hang on to the railing because my boot heels are high and the runner on the stairs is old and frayed. An arm snakes through the railing and grabs me around an ankle. I almost trip. I flush bright red at the thought that someone might have seen me stumbling down the stairs.

I peer over the railing and see Hector's face turned up at me. "You look amazing," Hector shouts. He is smiling up at me and I can't help smiling back. I thump down the stairs, the party noise getting louder with every step until the noise swallows me. Hector is blocking the bottom of the stairs, stopping me before I'm all the way down. He grabs me around the waist, pressing his face into my chest. He is holding me just a little too tight, but I let him for a moment, put my cheek on top of his curls.

Then I push him back and sidestep around him and down the last few stairs. I shout at him, "Have you seen my grandmother?"

"She's in the kitchen!" I think he says and I catch my breath. He reaches out to touch my hair and to maybe hug me again. But I am lurching into motion, shouldering my way through the crowd. Everyone is wearing the masks, but I still recognize them. They're all almost as familiar as the backs of my nontrembling hands. These are people I have known nearly my whole life. They recognize me, reach out, pull me into hugs and back pats and kisses. Ace shouts, "You look awesome!" and fluffy pink Jessica asks if I've seen Brandon, and Amy, the scariest volleyball player I have ever met, tells me I clean up pretty good.

I am turning away from Nicholas, who wants to talk to me about the budget for next year's dance because he was born to be a treasurer, and I bump into Morgan, still recognizable under her scowling half-Batman face. She points at it and yells, "Where's yours?"

I shrug. She's showing me her shark teeth, and I grimace back at her. She leans in close, and I wonder if she's standing on her toes. She still doesn't quite reach my chest. She shouts, "Oh honey." She's looking at my legs. "You forgot your pants," she says, and then she's smirking up at me.

I say, "I'm wearing a dress, Morgan," and step around her. She ruins my triumphant exit, though, the way she ruined my fourth-grade science fair project. Not exactly the same way. She doesn't "accidentally" lean her elbow on me and break me. She does stop me with a hand on my arm and beckons me to lean down, but I don't like getting closer to her face. I shake her off and leave her behind.

I make my way through the piles of people and streamers

and more people who stop me and kiss me and make me feel like they see me and are *happy* to see me. They're all shouting. I keep nodding and smiling and pushing my way through. I hold my hand up to Joseph, the assistant volleyball captain who has made many noises about asking me out. He nods at me enthusiastically as I backtrack around through the dining room and spot my father and half the neighbors in a semicircle. He's waving his arms around in that way he does, and I dodge back, swinging a circle around to the other kitchen door and at the threshold I stop because there is my tall, slim, elegant grandmother, wearing a red feather boa.

She is wearing a feather boa. Brandon is wearing an identical one. He is making her laugh. The fridge door is standing wide open, too, I notice. Half-filled plastic cups are on every surface, and she never lets cups stand like that. She's laughing at something he is saying, and her face doesn't change when she sees me. I see Brandon's eyes drop to my cleavage and I try not to smirk at him.

I open my mouth. I say, "You guys are certainly laughing!" I close my eyes briefly. It echoes in my head. Instead of looking at their faces I pull a Solo cup off the top of the stack and set it down on the counter.

Brandon says, "Laura said this was going to be fun. I'm glad I came."

"That's good," I say vaguely. I hoist up a soda bottle and try to twist off the cap but my hand is slipping.

"I'll get that for you," Brandon says. He reaches for it.

"No," I say. I try not to glare at him, because I am not twelve years old. "I mean, I got it." I untwist it myself with one sharp turn. My grandmother puts her hand on Brandon's shoulder. She says, "Will you excuse us?" She doesn't shout, but we can hear her perfectly well. Brandon lifts his eyebrows at me. I blink at him. Then she's leading me out the sliding doors, onto the deck where she gave me that first envelope four years ago. Tonight it is loaded with school people and coolers full of soda. It is that kind of early twilight where it is hard to see anything but shapes. I still have the two-liter bottle of Diet Coke in my hands. It's slippery with condensation and very cold.

"Is that your private stash?" Marc Alonzo says. I turn on him. He's wearing a pile of green beads. His mask elastic is snapped across his forehead because he's wearing it backward. He's in my history class and on the soccer team, and at my sixth birthday party he peed on the back lawn because he was scared to go into the house by himself. The whole soccer team is there and they're all holding Solo cups. I'm willing to bet they're filled with beer, the way they looked shifty when my grandmother slides open the door, but she ignores them.

"Drink up," I say, and thrust the bottle into the crook of his elbow, and shit, it splashes up over his chest and down his arms. The rest of the soccer team laughs at him. I can't stop to apologize.

I'm turning away because I have to talk to my grandmother. I have to be first in this situation. I have to take control of it. She is already a tall dark shape striding across the deck. Narrow shoulders and a long silver ponytail that glimmers in the deck light. "Goddammit," I say.

My grandmother does not glance back at me as she continues on around the side of the deck and down the stairs because she knows I'm going to follow her like a baby duck. My classmates are going to talk about this little outburst as soon as I'm gone but I can't stand there all night hoping to stop them. "Okay," I say, and sprint after her and of course they start talking as soon as I move out of the puddle of light on the deck.

I follow my grandmother down the steps, across the overgrown lawn to my father's studio. It was a second garage for rich people, built to look like a barn. We are not rich people, so it has become my father's space. No one's allowed to go inside. I recognize the smell of someone smoking weed around the back— probably someone's parents—and there are Solo cups scattered through the grass.

I have to pick my way across the lawn in my boots and around all the trash. On the brick path I can walk faster but I slow down instead. I realize that the calm and rational speech I had been planning is gone from my head. I have no blue index cards. I could improvise if we were in front of Rhetoric and Debate class, talk on my feet without stammering. But this isn't Rhetoric and Debate. People don't make out against trees in Rhetoric and Debate, at least not that I've noticed and you'd think I would. Some light is creeping out from under the garage's window shades. My grandmother is standing on the flagstones in front of the door, and turns to open it.

"I don't want it," I say. I'm surprised that I say it out loud. "Whatever you're offering me this time. I don't want it. Please don't give it to me."

"You don't know what I'm offering," she says. "Come inside where it's quiet."

"No," I say.

"Well then," she says. She slips the envelope out of her pocket, and takes my hand, putting it in my palm and closing my fingers over it. She says, "Open it."

"No," I say.

"You don't know what it is," she says again.

"What?" I look at the envelope in my hand, and then flap it at her wildly. "Of course I know what it is," I say. I'm having even more trouble keeping my voice low now. "It's the same thing every year, Grandmother. You know I don't want it. I'm not going to use it, so—" I stop because I can hear myself getting shrill. I can feel that temper shimmering at the back of my mind, insanely. I can't lose my temper at my grandmother.

When you lose your temper, she has always said, you lose credibility.

I swallow and try again, talking softly, urgently, at her very still and very reasonable silhouette. "I appreciate that you worry about me, you know, it's great. Thank you. But I don't want to go on a diet." I thrust my hand out and I can feel myself squinting, trying to see her face in the dark but she's just quiet, and my hand stays outstretched and we stand there for a moment.

Then she plucks the envelope from my fingers and I am filled with a relief so strong that I almost stagger under it. I can feel her staring at me and I know she's disappointed but she understands. She's a practical woman who knows when to press an advantage and when to retreat.

"Thank you," I say as she takes a step toward the shaded window and holds the envelope up to the light.

Her profile is sharp and her fingers are narrow and quick. She flips the envelope over and slides her finger under the flap. She rips it open with a quick tug.

"Grandmother," I say.

She slides the card out and holds it out to me. "Ashley," she says.

The card is yellow in the light from the window, and her handwriting is bold this time, big markered letters.

I step forward without thinking, and step forward again and

I'm taking it from her and holding it in the light and I can't stop myself from looking at it.

Ashley Maria Perkins.
Weight-loss surgery in exchange for four years of tuition at Harvard University.

CHAPTER 9

've dropped the car keys. All the lights back in my grandmother's house are on and the music is so loud it's echoing against the trees and I can't see anything out here and my keys are gone, lost somewhere in the dark. It's too noisy to think and even if I did have the keys, even if I did have them, there's a white Toyota with a faded COEXIST bumper sticker boxing in the Volvo. I don't kick their bumper. I come close, though. I'm grinding my teeth, which is a habit I thought I had dropped forever, and my ears hurt and my grandmother is saying again, "You know I don't joke, darling." The card is crumpled in my fist—no, I'm just making a fist. The card has disappeared somewhere. I don't remember if I dropped it somewhere or threw it away from me into the dark.

I didn't lose my temper at my grandmother. She said, "I don't see why you're so upset about this," but I didn't shriek and draw out crowds of people to see who was murdering us deep in the shadows of the back lawn. But there were still people watching us, faces around the corner of the garage peering at us, people on the deck. Brandon standing next to Laura on the steps down to the lawn. Looking our way, maybe. Laura can always tell when I am "considering acting irrationally"—that's what she calls it. *Considering acting irrationally, which is very unlike you, Ashley.* Maybe she can tell from a distance. We've never tested it. Why am I thinking about things like this?

Maybe they didn't see anything. Maybe they didn't notice me escaping down the driveway from my father's studio.

I'm pacing around the car parked behind mine and I think I see a glint in the grass, but my shadow blocks the light. I drop to my knees and search in the tall blades. The front lawn is too long because I forgot to remind my father to refill the gas tank on the mower, or maybe he just forgot to do it after I asked. Combing my fingers through, hoping Schatzi, the neighbor's French bulldog, hasn't been escaping through the screen door again, crashing headlong and leaving a big hole behind him because he's so excited to be crapping on our lawn. My dress is too tight to be kneeling on the ground like this and the urge to run away is swamped by a wave of tiredness. That's what this was supposed to be, running away—but just to take a breath, in and out, while I work out how I'm supposed to respond to my grandmother. To the idea of weight-loss surgery.

My grandmother thinks I need *surgery*.

No. My grandmother knows which buttons to push.

She knows that what I was looking at was the words *Full Tuition* and that my heart stuttered and leaped all at the same time before any other words on the card made sense.

I said, "Why? Why wouldn't you just pay for me to go to school if that's something you can do?"

She said, "Because it would be worthless."

"Worthless," I repeated. "I don't know what that means," I said.

"Ashley," she said, in the voice that can flay her residents at the hospital. "Think about it."

"About how I'm *worthless*?" I said.

As I'm kneeling on the lawn the front door opens, of course it does, and everything gets brighter and this dress is too goddamn tight to let me stand up with any kind of dignity, but I don't care. I haul myself up and run my fingers through my hair. I can't see through the bushes and over the railing from here, but I hear Laura say, "No, she didn't say she was leaving," and I sigh. She says, "I'll be right back," and I know she's coming to see if my car is still here.

She glides down the stairs in her heels and right past me. She says it's a life skill to always look graceful in dangerous situations. It is also a life skill to wear whatever you want with all the aplomb in the world. Laura's taste in clothing is "everything." She's dressed up now, changed out of her shorts and into a maxi-length red dress that makes her dark skin look like it's glowing from a fire beneath the surface, a sculptural dress draped down her body as if she were an artist's model. Fabric flutters over her shoulder. No mask, just a tiara. She looks like she doesn't belong here in this town.

She *doesn't* belong here in this town.

We all know every corner and hiding spot and person and secret here, and that's enough for most of us. That'll never be enough for her. Or me. I want to leave more than I have ever wanted everything.

Laura stands with her hands on her hips at the end of the walk, peering down the street like she's trying to decide which way to go.

"Hi," I say to her, and she spins around.

She sighs. She says, "Your zippers are shiny," and I look down at myself. I'm glinting geometrically. And my knees are dirty.

"I lost my keys. Do you have your phone?"

"It didn't go well," she says flatly. She pulls her phone out of the little silver furry bag she has dangling from her wrist and hands it to me.

"No. Is she looking for me?" I ask, turning the phone over in my hands.

"You're being illogical," my grandmother had said. "I'm not suggesting that you are worthless. I said no such thing." She moved toward me, as if she were going to put her hands on my shoulders and shake some sense into me, but I stepped back out of her reach.

"Then I have no idea what you mean," I said. "No idea." I cleared my throat and this was the exact feeling: my heart had dissolved so it was an acidic mess in my chest, leaking into the rest of my body. Just like that.

"Ashley," my grandmother said. And I had to turn and walk away from her. I was going to be the one to end this.

"Principle Simons is talking to your grandmother about the Organic Food for Every Neighborhood Initiative," Laura reports. "And she's *demanding* that your father feature the school in his real-estate listings. She's frothing about it. Waving her hands around. She's very worked up. Her teeth are huge, did you ever notice that?"

"Wait, my grandmother's?" I think maybe I've lost the thread of the conversation. I can't focus very well on what Laura is saying.

"No, Principle Simons." Laura waves her hands around and her wrist bag bobs and dives.

"Okay," I say. "I need to find my keys."

Laura pulls me into a quick hug. She's as tall as me in those heels. "We'll find them," she says.

"Okay," I say. I pick my way out of the grass and head down the walk, using Laura's phone screen as a flashlight. Nothing is glinting.

"This is perfect," I say.

"Ashley," Laura says, spreading her arms wide, her purse swinging in circles from her wrist. "It's a beautiful night and every single person in this town is trying to fit in your living room. They all love you, and they've eaten all your tamales."

"All of them?" I say. I stop in the middle of the road. Both ends of the street are dark and I realize I hadn't picked a direction to go in anyway.

"I got one but Morgan ate most of it while she was trying to sell me on being treasurer this year, which is really highly unlikely and she knows that. Pretty sure the girl was after my food, which is immoral and not behavior suited to a class president and future legislator."

That's something Laura's dad says when he's moved to act like a father in the brief glimpses she gets of him. *Young lady, that dress is not suitable for a future legislator.* As if her dad is not perfectly aware that Laura is not going to be legislating anything except her own life.

"At least he thinks I'm smart enough," Laura sometimes says.

"I want to play skee ball," I say now.

Laura claps. "Tickets! I will win all the tickets and we will get pirate hats. I'll text Jolene. Let's take my car." She's fumbling in her furry bag again and produces her key fob. She is not going to press further, she is not going to ask me more, she is not going to give me advice. She's heading down the block to her MINI Cooper and she's walking like a supermodel down the middle of the pockmarked road, her heels ticking off the beat of the music inside the house.

"Should we change?" I say.

"Never change," Laura calls over her shoulder.

Again I hear my grandmother saying, "You're being illogical. I said no such thing. You know exactly what I mean."

She had moved toward me, as if she were going to put her hands on my shoulders and shake some sense into me, but I had stepped back out of her reach.

"I have no idea," I had said. "No idea."

I had been ready to walk away, but then my grandmother had stepped forward so I could see her face in the light. She had cupped my cheek, squeezed my shoulder. "I love you. You know that." She had stroked my hair back from my face. "I want you to think about your future. We'll talk about it tomorrow. Go enjoy your party." And then she was the one who had walked away.

I've stopped in the middle of the street and Laura is almost around the bend ahead of me. I want to run after her, so I do. I race down the street with my hair flying and bump into her with a hug and she laughs.

"See? I told you things were perfect," she says. She throws her hands up in the air. "All the things." Her face is bright in the moonlight and sparkly with makeup and her tiara is askew. Jolene is bounding toward us, her face alight. "You're perfect," Laura says. When she hugs me I'm glad they can't see this sudden, unfamiliar doubt I feel twisting my face.

CHAPTER 10

Monday and the test both come too soon.

My test-taking ritual, especially for physics: I get up two hours early. I put my hair in a giant messy bun on top of my head so that it is all out of my way, and I wear something pretty close to pajamas, only marginally more socially acceptable. I swing through the Beans There Done That drive-through, which is the only place open at four in the morning because otherwise I would boycott it for the execrable pun. The exhausted dude at the window always blinks at me when I order an extra-large, extra-hot black coffee (the mocha with whip is my reward for getting through the test), as if he can't believe he gets to avoid using the espresso machine. The paper cup is always too hot to handle for long, even with the heat sleeve, but I take a tiny sip anyway as I pull forward. My whole body and every part of the inside of my head jerks awake, glowing red and warm and bright.

The car windows are all rolled down and I take a sharp left

out of the parking lot, balancing my cup and hitting the gas hard to shoot through the middle of downtown and veer onto the coastal road that will take me through three towns and back, just barely in time for class. My ritual is that I don't think—I have been thinking a lot, too much, all the time, for the previous week, all the way up to the test. Now I need that drive to clear it all out, to breathe in the dust of the universe and breathe out the shards of stress or whatever our yoga instructor is always saying. All I know is that rituals are important.

But I can't make myself stop thinking this time.

We ditched the rest of my birthday party and drove down to San Luis Obispo, all the windows open and blowing away all the things I didn't want to admit to them. I felt cold and clear and cleaned out by the time we reached the all-night diner, filled with local college students who hooted as we walked in. Over disco fries, I said the words—*weight-loss surgery*. I didn't look at either of them. Jolene touched the back of my hand lightly, and Laura made an angry noise.

"No," I said. "Not right now. We can talk about it later."

"Skee ball?" Jolene said, and we walked the three blocks over to Dizzy's. She bought us all foam pirate hats with the tickets she won. We had more coffee at the diner when we realized none of us wanted to go home. We drove back as the sky was getting pale and bright.

Sunday I stayed in my room with my textbook in my lap and

my phone turned off and my door locked. "She's got a test," I heard my father explain to Lucas when I dashed from my room to the bathroom across the hall, into the kitchen, and then right back up the stairs. Everyone knew the ritual and I was taking a lot of grim satisfaction in the idea that I wasn't hiding from anyone, just doing what I always do. I forgot to say good-bye to Mateo and Lucas when they were leaving, or I didn't hear them go.

I spent Sunday thinking about nothing but differentials, and now that there was no book in my lap, just endless empty space stretching ahead of me in the dark, my brain seizes the opportunity to drive me crazy. Dragging me through scenarios— where I told my grandmother off; where I ripped that little slip of paper up and threw it in her face; where I announced to the party that my grandmother was trying to bribe me (public shame is intolerable for her—there's a reason she refused to accompany my brothers into town until they were of legal age); where she handed me an envelope with the business card of a used-car dealer tucked inside, no strings attached to trail on the floor between us and trip me up.

Worse: Picturing surgery. Weight-loss surgery. Doctors opening up a flap in my gut and lifting it like the hood of a car, digging elbow-deep inside of me. Hauling out all the broken parts and leaving them in a steaming heap on the floor of the operating room. Me sprawled on the operating table, helpless and huge. My grandmother standing next to my limp, torn-open body with a mask snapped over her face, in pearls and scrubs, looking terribly satisfied.

I'm cresting a slope, swinging around a sharp turn where the road feels carved into the cliff over the sea, and then I find myself abandoning my ritual, skidding into the turn-about, flipping a U-turn, and peeling out to the sound of clattering gravel. Heading back into town, past my house, pulling into the parking lot of the school. It's still empty except for the janitor's car. I know she's smoking by the gym doors. She doesn't look surprised when she sees me coming.

"Tonya, can I go in?" I say, and she smiles at me. She's let me in before.

She says what she always does, which is, "Don't tell Simons," as she stands and swings open the door, gestures me ahead of her. "And don't break anything."

"Why would I ever talk to Principle Simons?" I say, as I always do, and then "thank you!" as I'm racing up the carpeted ramp toward the library.

The library is kind of like an aquarium: a couple of thousand square feet staked out by floor-to-ceiling glass walls. People who are less studious can stop and stare at the very studious people inside with the drooping mouths and the sense of being trapped underwater forever in a hell not of their own making. I don't like the library very much. But it's got computers—in fact, it's mostly computers, because Principle Simons believes in the information superhighway more than she believes in most things except a Whole Spirit and a Healthy Mind. Maybe that's why the door is locked. I rattle the handle, and then again, and then I step back and notice my reflection in the dark glass. My hair is sticking out of the bun and there's a curl that's fallen down my neck and my glasses are slightly askew and then a face is superimposed on mine and I scream as it comes at me.

"Oh man, I'm sorry," Brandon says when he swings open the door, reaching for my shoulder. "I thought you saw me coming. I thought you were waiting for me to open the door." I start to giggle helplessly and then he is giggling too, both of us giggling like idiots in the dark together.

"No," I say, catching my breath. "No, I wasn't expecting you. I wasn't expecting anyone. So, you know, the screaming. But I'm—I'm good. I'm jumpy. I'm just. I have a test." I realize he's still got his hand on my arm and I duck around him into the dark library. We do have chemistry, no matter what he said last year. He'll never find out that I cared, even briefly, what he thought about my size. "Thank you," I say. Then, as it occurs to me, "Why are you sitting in the library in the dark with the door locked?"

"I didn't realize it locked like that," he says, and in the low lights from the hallway I can tell he is embarrassed, the way he ducks his head and scratches the back of his neck. The way he used to get embarrassed when we were kids and my mom teased him about how much he must love her beans and rice, since he was coming over for dinner every night that summer while Laura was at art camp. That was the summer he asked if he could kiss me and I shouted *no* and threw my plastic shovel at him and ran down the beach, my hair streaming behind me. I never told anyone about it. Does he even remember?

Instead I say, "I don't know, you seem kind of suspicious." It comes out accusatory and I cringe.

"I'm just studying," he says, smirking, with his hands in his jeans pockets.

"I'm sorry," I say, and he laughs.

"It's only Literature," he says. "Joyce. It's just quieter here. Laura's always—" He waves his hands around.

His gesture is the international sign language for, *She's always up until four in the morning painting and playing house music way too loud.*

"I'm here for that, too," I say stupidly. "But physics." Why else would I want to break into a locked and dark library myself?

"I thought you usually drove around before a test," he says.

I blink. "How do you know that?" My hand goes up to my messy bun, which is collapsing under the weight of its own gravity, and I can tell I look insane.

"Well," he says. "You know. I think you've mentioned it. Laura's mentioned it."

I feel the giggles rising back up and I clear my throat hard and awkwardly.

"Okay," I say. "So, uh, I just have to look something up." I march past him to the bank of shiny Macs sitting in formation up and down the center tables. His bag and books are at the far right near the printer banks, so naturally I head to the far left and smack the mouse to wake up the monitor. And then I smack it again. And then I pound the space bar on the keyboard.

"You have to turn them on. Dr. Trujillo shuts them off before she leaves at night," he says. I hate him a lot for a moment, and then sigh.

"Thanks," I say, because I am not unreasonable, just awkward.

"You know, you can log in at home," he says.

"Oh?" I say, as the library page comes up.

We're both silent for a moment, and then I say, "I never like to do things the easy way."

"That's what Laura tells me," and he's smiling at me in the bluish light of the computer.

"Oh," I say cleverly. "Well. I'm going to look things up now."

"Okay," he says, nodding, and he doesn't move.

"Okay," I say. "Good luck studying."

"Right," he says, and shakes his head and lopes back to his chair. He picks up his book but he keeps glancing over at me. I don't know how I'm going to concentrate, but my hands are steady when I type in my log-in info, scroll down through the database listings to medical journals.

When I am certain he can't see my screen, I type *weight-loss surgery* and hit enter.

Brandon leaves before I do, but I don't pay much attention. I don't look up from the monitor until the lights flicker on and then Dr. Trujillo is saying, "What are you doing in here so early? Did I give you a permission slip? I don't remember giving you a permission slip," in her slightly befuddled way.

I've taken notes. Almost automatically I reached for the stack of scrap paper and started writing down words like *malabsorption* and *gastroesophageal junction* and *duodenum*. I've gone beyond basic biology and how food proceeds through your body and then out, and now I'm deep in the minutiae of digestion and all the ways you can prevent it. All the ways you can starve your body with a surgeon's knife. Right now I know what my stomach looks like, in cartoonish flat profile helpfully color-coordinated in primary colors, with arrows pointing to all the parts that can be improved, and dotted lines indicating which parts will instead be sliced off and discarded.

I know how digestion works, and how we can fool it. I know that the body is smart, and the body is adaptable, and the body will always try to find a way, but we are smarter. We are smarter than our bodies and science has figured out a method, a clumsy method full of hacking and stitching back up, to undo biology and remake it. A messy sewing project that's designed to circumvent nature, bypass evolution, fix everything that went wrong with your guts somewhere along the way. Because that's the overall message. Your digestive system might look like everyone else's digestive system—side by side with a skinny person's stomach diagram, your colors would match and your arrows would point to the same things and you could never definitively choose one and say, "There. That's the gut of a person who never second-guesses her ass in skinny jeans." But a fat person's digestion is invisibly broken.

I understand the basic process of digestion now. I can draw you one of these gut diagrams. I could waltz into an operating room and announce that I'd take it from here, I've seen the pictures. I understand what weight-loss surgery does and why it works—because your stomach can't fit any food inside it when it's been cut down to a quarter of its original size. Because your intestines can't absorb calories and fat when you've rearranged them to bypass those mechanisms that happen naturally (oh, the aha moment when I realize that that's where the *bypass* in *gastric bypass surgery* comes from).

I can't find any photos of real stomachs. I want photos of pink and glistening organ meat. I want pictures of torn-open guts. I want to see stitches and staples but these studies don't offer anything but pages of statistics and diagrams and medical words.

All of it seems one clean, logical step removed from reality. Dieting is a messy solution full of *what ifs* and possibilities and so many pitfalls, a thousand of them, and all of them assignable to personal failures and human weakness. A dieter can try and a dieter can fail—and does most of the time—and dieting doesn't work because it's more than calories in and calories out, these journals tell me. Dieting doesn't work but it's not the dieter's fault that they're weak. And it's not the fat person's fault they're fat. But that can be *fixed* and that can be rearranged—literally—and everything and everyone can live happily ever after.

I can see clearly—oh, so clearly—why this appeals to my grandmother. The numbers, the biology, the idea that there is a simple solution to the endlessly vexing problem that your granddaughter refuses to even acknowledge exists. Just send her in to the mechanic, get her back the next day with her digestion hosed out and her windows washed and fluids topped off. It's cleanly anatomical, filled with neatly delineated starts and stops.

I was tempted to print out all these studies, all these articles about weight-loss surgery, and carry them around with me but I was already carrying it around. I could feel all that information, all those words and pictures growing huge in my brain, making me feel larger and heavier than ever.

I drag it behind me out of the library and through the halls, weaving between all the people who have always known me and wouldn't know what to do with a different me, one that had been tuned up and turned back onto the world with a whole new circuit board. The warning bell, and I start running because the word *test* flashes bright in my head. I have a test, something real, something I need to be present and focused for, something that is happening now.

Dr. Reinhart is closing the door of the classroom as I fling myself at it, red and damp and feeling all that tiredness crashing against my back as it catches up to me. And my head feels stuffed with everything I hadn't gotten rid of, that was supposed to be blown out and cleared away by a fast drive down the coast. Full of everything I've added, things I need to think about, things I can't think about right now because there's too much that's more important and I don't understand enough about this feeling in my gut—my actual gut, the maladjusted lump inside me that is twisting in knots like it was aware it was being talked about. Aware that things could be coming down the pike if my grandmother somehow got her way.

Everyone in class has got their books away and their calculators and pencils on the desks and they're all staring at me or whispering to one another, a little hum and buzz rising up that sounds like the fluorescent lights Principle Simons had all torn out because she was convinced they cause cancer. It's like they've never seen someone late to class before. Reinhart says, "Nice of you to join us, Ashley," as if no one has ever made that joke and she is the funniest person ever.

I face front, and the test is passed back along the rows; Emma, in front of me, turns to hand me the stack, smiling at me warm and friendly-like for no good reason because seriously we're about to take a test, and then settling back in her seat. I realize I'm frowning at the back of her head as I drop the stack over my shoulder without looking, and I know I need to get some sleep before I start trying to set everyone on fire with my mind just for glancing sideways at me.

Reinhart says "Go" and I flip over the sheet. Feel better almost immediately. Everything here is familiar. It is easy to settle into the things I know and the things I understand. Things that are real, unequivocal. Things that can't be broken.

CHAPTER 11

Brandon. Brandon again. Brandon suddenly everywhere. He is staring at me when I push through the glass doors of the cafeteria, which is essentially a greenhouse filled with café tables and organic vegetables grown in waist-high poured concrete planters that alternate rows with the seats. He leaves the restaurant line and heads directly over to me. I resist the urge to dodge behind a tomato plant.

He skids to a stop and leans forward, his voice just barely above a whisper. "Did you find what you were looking for?"

I realize I'm staring instead of answering, and just shake my head no. He's talked to me more in the past few days, at the party, this morning, than he's talked to me since I asked him out. He had promised me we were great friends, but somehow we just stopped. Now I have the urge to confide in him, though I never have before. *I found everything except what I was looking for,* I could say dramatically. Sometimes I worry that I have poetry in me, the kind that makes you sentimental and sappy and vulnerable.

"I'm sorry," he says. He hesitates. His eyes go soft. I've seen that look on boys' faces and I think I'm panicking about it.

"Okay, bye!" I shout, and dodge around him, fast-stepping it to our regular table.

"Where'd you go Saturday night?" Hector says, dropping his recyclable organic corn-product tray on our little café table just as I sit in front of the latte Laura's already gotten for me. The bamboo centerpiece wobbles and falls over, but Jolene catches it. Hector has stacked three slices of vegan pizza on top of one another, with extra soy sausage on the top. The chefs give him extra anything he wants. He just thinks they're super nice and friendly. If he were more self-aware he'd be dangerous. *If he were more self-aware, he wouldn't be with*— I stop myself in the middle of that.

He says, "You left your own party. I was looking for you." When he hauls out his chair he knocks into the table behind us. The Rebus Club kids glare at him.

"I texted you," I say. "The house was crowded. I had to go."

"Yeah, but for the whole night?" he says. His eyebrows are all rumpled up and he looks puzzled. "You didn't even find me before you left. And then you were gone for the rest of the party. I called you." He looks sad. "You didn't even text me back Sunday. I wrote a song about it."

My heart squeezes. I rest my head against his shoulder. "I'm sorry," I say. "I needed to go." I had ignored his calls and texts. I couldn't have told him about weight-loss surgery. No matter how well I know him, how much I love his arms around me and his kisses on the side of my neck—I would have been afraid to see his face. A part of me, the part that understands how the real world works, might have been scared he'd agree.

"Skee ball is a dangerous sport," Laura says. She leans forward and the tips of her scarf are dangling so close to her pile of greasy fries. "Dangerously addicting. We couldn't stop. We sold all our belongings and camped out at Dizzy's until closing and then we had to sleep in the ball pit because we couldn't afford gas."

"I would have come and got you," Hector says.

"No one can save us from ourselves," Laura pronounces solemnly.

Jolene is keeping a very straight face. She pats Hector on the hand. "You're a good boy, Hector," she says. Teasing Hector is too easy sometimes. We fall into it the way we fall into formation when we walk, the three of us in a line and our heels clicking in the same rhythm.

He looks at Jolene, and then at me. His eyebrows are pulled together and he looks kind of lost. "Okay," he says. "You don't have to tell me anything."

"She tells you everything," Jolene says comfortingly.

"She's an open book," Laura says. "She can be checked out of any library."

"I wish you would have come to find me," he says to me. I lift my head up. Before I can say anything, he continues, "Your grandmother was looking for you," and then folds half his pizza slice into his face and chews with enthusiasm.

"That's what Brandon said," I say, and then glance at Laura. She doesn't look surprised. She is squeezing a perfectly straight line of mayonnaise across her french fry, but she sets it down instead of eating it.

"Brandon found the note," Laura says, looking at me steadily. I make a choking noise and she keeps going fast, not dropping her gaze, "He was looking for my car and he saw your name on the note and he picked it up because he thought it was important."

"What note?" Hector says.

I close my eyes.

"He read it," I say. Because of course he did.

"Well, he couldn't help it," she says. She is squeezing mayonnaise on another fry and lining it up next to the first one. It looks like she's building a log cabin.

"What note?" Hector says again.

"The birthday note from my grandmother." I say. This feeling in my stomach (*the stomach my grandmother wants me to get sawed into pieces,* I think) is humiliation. Exposed and without a way to defend your vulnerable, squishy parts that are suddenly available to judge.

Did you find everything you need, Brandon had asked so solicitously. Pityingly.

"Oh yeah!" Hector says. "The car, right? Are you getting a car? What's she going to give you if you take her up on it?"

I shake my head. I can't look at him.

"Tuition," Jolene says.

"Tuition. Like for Harvard? Oh my god! That's amazing," Hector says. He takes another outsized bite, and he's smiling so his cheeks bulge out as he chews.

"Yeah," Laura says. "She gets to go to Harvard. In exchange for agreeing to her grandmother's unacceptably controlling attempts at changing her for no good reason whatsoever." She's leaning forward and her voice is rising. Jolene is keeping her head down, but glancing over at the table next to us. The entire Rebus Club is staring at us. I have never been stared at by an entire Rebus Club before and I don't like it.

"Laura, I don't want to talk about it," I say.

"It's not right," Laura keeps on. Her cheeks are darkening and soon the color will start to creep down to her chest.

I say, "She is trying to help." What I have always said.

"What?" Hector says. He's finished chewing. His last pizza slice hangs from his fist. "What is she trying to help with?"

He looks at me as if we have never had this conversation. It is maddening.

Jolene says, "Her grandmother wants her to get weight-loss surgery."

I groan. I want them all to stop talking now.

"What the hell is that?" Hector says before I can respond. He hasn't stopped staring at me. I want to ask him to keep up with us, just this once. I shake my head. This never works to clear it.

"Hector," I start.

My voice must not be clear of irritation because Jolene says, "I didn't know what it was either, Ashley. It's a fair question."

"It's mutilation!" Laura snaps. She slaps her hand against the table. Her rings clatter on the Formica. The Rebus Club is still staring. "Weight-loss surgery is a brutal maiming of the body's natural digestive system."

"What? You shouldn't do that!" Hector yelps. He puts his pizza down and his eyes are huge. "Why would your grandmother want you to do that?"

"It will make her lose weight quickly and help her keep it off permanently," Jolene says.

My friends have both done their homework, but apparently they used completely different Google searches.

"Please don't talk so loudly," I say. I've never noticed how crowded together the tables are in here.

"Right. Okay, so, what does Brandon have to do with this?" Hector asks.

"He knows about it," I say.

"Why would you tell *him* but not *me*?" His voice is plaintive.

"I didn't tell him, Hector. He found out." The exasperation and anxiety is shimmering right there at the surface of my voice and I fight to keep it from bubbling up and spilling over. He gets so hurt when I snap at him.

"He told *me* he found the note because he didn't want to make *you* feel like he was lying to you or something," Laura says, quieter now.

"I might have preferred being lied to!" I say, and now I'm the noisy one. I suck in a breath and take a sip of my latte to distract myself from trying to see who is watching us. We're a tiny school full of people who know everything that's going on with everyone. This wouldn't be a good thing to miss.

"He's probably not going to tell anyone," Jolene says.

"Probably?" I say, and I look at Laura.

"Who would he tell?" she says. "He doesn't tell people things. You know that. I mean, besides me. I'm obviously a special case because I'm his sister."

"Why does it matter if he tells anyone?" Hector says.

"Because it's nobody's business," I say. And there it is, skipping over irritation and heading straight toward pissed off. I can hear the anger in my voice. A spitting, hissing kind of thing. I can't stop myself from saying, "Do you really have to ask that?"

"Apparently," Hector says, and pushes his chair back. His face is calm and he doesn't meet my eyes. He bumps into the

Rebus Club kids but does not look at them. He rises and shoves through the tangle of tables and chairs and now even more people are looking over at us. Not in the way you always unconsciously assume that everyone is looking at you. In an absolutely concrete, all-eyes-here sort of way.

I take another sip of my latte and realize I'm trembling. "Shit," I say.

"He's mad, but he won't stay mad for long," Jolene says.

"I've never seen him *get* mad," Laura says. "I mean, I don't think I could imagine Hector being mildly miffed. Or vaguely concerned. Or even sort of irritated before now. Wow."

Never at me. He never gets irritated with me. "You are not helpful," I say to Laura unsteadily.

"You could follow him and apologize," Jolene says. "I think he'd appreciate the gesture."

"Or you can let him go off and experience for the first time what it's like to be emo! It'll be good for him. He can write a song," Laura says.

I don't want to see the look on his face. I can't talk to him right now. "I'm going to go to class," I say. Guidance is next period. It's the thing I would like to do least in the world. Thirty-five minutes of Positive Thinking and Visualizing the Future. It has finally happened—I'm tired of thinking about the future. And I don't have my essay. And Ellman is going to scold me again and talk about my grades again and *there is the chance that I can actually go to Harvard now if I finish my essay* and I cannot, cannot think about that.

"I have to skip," Laura says.

"Why do you have to skip?" Jolene asks.

"Drama club is dramatic. Wellesley wants me to come talk seriously to everyone about serious things and how we have to take everything seriously because *art*, or something like that." She waves her hand around her head like she's shooing away gnats, and then frowns. "I hope I don't miss chi breathing this time."

"I hate chi breathing," Jolene says, poking through the edamame shells in the bowl in front of her.

"You're good at it," I say. I can never bring myself to close my eyes for very long. Jolene's face is always serene and smooth and open and she is still. The only time I ever see her still.

Jolene shrugs and the chimes that signal the end of the period start to toll and it's too loud to talk anymore, with scraping chairs and everyone yelling at each other. Jolene vanishes ahead of us instead of walking with me to class, Laura peels off to go out the side door and through the courtyard, and I am left alone to weave through the maze of chairs. I keep my head down. I make it to the main hallway and the first thing I see is Brandon. The second is Morgan, next to Brandon. Morgan turns her head slightly as I pass and smiles at me. It is her wide "I am totally sincere" smile with *all the teeth. They're going to be late to Guidance,* I think, instead of worrying about how she's looking at me, how he might be looking at me.

Speculation is worthless. Maybe my grandmother has told me that.

I take careful, measured steps, because I refuse to run away. I walk until I hit the lobby and then I burst through the front doors and I can feel myself getting ready to keep walking through the parking lot and out and all the way across town and off one of the jetties into the ocean. Walking along the bottom of the sea until jellyfish sting me to death.

I stop at the curb because I don't retreat from things. And then tiny round Principle Simons is at my elbow, and hooking her arm through mine and saying, "Fresh air is always so good for the soul, isn't it?" She smells like baby powder and incense and I have to try not to sneeze it out of my nose. She gestures her administrative assistant away. "Excuse us, Quincy," she says. "I need to take a private moment here."

"Oh sure," Quincy says. He's smiling at me kindly. "Anything for rock-star Ashley, you know that." He pats my shoulder almost sympathetically and taps briskly back down the hall, shuffling through his stack of folders and never looking back. I watch his blond-and-silver head recede and my heart recedes right out of my chest when I glance back down at Principle Simons.

"Well then," Simons says. "It's a beautiful day to talk about beautiful things."

"It's too hot," I say.

She throws back her head and laughs heartily. She's got huge white teeth and short-cropped silvery hair and as always she's draped in cloth—a fluttery tunic and a flappy cardigan and wide-legged pants in maroons and reds and blues and golds and purples and greens. She is about as wide as she is short. She looks like a series of soft round bean bag chairs stacked on top of one another, comfortingly yielding.

"Oh, Ashley," she says. "Your spirit is a wildflower."

She says things like that a lot. She pats my forearm. Her hand is tiny, and her feet are tiny too.

"Thank you," I say. There is not much else to say except for that.

She swings me around and steers me back through the entrance doors. She stops in the vestibule, before the doors that open into the hallway, and the main doors close behind us. We're trapped in a little airlock.

"Your grandmother says your birthday was a smashing success," Simons says, releasing my arm and clasping her hands in front of her. "You have greeted your seventeenth year of life with great joy and new possibilities!" She smiles up at me, the skin around her eyes crinkling. The sun glints on her tiny round glasses and I blink. I can feel myself edging away from her.

"Yes," I say. "It was very nice."

"That warms my heart," she says. She puts her hand on the spot where I imagine her heart is to indicate its location, and I guess to signal the warming of it.

"Thank you," I say again, though I think I sound a little panicked this time. I step back slowly, saying, "I have to go to class now! Because my birthday is over, ha ha." I sound like my father.

"Nothing ever ends, Ashley," she says very gravely. She swings open the doors to the hallway and waves me ahead of her. "That is the nature of our journey."

"Okay," I say.

"I understand you have some big events coming up," she says. She's staring up into my eyes, unrelenting eye contact, and I flush all over, painfully too warm. She pats me on the shoulder. "Your life will change, Ashley. Your whole world will open up into a new one. Blossom like a rose or a similar flower that is yet still completely unique."

She keeps me immobile with the barrage of words that I want to swat out of the air as they come at me and wrap around me and pull tighter and tighter so it feels like my skin doesn't fit anymore and I can't possibly get more uncomfortable.

"I don't know what you mean," I grit out. And I pray silently, *Please don't tell me she means what I think she does.* My cheek twitches, and I curl my hand hard around the strap of my messenger bag.

She glances around us and pats my shoulder again. "Bariatric surgery." Simons leans back a bit and peers into my face. She looks puzzled. "Or did I misunderstand Clara?"

"Many people do," I say. I'm proud of my impression of a person who doesn't desperately want to run shrieking down the hall away from this.

"Bariatric surgery," Simons says. "It's an extraordinary opportunity. It's not too late for you. Think of what you could do."

"I'm not doing it," I say.

She doesn't stop smiling. "That would be such a mistake."

"It would be a mistake *to* do it." I am trying hard not to let my voice get loud.

"You're being shortsighted, Ashley. It's my job to point out these things. To point out that it's for your health."

"It's your job to run the school," I say.

She doesn't even blink at that. "And part of that," she says smoothly, "is helping my students understand their life paths."

"My life path is set," I say.

"It is," she says sadly. "But it's not too late."

I step back from her overwhelming smell and her teeth and her little silver glasses. She's silent with her hands still clutched in front of her, her lips pursed. And then she smiles, bright and happy.

"Come see me in my lair!" She winks. "My office, you know. After school. Let my gift of healing be my gift to the very gifted you."

"I'm fine," I say because that's the best I can do. I can't take another step back. I'm still pinned into place by her eyeballs. The bells rings, *finally* the bell rings. She twitches slightly at the noise and turns her head and that's when I flee, fast-stepping it down the hallway.

When I look back, I see of course that Simons hasn't stopped smiling. She's lifting her tiny hands in the air and all her rings are glinting as she cries out, "Oh, Tabitha! Tabitha you angel fruit, stop just a moment—" And I keep going, feeling sorry for Tabitha all the way to class.

In Guidance class we've already been broken into small groups. A more intimate way to nurture our growth as individuals and respect each other as human beings, we're told. Morgan made it before me. She's leaning into Brandon's shoulder and looking at her phone. He is sitting right next to her but he's got his hands in his pockets and is looking out the window.

Dr. Ellman does not seem to notice me gently easing the door closed. I think I've managed to sneak in, but then she spins and beams all her light at me.

I am tired of being looked at. I'm rubbed raw by it.

"You're just in time!" Dr. Ellman says. "Find a group. We're doing groups." She points at a table. "Here. This one," she says. She pulls out a chair across from Ace, who tries to high-five as I drop my books on the desk.

"No," I say.

He shrugs and leans forward and shout-whispers, "You're a goddess." He winks, except he closes both eyes. He's never been able to wink. "Ellman was just about to group with us." He rolls his eyes over at Louis, sitting next to him, hunched over his page, his pen scratching. "Which would have been lively."

To me, Ace looks just like he did when we were thirteen. I kept growing and he stayed small. He still wears Converse high-tops and skinny jeans and T-shirts. His hair always looks long, even right after he gets a haircut.

Louis doesn't look up while Ace is being noisy. His hands are covered in Sharpie lines and swoops. I don't think I've heard him say anything since the sixth grade. He is a math prodigy, happily lost in the calculations that describe the world the rest of us only live in.

I shake my head at Ace. "What are we doing?" I say. "Do not say groups."

"In a group," he says, grinning at me, "we are brainstorming our personal essays. We are coming up with five excellent subjects and then a topic sentence for each one."

I stare at him. "Not again," I say.

"Seriously," he says. He points at the board. "It's there. She wrote it down."

"I believe you," I say. "Why are we doing this? We've already written our essays. I mean, I haven't written my essay but everyone has written their essays."

He stares at me for a second. "You haven't? I thought for sure you'd have it done by now." He pauses. "I thought you'd have done it last year."

"I didn't do it last year," I say.

"Okay," he says. "You can just make stuff up, anyway." He tears a sheet out of his notebook and pushes it over to me. "Okay, write down 'essay topics' on the top line." He points at me with his pen then prints in block letters on his own page, "ESSAY TOPICS ON THE TOP LINE," and then grins at me when he turns it around to display it. My father has always liked him.

"Hey, this isn't a big deal," he says. "Don't look so worried." He's another one not going to college right away, so he can say things like that.

"I know how to make lists," I say to him.

"This is a snap then, right?" He gives me a thumbs-up.

Dr. Ellman is pacing around the perimeter of the room, her hands behind her back. She stops at the board and clears her throat. "I want you to let yourselves go for this one," she says. "I've always said that this is the only part of your application that matters. That sounds irrational, doesn't it? I know you're thinking, 'Doctor Ellman, stop being so irrational.' Or maybe, 'Doctor Ellman, it is so irrational to be coming up with more essays because we've already *written* a draft of our essays.' But that's the key here. That was for a grade. This is for your *heart*."

"Oh god," I say, and she pauses and looks around. Ace snickers.

"Your heart," she continues. "Once you let go of your ego and write from the heart—write what really matters—you'll find your real essay. Your true self. So many of you are so worried," she says, conspicuously not looking at me or maybe it just feels that way. "I'm saying—you've tried to write what you thought I wanted to see. What you thought your college wanted to see. *Now* is the time to play. To experiment. To write about what you wish you could write. Let yourself go." She throws both hands in the air and I can feel myself shaking my head so I stop.

Ace is grinning at me. "Let yourself go," he whispers.

I pull my sheet of notebook paper closer and concentrate on tearing off the spiral bits on the edge. I underline the word *essay*. I underline it twice. I write the number *1* on the first line. This is ridiculous.

When I look up, Ace's page is full. And he's got another, which he hands to me. He leans forward and says, "So I think we've come up with some really good ideas for you. The first five are a little weak, but I think we really started to get somewhere toward the end."

I look at Louis, who is still drawing and not looking at us.

"He was very helpful," Ace says, nodding. He hands me the sheet.

IDEA ONE: Valedictorian.

"No," I say.

"You haven't even read them all!" He is mock outraged, bouncing around in his seat. He takes it back from me. He starts reading but I interrupt him.

"One, valedictorian. Two, volleyball. Three, doctor. Four, rescue dogs. Five, my dream is to be a valedictorian volleyball-playing dog-rescuing doctor."

He looks at the page. "Well, not in that order."

Dr. Ellman claps her hands. "Fresh air," she says. "Switch seats with the person behind you."

It is hard to make myself stand up and turn around, but Brandon has already switched seats with the new girl. Morgan's still sitting there with her cheek resting on her hand, smiling up at me. "I had the best idea for you," she says. Next to her Jessica is doodling flowers and hearts and stars and kittens.

I frown at Morgan. "I'm sure you think so," I say. When I pull out the chair she reaches over and grabs my sheet of paper, snatching it out from between my fingers. I stop and hold out my hand.

"That's mine," I say pleasantly.

"We're swapping, Ashley," she says and pushes her laptop over to me. "I'm very helpful."

Jessica looks up and tucks a blond curl behind her ear. "Oh, she really is! Brandon is helpful too."

Morgan rolls her eyes at the same time I do and I spin her laptop around before we start giggling like schoolgirls and exchanging BFF bracelets. "Yes, super helpful I'm sure," I say. On Morgan's laptop screen, in curly font, she's telling the academic committee at NYU exactly what they want to hear. She's an athlete and so she understands drive and commitment. She believes in focus. She is a winner. She's got more than five topic sentences that all say the same thing. I say, "You've got more than five topic sentences."

She looks up from my sheet. "I've got a lot to offer," she says. "I don't need weight-loss surgery just to be normal. Which reminds me!" She slides the paper back. She's added number six to my list, and it's just that. She helpfully reads it out loud. "'Six. Getting weight-loss surgery as an inspiration to fat and poor people everywhere.'"

It feels like a camera flash has gone off in my face—violent, bright, painful. I see nothing but red and black for the longest moment and I can't hear Morgan's drawling voice and I can't make my mouth move or my lungs suck in air but I clench my teeth and I shake my head. My voice comes out rough and low. "How do you manage to be so offensive on so many levels in just one sentence?"

Morgan says, "The truth isn't offensive. It's just true."

I can feel my teeth baring in a shark smile just like hers. "So did you hear a rumor and decide it was true, Morgan? Or are you just making shit up?"

"I have my sources," she says stubbornly.

Sources. I glance one table behind ours. Brandon.

I stand up and hold out my hand to her. She flicks my paper back across the table, but I can't catch it before it flutters to the floor and slides. Ellman stops it with her foot and picks it up.

"Would you look at mine too?" Jessica says to Morgan.

"That's mine," I say to Ellman, shuffling between the tables, my hand out. "It's not ready to be looked at. I'd prefer if you didn't look at it." But she's already glancing down the list, and then back up at me with her eyebrows raised.

"Is it true?" Ellman says.

"No," I say.

"Because it could be powerful."

"It's not true," I say.

"It is a visceral subject, fraught with a lot of fear and pain and anxiety," Ellman continues. With every word she waves her hand, *fear, and pain, and anxiety*, like she's conjuring it all out of the air.

"That's not what I'm writing about."

She smiles and pats my arm. "Let's talk about it after class," she says, and hands the paper back to me.

Morgan looks like she's actually helping Jessica with her topics but I can't go sit back down with them. I fold my paper in half, creasing it hard with my fingernails and I have to find another place to sit but then I see door swing open and Jolene's face peering through the crack. I drop the paper on top of my bag and hurry over. She's leaning against the wall when I open the door. I let it fall shut hard behind me.

"Can you drive me home?" she says, straightening up. "Please drive me home. I need to go." She starts down the corridor ahead of me because she knows what I am going to say. I've left my bag behind but Dr. Ellman will hang on to it, or Ace will grab it. I imagine someone opening up that list of essay topics and I stop.

"Jolene," I say. "Jolene, I need to get my bag."

She spins. Her face does not look right. Her face does not look anything like her. "Your *bag*?" she says. "Sure, yes, please do get your bag. I'll walk home. I didn't mean to bother you in the middle of chatting with *Morgan*."

She turns again and is walking away from me.

I fly inside. When I run back out of the classroom with my bag under my arm, she's gone.

CHAPTER 12

She's not picking up her phone and she's not reading her texts and she is not appearing by the side of the road as I creep down every street that leads away from the school, leaning over the steering wheel as if that will help me see better. Jolene never has outbursts. Jolene never disappears. We're supposed to protect her, but she's vanished.

I leave Laura voice mails. I drive downtown and walk up and down Main Street. I look in the coffee shop. I head down to the jetty but she is not on the public beaches. I wade into the water to look down the shore to see if there are any small figures on the private beaches. It is too cold for anyone to be out. I get back into my car with sandy feet and make wide circles through the neighborhood, looking for her bright hair and her khaki shorts, until school is over and I've been driving forever and I still can't find her.

I have to pull over when I think, *Should I be looking for a pile of cloth by the side of the road?* I have to get out of the Volvo and rest my head against the hood for a moment. I shut my eyes and listen to the ping of the engine as it cools down, smell the familiar sun-warmed metal and rust. I think about calling Hector. He'll reassure me. Tell me this isn't my fault and I am a good friend. And then I remember him walking away at lunch.

I straighten up and look at my phone. Laura picks up on the first ring. "God. There you are. Have you heard from Jolene?" I say. I lean against the side of the car and look up at the sky, which is a blue that does not look real.

"She called me," Laura says. "But she didn't pick up when I called her back." She stops. "She okay?"

"No," I say, and I hear Laura draw a breath.

"What's going on?" she says. "Oh god I should have called her back right away. Why am I such a shitty friend?"

"You're not," I say.

"Omar's stupid studio time is pointless," she says. "I could have just picked up the phone it wouldn't have even mattered she's more important than modeling, oh shit Ashley."

"I thought you were in drama club. Or did you drive all the way to San Francisco?"

"I didn't feel like going to drama club," she says. I can hear voices in the background, Laura responding.

"Laura," I say. "Where would she go if she were upset?"

She comes back. "Home?" she says.

"She *wouldn't* go home," I say. "She would *never* go home when she was upset."

Laura is silent. We both know that Jolene's parents treat her very gingerly. They are friendly to her—I'm reminded of someone being polite to a stranger on a bus. They ask after her well-being. They tell her that they would like her to be happy, Jolene says, but they don't know what that means. And they don't care about finding out.

When she was seven and said that she was not a boy, she was not David, they took her very seriously. They thought that there was something wrong with her. That she was broken and delusional and that they had done something to her. Had twisted her somehow. They said, "Is it because we are divorcing?" but that was the first time she had heard about that. They pretended they had never said it and they might have been relieved.

Her parents made appointments with the counselors at school, and they got another copy of the *Humanism Handbook*. I remember running to find her after that appointment, and stopping short when I saw her father tearing it in half in the parking lot, Jolene just watching him.

Her parents made appointments for her at psychiatrist offices, and took her to a new one every time a doctor said that there was nothing wrong with her. They would not listen to a doctor speak about transition strategies, or support groups, or anything that suggested she was normal but struggling. They wanted to hear that she was damaged, that "sex is a biological reality not subordinate to subjective impressions," etcetera, etcetera.

At school, she changed every morning into a dress in a bathroom lounge near the counselor's office because she felt she had to convince everyone she really meant it.

She told me about all of this only in bits and pieces and during quiet moments.

What I really remember was that one day, she was not in school and then after that she wasn't there any other day for a month. When I rode my bike over to her house her parents told me that she was sick. They wouldn't say with what. I remember my grandmother leaving the house with a plastic container of chicken soup. She was gone for hours and when she came home, Jolene was in the car with her. She had her pillow and her blue denim duffel bag.

My grandmother had said, "She just needs to rest for a while."

Jolene stayed with us for a week. She slept in my trundle bed. After we turned out the lights, if I looked over the side I could see her lying on her back with her hands folded at her waist. Her eyes were open and she was staring at the ceiling. She would never say anything. I never knew what to say and I did not know how to help and I called her Jolene like she asked because she was still the same person I knew. Sometimes I wished she wouldn't keep doing it. She didn't have to let anyone else see, I thought. I didn't understand.

Her parents didn't call her at all that week, or come to see her, or demand that she come home. When I was seven I did not think about that.

When we met Laura in fifth grade, Laura told Jolene she liked her dress. She was outraged that Jolene couldn't wear it after school. But with Laura there, Jolene felt safe. Laura, flashing braces and a head full of perfect tiny braids, strange to the upper-middle-class white teachers who couldn't figure out how to treat her like a student instead of an opportunity to demonstrate their open-mindedness. My temper; Laura's quiet force, standing straight and looking them in the eye and telling them exactly what she thought. Jolene always there between us, the tiny figure with the serene face, twisting her hands in her skirt, safe. Our job.

I pull the phone away from my ear and check the time. "It's been hours," I tell Laura. "Come over. Maybe we can figure out where to go."

"I can't yet," she says. "Wait, maybe. Hang on." I hear her talking to Omar in the background and I hang up and get back into the car. I sit there for a minute. I stare through the windshield and then start the car because I am not sure what else to do.

I think about that as I drive down the back road to Jolene's house. They live in a development with an iron gate all around it. Every house is the same as the one next to it. The lawns are very green and the stucco of each house is one of three shades of brown.

That week Jolene stayed with us we ran down the beach every morning and went swimming and climbed the trees in the yard and we told each other an ongoing story, about an undercover princess who travels the world righting wrongs and unleashing justice and we ate a lot of Otter Pops. That is my strongest memory, the taste of salt on my lips, sweet, slushy ice pops, how hot it got that summer. Plunging into the water together, holding hands. The shock of cold.

Jolene had not slept at night. But when she went back home, she was wearing the clothes my grandmother had taken her shopping for. We dropped her back at her house and watched her carry her duffel bag inside, her narrow shoulders squared and skirt swinging.

My grandmother's mouth was grim. She said, "The world can be a cruel place, Ashley."

Now at Jolene's house, there are no cars in the driveway. I stab at my phone keypad. Jolene still doesn't pick up. Laura doesn't pick up. My grandmother picks up. I didn't mean to call her but her number is in my head whenever I am lost.

She says, "Ashley, are you on your way home?"

"No," I say. "Jolene is missing."

"She's here," my grandmother says.

"Oh god," I say, my breath coming out with a whoosh like I've been punched. "Oh, okay yes."

"Come home now," she says. I hang up the phone but she calls back immediately. "Bring sugar," she says. "She likes her tea sweet."

"I know," I say.

"Then bring it home," my grandmother says. She hangs up on me this time instead.

When I get home I find Grandmother and Jolene in the parlor off the kitchen. My grandmother has set out the formal tea service. Four cups and the serving bowls. She must know Laura is on her way too. Jolene is a ball tucked in the corner of the couch. She looks like she is the size of one of my grandmother's scratchy, musty embroidered throw pillows that my mother used to hide.

"Jolene," I say. I have the bag in my arms. I hold it up. "I brought sugar."

She looks at me. She's been crying. She looks at the sugar in my hands and her face contorts and she starts crying again. My grandmother sips her tea.

I rush over to sit next to Jolene. The couch dips down, bouncing her so her sob hiccups slightly. I put the bag of sugar in her lap. She looks at it and looks at me and she laughs. It's a short laugh that sounds like the rest of her crying. She does not stop crying. She puts her face down on top of the bag.

My grandmother catches my eye and nods at the sugar bowl

on the coffee table. Jolene has her arms around the bag of sugar now. Holding it like you would hold a teddy bear.

"Darling," my grandmother says, leaning forward and putting her fingertips on Jolene's knee. "Won't you let Ashley make you a cup of tea?" Jolene looks at each of us, and then down at the sugar on her lap.

"Right," she says.

I pick up the sugar bowl. "I'll just. I'll fill this."

"I'll go with you," Jolene says. My grandmother raises her eyebrow, just one, at us. She sips her tea again.

"Cookies," my grandmother says to me. "Cookies are quite good for this sort of thing." She adds, "Not too many, Ashley." I turn abruptly away.

Jolene is still holding the bag of sugar. She hauls herself off the couch and starts for the kitchen ahead of me. She seems so small. Why does she always seem so small to me? Things that are small are breakable, I think. They're delicate. They're precious.

"I'm sorry," Jolene says when we are standing in the kitchen and I am tipping the sugar into the bowl. She won't meet my eyes.

"What are you sorry for?" I ask. "You shouldn't have run off like that. You scared the shit out of me. But you don't have to be sorry for it."

"I'm sorry!" she says. Her face is doing that thing where it falls apart again and I cannot stand it.

"Stop that," I say. "Please, just stop."

She looks up at me and I have to drop the sugar bag and put my arms around her shoulders. I have to hug her even if my hugs are awkward and unhelpful. Even if I am unhelpful.

"I'm sorry," she says again and then, "I'm sorry I didn't mean to be sorry!"

"Okay," I say. "It's okay."

She lets me hug her for few moments before extracting herself. I finish filling the sugar bowl, and then hand it to her.

"What happened?" I say. "What's going on?"

She looks at the sugar bowl and then sets it down on the counter. The front door opens and I know Laura is making her way directly to the kitchen. Jolene tilts her head and I nod. She turns when Laura walks in, lets Laura hug her for a long time.

"I was scared," Laura says simply.

"I was too," Jolene says.

We're all silent. Jolene picks up the lid of the sugar bowl, spins it around in her hands. "Simons stopped me in the hallway when I was on the way to class." She is biting her lip and her foot is tapping fast. "She stopped me and she said she was worried about my happiness."

"She did that to me too today," I say.

"How is that her business?" Laura says.

I turn on the water in the sink and hold the kettle under the faucet, flip the burner on, and set the kettle down.

Jolene shrugs, and her face is on the edge of falling inward again. She grips the edge of the counter. She says, "She said my parents called."

"Why would they call?" Laura says. "Why now?"

I inspect the excessive number of tea varieties in the cabinet. My father collects teas with pretty boxes or weird names or strange flavors. No one needs to drink chocolate tea. I am trying not to look at Jolene, to just let her talk, but I sneak a glance. She's clenching her jaw and bouncing just the tiniest bit on the balls of her feet. Laura is sitting cross-legged on the counter, looking at her hands.

Jolene says, "My parents asked me my plans. My plans for— for my life. For everything . . ." She trails off.

Laura and I are silent. When Jolene looks up, her eyes are huge. She opens her mouth, and closes it again.

"What did you say?" I can't stop from asking. She is fierce about her desire never to talk about the "Next Steps," that section every website and flyer and pamphlet includes at the end. *You are transgender. What do you do next? What do you do about this body you have?* And I have gotten loud, furious at the curious people who want to talk about what's under her clothes. I realize I have always assumed that she'd take Next Steps. That it's what you're supposed to do.

Jolene shrugs.

"I hope you told them it was none of their business," Laura says.

"You're the only one who can get away with that," Jolene says quietly.

"Fuck," Laura says. I glance over at the door to the parlor, where grandmother is sitting. I don't know if she can hear us.

"What did—what did your parents say?" I ask.

Jolene's face twitches and she is on the verge of tears again. "My decisions are 'unacceptable,' they said. And they called the school to tell them—to tell them that their policy is unacceptable. That I am David. And if the school doesn't comply—" She takes a deep breath. "I won't be going back to school. And if I don't comply, I won't be going back home."

"No," I say. *"No."* I take two big steps over to her and she's smiling at me, just a small smile. She shakes her head, a quick fond, *Oh, Ashley.*

"Oh yes," she says. She swallows and says, "So, Simons wants to step in. She wants to *intervene.* She wants to *mediate.* She wants to get me into a program that can support me through the preliminary steps."

"Well that's good . . . right?" I say hesitantly.

She goes on. "And my parents want to send me to—to an inpatient program."

"Oh hell no," Laura says. Her voice is low and furious.

"Simons can help, though," I say excitedly. "I mean, we can fix it so—"

"No," she says. "You can't fix everything. Especially me."

"I don't think you need to be fixed!" I say. "I didn't say that."

In the next room my grandmother says, "Ashley?"

I lower my voice. "I'm sorry. I just." I don't know what to say.

"Everyone wants to fix me," Jolene says. She has gone perfectly still, staring at the counter with her arms crossed over her chest and her narrow shoulders hunched. I put my hand out and then pull back when the kettle goes off. My grandmother calls again when I lift it off the stove. I step around Jolene, who hasn't moved at all, and peer into the parlor.

"The tea?" grandmother says.

"Almost done."

"Your voice."

"Okay," I say.

"But how can they do that?" Laura says behind me. "Any of them?"

Jolene shakes her head. One shoulder goes up. "My parents tell me that while I am under their roof I am subject to their concerns about my psychology and my perversion."

I grimace and Laura yelps at the word. "They're just going to have to—"

Jolene interrupts hard. "I didn't tell them what I wanted to do. I *don't know* yet." Her face is miserable, her hands twisting. "But they want to know what I think transitioning will accomplish. 'Do you really think you'll be happy when you're a real girl?' my father says. Just like that."

"Oh Jolene," Laura says. "No."

"Principle Simons told me all about what she said to them. She said that my parents can't hold me back and I am a butterfly and George Love Academy is a chrysalis and I am meant to be free but it would be cruel to let me do it alone."

I turn back to the stove, drop a handful of chamomile bags into the teapot to steep.

"And my mother said that it would be kinder to be cruel," Jolene continues. "At least until I come to my senses."

She slips between Laura and me. She picks up the teapot with two potholders. I don't know what to say to her. She carries it out of the room cradled in both hands, and I hear my grandmother say, "Ah, Jolene. Thank you, darling."

Laura looks at me and turns to go into the parlor after her.

I pick up the sugar bowl and follow them. Jolene's already curled up into a small ball again at the farthest corner of the couch. Laura is sitting on the other side of the coffee table with a cookie in her mouth.

"You'll stay in the guest room of course," my grandmother says, holding her hand out to me for the sugar bowl. A sleepy Soto pads into the room and circles around me, bumping her head into my knees and under my hand. Her fur is warm from the sun. I sit on the floor and put my arms around her neck, but she pulls free and jumps onto the couch, circles twice, and puts her chin down on Jolene's knee with a sigh.

Jolene says, "Thank you." I don't know if she's talking to Soto or my grandmother. She reaches out and runs her fingers down Soto's nose, again and again, and Soto closes her eyes in bliss.

"You can stay wherever you need to," I say. My grandmother leans forward to start pouring the tea. "You can do whatever you want to, you don't have to—"

"I know that," Jolene says. Serene face.

"You're brave," I say. My grandmother holds out a cup to me and I climb up off the floor, sit next to Jolene on the couch and pick up the teapot.

"Shut up, Ashley," Jolene snaps. "Don't do that. Don't be the same as everyone else."

I jerk and slosh the hot tea over my hand. "I—I don't want to be," I say.

"The couch, Ashley," my grandmother snaps.

Jolene and Laura watch me set the pot down and dab at the brocade with a napkin. "You're not," Jolene says, and I look up at her, Soto snoring in her lap. "Usually."

Jolene has given me that gift our whole lives—that forgiveness when I am wrong. I can feel the backs of my eyes prickle like I'm going to start bawling too.

"Okay," I say.

"So, then," my grandmother says. "I can send Ashley's father over to fetch your things once he's back from the"—she wiggles her fingers in the air—"the whatever it is he's doing to occupy himself today."

"I can go," Laura says. "I'm extremely diplomatic."

"No," Jolene and I say at once.

"I hope you stay," I say to her.

She nods.

Grandmother says, "Good," and sets her empty teacup down, lifts herself from the armchair. She pauses at the door. "You'll be just fine, Jolene darling."

Jolene has both hands wrapped around her teacup, closing her eyes as she takes a long sip. I reach out to pat Soto, curled up against Jolene's body like a parenthesis, setting her apart from the rest of the couch.

I want to smooth Jolene's hair back and squeeze her hand and promise her that everything is going to be okay. That everything's fine and no other alternative to fine is possible. But I can't lie— even for Jolene.

CHAPTER 13

The week crawls by. I avoid Hector, and skip lunch, and watch Jolene wilt. By Friday morning I cannot stand it anymore.

Omar has a show tonight—in an actual San Francisco gallery, Laura says. She was ready to take off herself, speeding up the highway and leaving us all behind, but I had that overwhelming impulse to sweep us all away. Shoot past school and keep going, catch Highway 1 and drive until we see the city lights.

So we are playing hooky, as my grandmother would call it, on a Friday morning. We're driving fast and furiously up the coast, taking the long way to San Francisco. I don't think I've ever deliberately made the choice to reject all the things I'm supposed to be doing, leaving behind the *should* and barreling directly into the *want*. It must be what Laura feels like all the time.

Laura is in the passenger seat next to me, her head bumping against my shoulder and her feet, both of them, out the window. Her long, graceful toes look like they should be dragging across the cliffs that loom up on our right, scraping across the tops of the pine trees that crowd us up against the bluffs, dropping straight down into the sea. Black water, white froth, a wide-shouldered blue sky, it's everything, rushing right through us so it's everything we feel. Jolene is curled up at the back door, both arms crossed on the window ledge. Her eyes are closed and her face is turned up to the sun. Her hair is just as gold and white as the clouds and it is whipping around her head, streaming along the side of the car like a torch. I can feel my hair in a nest around my face, a cloud of salt smell and tangles, and I laugh.

We've been quiet for a hundred miles, the wind scouring us clean and everything strewn behind us, left to scatter in the wind, melt in the seawater and dissolve in the sun. I drop my foot harder on the pedal, take the series of curves ahead of us in long, languid loops. Jolene smiles but doesn't open her eyes.

Home is hours away and the ocean is so close I could run my fingers through the waves and I am almost convinced that we will be all right.

I thought about calling Hector—this is the kind of thing he is best at, this driving-too-fast kind of freedom, and that is when I like him the most. When he grins at me and his face is exactly like a thrown-open window and there is nothing but pure happiness in him. It opens something in me, too. Just for a little while. But he still hasn't called. It feels like he should know everything that's happened, but he's too far away to talk to. He'll come find me when he is ready. At least, I think he will. I'm not sure how else to handle it. We've never had an argument before.

I have only been to San Francisco with my grandmother, for her conferences. I don't know the city well, and there's a frisson in my chest that feels a tiny bit like fear. We're plunging right into the middle of a place I don't know, crowds of people I'll never see again. Laura's father gives her his platinum credit card and sends her there for every holiday and birthday because he's too busy to shop and her stepmom is somewhere tropical. Laura knows the city almost as well as she knows San Ansia, which seems like an overwhelming amount of information to me. And Jolene does not seem nervous at all. I keep glancing in the side-view mirror at her peaceful face, which is the best part of the trip so far.

We're supposed to be in the Tenderloin, somewhere in the middle of the city, but I automatically take the exit to the Great Highway, which runs up the side of San Francisco like a hand on a thigh. It's getting dark earlier; the sun is casting a redder gold, bright on the sides of our faces. I squint against it, glancing over at the ocean, all tumbling sparks of silver.

"We're here," I say, and nudge Laura, who's slipped into a nap with her head against the window, her mouth slightly slack and her sunglasses sliding down the bridge of her nose.

"What? No," she says, peering past me and out at the ocean. "Oh," she says. "We're supposed to be downtown. Are we late? I think we're running late, the show is at six and I knew we weren't going to make it if you took the One, shit." She's lifting her butt off the seat, digging through her pockets to find her phone.

"We're not late," Jolene says, sitting up and yawning. "We're really early, aren't we?" But Laura is texting rapidly, biting her lip and squinting at the screen as we swoosh by the Beach Chalet's long row of glinting windows and swing a right at the rickety windmill. "I wanted to go to the Camera Obscura," Jolene says wistfully, looking behind us like she could see the beach behind us over the trees.

"Maybe on the way back?" I say.

"We're not going to have time to see it," Laura says, still texting. She's frowning at the phone now.

"Maybe we can drive up again soon," I tell Jolene.

"The shorter way, maybe," she suggests, and I snort.

"Omar's taking the bus," Laura says, sitting back in her seat and dropping the phone in her lap. "I told him to wait, but he's loaded up everything into a duffel bag or a rolling suitcase or something and he's taking the bus from buttfuck nowhere and then walking."

"You didn't tell me we were going to give him a ride," I say to Laura. We're cresting the hill at the top of Golden Gate Park, and I just miss the yellow light.

The brick church at the opposite corner squats and scowls, and it looks like all the condos across from the park are for sale. I can't picture Laura living in one of them with Omar, kimonos nailed over all the windows and streamers of photographs clothespinned to strings crisscrossing the ceiling and Omar cooking rice and vegan tortillas while Laura—I can't imagine what Laura would be doing or why she'd want to live surrounded by bad photos and with someone who smokes all the time and never eats cheese. I'm not even sure she likes him. I secretly think he's just a place far away when she needs to escape.

She met him on one of her shopping trips, at a coffee shop where he was chain-smoking American Spirits. Just two years older than us. She ended up staying overnight with him. "Nothing happened," she told me breezily. She just slept really well on his roommate's futon. I, on the other hand, couldn't sleep that night, not knowing where she was. In the morning, she arrived at my house with lattes, still wearing her sunglasses. She went "Oof!" when I hugged her tight.

"No one ever notices when I'm missing." She had laughed at me. "You know I'm always okay." The elegant, dismissive flip of her fingers.

Now we shoot through the light as soon as it turns green. Laura says, "Well, I told you I had to help him set up. He's bound to get lost or lose something."

Jolene leans forward between the seats. "You are nice to him," she says. "But I thought he had roommates or bandmates or something?"

Laura shrugs. "Maybe. But I promised to help and now he's

getting really sad at me and saying I don't even have to come and the worst of it is that he isn't being passive aggressive, he thinks I don't want to go and it's really okay with him even though it hurts his feelings."

Jolene says, "That sounds like the definition of passive aggressive to me," and I laugh.

Twisting around in her seat, Laura glares at Jolene and then at me. "It's not," she says. "I know him better than anyone. He's got a really good heart. He's sincere. He's respectful."

"He's kind of helpless," I say.

"Like a kitten," Jolene says.

"Not super cute in a grown dude," I say.

Laura flops back in her seat and crosses her arms over her chest. "Yeah," she sighs. "At least he's talented. Sort of."

"He's in a show," Jolene says, all encouragement. "Doesn't that prove something?"

"I don't know," Laura says. She's gnawing on her thumbnail. "I don't know how it works."

"Guess you'll find out," I say.

She glances over at me sharply. "Yeah," she says. "Guess I will."

We hit the Tenderloin. I've always been shit at parallel parking but I manage to wedge us between a rusted-out scooter and a Smart car without knocking either of them over. The Smart car's got its windows busted out. The smell of pee, which is the first thing that let us know we had definitely crossed over Van Ness and were in the heart of darkness, is even more violent out here. Jolene is gagging and Laura is texting and my fingers are tight around the steering wheel. There's a man sitting on a folding chair in front of a bodega called Grand Liquors that fills half the block and he's hunched over with a towel draped over him. He looks like he's breastfeeding under there but I know—and I cringe when I realize it—that's really not what he's doing. Laura would laugh at me if I pointed it out. I don't like how lost I feel out here.

I don't want Jolene to notice him, or the white woman next to him wearing flip-flops. Her feet are black all the way to the ankles, and then she is the palest blue-white I've ever seen, with eyes as watery as skim milk. She's staring at us. I turn around to make sure the car is locked but I catch sight of the glass littering the street and sidewalk around the Smart car, and realize it doesn't matter out here on this stretch of block where everything is gray and greasy and shimmering with a kind of sadness and stink.

"Are you sure this is it?" Jolene says. She seems calm. Happy, even. "I mean, did Omar tell you the right address?" She's shrugging into her cardigan. I realize that I forgot my sweatshirt, and I can see the goose bumps on Laura's shoulders.

Laura looks up. "He didn't have an address, he said. He said to 'come find it off Turk and Taylor.'"

I point up at the street signs on the corner. "There you go," I say. I am jittery, and trying not to look back at the people on the street. I can feel them staring at us and I wish I could assure them that I know exactly how much I don't belong here.

"No, there he is," Jolene says. We turn to see Omar huffing down the block toward us, his head hunched over and his lank black hair flopping in his face. He's hurrying with his arms wrapped around a pile of frames and a duffel bag bouncing on his back. He is scrawny and his little legs look hilarious, pistoning down the street. I cover my mouth so I don't start giggling hysterically.

Laura takes off, her sandals slapping against the pavement, and I hope she doesn't step in anything.

We start after her, not wanting to be left behind. She pulls the bag out of Omar's arms and scolds him for not listening to her when she said to wait for us. He's nodding with his head down, and then points at the busted grate they're standing in front of. Everyone on the block can hear her say, "Seriously?" even from all the way back here.

Two boarded-over windows are barricaded by metalwork. The gate in front of the door is hanging from its hinges and the entranceway seems to just be covered by a few more boards. It is dark in there. I have never seen anything like it in real life— maybe in gritty movies, or cop shows with a lot of angry people yelling. I didn't think places like the entire Tenderloin existed in *real* life, really. But Jolene is grinning.

"Guerilla art," Omar is telling Laura earnestly. He sets

everything down on the sidewalk and starts to drag the limping gate open and I cringe because I would give up my hand-sanitizer-is-killing-the-planet stance in favor of drowning everything that has touched this sidewalk and that gate in gallons of the stuff about now.

I had planned to revel in the gritty realness of a life that is so far removed from our precious, tiny little town, but now I am wondering if I am not as resilient as I thought I was. The sky is still blue, I remind myself. The buildings are settled against the exact same clouds and the ocean is just twenty minutes away. This is the same planet and I am the same person and we are probably not going to catch any diseases . . . if we're careful.

Jolene pats my arm. "We're not going to catch any diseases from the sidewalk," she whispers, and I wonder if I had said that aloud or if my twitching is that easy to read. Jolene pats my arm again soothingly like she is trying to settle down all the words that are bubbling up looking for a way out of my mouth. "Lots of people *don't* get diseases here," she says.

"Statistically speaking that is really unlikely." My voice is very grim.

She's still grinning. I'm disconcerted.

A woman in red shorts and a tube top stops next to us, snatches up a cigarette butt from the stained pavement, and pops the end in her mouth. I shriek, "You have got to be kidding me!" She stops short and looks at me hard with one eye screwed shut.

"I didn't mean to get upset," I say to her. She grunts and walks away and I put my hands over my face and Jolene is giggling at me. "Oh god," I say.

When I pull my hands away from my face Jolene is grinning at me. "I don't think I've ever seen—you don't like this place very much, huh?" she says.

My fingers are twitching around the car keys in my pocket. "I want to go," I tell Jolene.

"You're fine," she says, looking very reassuring. "It's okay. We're all here together and it's not like—" She pauses and frowns. "Nope. I don't have anything worse to compare it to right off the top of my head."

I choke on the unexpected laugh, and cough, and then I'm breathing normally again. She pats me again, a little more firmly, and picks an armful off the pile of Omar's stuff on the sidewalk.

"I'll wait out here with the stuff," I call, but then I scoop everything that's left and bolt inside behind her.

By eight, the dirty, windowless store with the torn-down interior walls is packed. There are Christmas lights attached to a chugging generator that drowns out the yelling on the street and the traffic noise and the random cop-siren *whoop-whoops*. There are bunches of candles stuck on folding chairs, with sticks of incense stabbed into them and dropping big columns of ash. Bare bulbs swing dangerously low over everyone's heads, turning the clouds of pot smoke and incense smoke and cigarette smoke and smoke-machine smoke a jaundiced yellow that looks like it ought to smell worse than it already does. The smells mingle and disappear into the jangling, screeching noise coming from the CD player that's sitting in the corner, one that looks like my mom's with the two attached speakers and the handle. It fits here, though. Everything fits here, the stained concrete floors and the graffiti on the walls and greasy scraps of the *SF Weekly* scattered like someone was trying to house-train a puppy. Everyone is wearing heavy black glasses and the dudes all have button-down shirts and tight jeans in primary colors. Most of them have beards. They're all even slimmer than Jolene, elongated like fun-house mirror reflections, and they're drifting gently around the room like they're dandelion fluff being wafted by a steady wind.

Now, with all of this smoke, I start to wonder if I'm high.

Yep, I definitely think I'm high.

There's a mattress in the center of the floor, blue satin and sagging in the middle, with a dark stain that's shaped like Uzbekistan, and it's clustered around with candles to make it . . . festive, I guess? Jolene keeps flickering in between all these people, and I think she is flirting with one of the beard group. She actually has a beer in her hand, and she's waving it as she talks animatedly. I am in the corner and I have to keep reminding myself not to lean on anything. I keep reminding myself to stay here and stay quiet. It feels safe here.

Laura is chattering to the group of dudes surrounding her, a beer in her hand too. She is glowing—I am surprised not everyone is surrounding her. Omar stands there with his hands in his pockets, looking down at the dirty floor with a small smile on his face. You can't see any of his photographs. They're all leaning against the walls. The light of the candles next to each of them and the overhead bulb glares off the glass and casts shadows and no one is even bothering to lean down and squint at them. I argued about it the whole time we were unpacking his bags, but no one listened to me.

Everyone is happy. You can see how happy they are just surrounded by art or by one another or by this, all this, whatever *this* is that fills up the room and keeps me backing away from it. I wonder where Laura got her beer and Jolene got her beer and I want to ask someone where to find a beer. I really feel like I've had a few already. I reach out my hand to touch the sleeve of a small, blade-thin person. Their hair is shaved all the way up the back and wisps on the top spill down over their bare skin like a fountain. I miss but I reach out again and they turn with a jerk. They're wearing a lot of eyeliner, winged up and out in gorgeous swoops and I want to touch that too. I think about putting out my hand to touch it and I must have because they look at my outstretched hand and sneer at me. That's what it looks like to me. But then they say, "Oh, what? You want?" and hand over the joint. I am good at pretending so I inhale smoothly and hold it.

They say, "I like your necklace!" and I have to touch my neck to figure out what they're talking about. My DNA pendant.

I cough out smoke in a stream. When I can breathe again, I shout "Thanks!" I'm too loud. "My grandmother gave it to me! I'm going to be a doctor! At Harvard!" I lift the pendant and smooth it back down. She is not listening. She turns away and leaves me with the joint. The tip is still glowing red. I'm not sure what to do with it so I take another drag so my lungs are full and I wonder why I can't just enjoy this feeling of being full, my lungs inflated with smoke and the noise and the dark. I don't know how long I stand there. My eyes flicker around the room but keep getting caught on each of the bulbs of the Christmas lights. I realize, suddenly, that they're beautiful. I smile at Jolene but she doesn't notice me, so I push my way around and step on the mattress. I bounce across it in three steps and people are looking at me and I laugh as I stumble off because my knees are made of marshmallow candy. I throw my arms around Jolene and curl in a comma to put my face down on her shoulder.

"Oh, Jolene," I say. "I love you. I think you are really the best and I will always try to take care of you because you are so fragile like a flower or a small bird."

She pats me and rubs my shoulder.

"You should just do it," I yell in her ear. "You should just say, 'Fuck all the haters' and do your thing. I mean, whatever your thing is. You know I'm right. I'm always right. I got your back,

Jolene, I got you, you got this. You have to do it, you have to take the steps you need to take." Jolene is pushing back from me and I hear the person she's talking to say, "Oh, is she yours then?"

"No," Jolene says. "She's—"

"Yes," I say indignantly, standing up straight, keeping my arm around her neck. "I'm hers."

"Really?" he says. He has a beard. "I think she could do better than a land cow." He smirks and takes a swig of his Hamm's.

"What?" I say. "What? I don't even know what that means. That makes no sense."

He leans forward. His eyes are very black in the light. "A land cow," he says. "A *land cow*," he shouts in my face and I feel cold and flushed and too warm shivering cold and it's hard to breathe. I'm staring at him wide-eyed, and the smoke stings. Jolene is shouting too. I can't hear her but the guy is just laughing. "Moo," he says, and grins a great gaping grin that looks like a hole in his beard.

I can't breathe. I say, "I have to go," and push past Jolene. She's still trying to say something but I still can't hear her and the guy is laughing. I push my way through the crowd and stumble over the mattress and kick it, but I'm kicking candles over and I don't care because it is so satisfying, and I'm almost falling on the mattress and then I've fallen on it and it smells as awful as I thought it would and I lie there thinking, *You have got to be kidding me. This is not even real. None of my life is real. All of the shit that keeps piling on. That I can't handle. I can't handle any of it. That can't be real. That can't happen.*

And then there's the smell of fire.

Laura bounces on the mattress and her mouth is close to my ear and she says, "Hey, hey, let's get up, okay? Let's get out of here, okay?" She's helping me up, and Jolene is standing there. She gives her beer to a guy in red gym shorts and a sweater vest and takes my other hand. I stand up gracefully, and the guy says, "Hey, you okay?" and I say, "No, not really," and Laura says, "Shit," and I say, "There's a fire," and we're moving down the dark corridor and back to the boarded-over door and through it, where it is not much brighter out. The sun is down and the sky is a hazy black and orange. All the lights of the Grand Liquors are bright and streaming onto the street, but the lampposts aren't illuminating much at all.

"Oh god, it's worse," I say. The smell of pee is stronger in the dark.

"How was your night, honey?" a woman croaks, leaning against the bars over the window. She's got a crack pipe. I am pretty sure that is a crack pipe. Not that I have seen one in person. "It looks like it was pretty rough."

"I set that place on fire," I whisper, pointing at the door behind us.

"Be quiet, Ashley," Jolene says. She doesn't look happy or relaxed anymore and it's all my fault.

I try to be dignified. No one can know that I am probably

high. "I don't even know what happened," I say very carefully. "This is very unusual."

Laura is patting my pockets and Jolene is saying, "I don't think I'm okay to drive and I don't think you are and she is a mess and we have got to go." And Laura says, "Well fuck," and she's dialing 911 and reporting a fire and the woman says, "You need a hit, honey?" and she's so sympathetic I want to cry. And then Omar is out here with us.

"Hey, baby," the woman says.

His eyes are huge and he says, "Laura. Laura, practically everything is on fire. Where are you going?" He is teetering on the edge of a whine. People are pouring out of the door, and there's smoke unfurling behind them. We all back up together.

Laura swings around, still on the phone. "It's not really *on* fire," she says. "There's just *some* fire."

"That doesn't even make any sense!" He's shouting.

"I'm on the phone with the police," Laura says.

"What the fuck, Laura? My show is on fire! My art!" he says, and looks back at the building like he's a helpless kitten.

"They're prints," Laura says, covering the mouthpiece with her hand. "Aren't they just prints?"

"Just prints?" he says. "You don't even know how this works! Just prints." The smoke is silhouetting his wan, sallow face and his huge sad eyes. And he says, "Sure, yeah," he says. "Sure. Okay." He runs his hands through his hair.

"Look, just give me a second here," she says, looking at the screen of her phone.

"Whatever," he says, and pushes back through the crowd of people coughing in front of the gate.

Laura looks at both of us, gestures back at the door. "Is he serious? I'm trying to fix this for him!" She starts after him, but stops after a second. "Omar!" she shouts.

"You guys, I think he sucks," I say. "And I hate his stupid art party. His art wasn't even there. It wasn't even the point. It was an afterthought almost like it didn't exist and it was just an excuse. And I hate that guy I really hate him."

Laura rubs her eyes with her fingertips. "I can't handle this right now."

"No, not Omar," I say. "That other guy. 'Moo.'" I sway a bit and catch myself on Jolene's shoulder. "Oh no I'm sorry. I don't want to hurt you."

"Were you drinking? Were you smoking?" Laura asks me. "Are you okay?"

"We have really got to just get away from here until someone can drive, okay?" Jolene says. "Can we go?" They both propel me forward down the street away from the confused hipsters.

"What happened?" Laura says to Jolene. I'm between the two of them. I'm taller than both of them. They're smaller than both of me. Both of them are one of me. One of me is—it is too much.

"Where's the car?" Laura asks.

Jolene says, "I don't know!"

"It's behind us," I say. "It is back there." I wave my hand.

"This is not safe," Laura shouts. I can't tell if she's talking about the neighborhood or about me.

"Let's find a coffee shop," Jolene says. "Or a restaurant or something. It's still early. It's not even nine."

"Let's just keep walking into the sea," I say. "Just walk in and keep going until we are eaten by sharks." I stop and try to spin around, but Jolene hauls me forward. "No, wait. Is this the way to the sea? One way is the sea and one way is the bay so you're fucked in both directions." Everything is blurry and there are so many people on the street, traveling in packs and all interested in one another and they're shouting and there are a lot of car horns and bass goes booming by, rumbling hard in all my joints. "Oh what is wrong with people," I mutter.

"I think if you go up you get out of the Tenderloin," Jolene says.

"You guys," I say. "I forgot about the map Grandmother gave me, the first time we came here. When I got my license." I am giggling again. That was a quieter trip, with the Japanese tea garden and the new natural history museum with the stingray in the shallow pool. Dragging my fingers across the surface of the water and then she was there, unexpectedly yielding and soft under my fingertips, brushing quick and fleeting and then gone. "Grandmother gave me one of her big folding maps of the city and she circled the museum and she circled the tea garden and she drew an arrow to Golden Gate Park like we wouldn't have noticed it and she drew a box around the Tenderloin."

"She wanted you to visit the Tenderloin?" Jolene says.

"No," I say, and I start to laugh. "No, she drew a big box around it and then she scribbled it all out. She scribbled out the whole Tenderloin and she said, 'Don't go there, it's Murdertown.'"

"She didn't call it—"

"No, I guess she didn't call it Murdertown." I sigh. "Maybe she called it Dieville."

"Crack Village," Laura mutters, hurrying us past a group of guys turning to watch as we pass.

"Urine Nation," Jolene says, and we all pause for a moment and then I am helplessly laughing, collapsed between them, tears streaming down my cheeks as I giggle.

"I can't breathe," I gasp. Laura is urging us forward. "Oh god," I say.

"You never laugh at my jokes!" Jolene says.

"We have to go before we are murdered in Murdertown," Laura says under her breath.

"I don't want to be a citizen of Urine Nation," I say, and I have set myself off again. They're both prodding me down the street and I link arms with them, drag them forward. We're passing ripped up awnings and neon signs and more people with beards, spilling out from behind swinging wooden doors that bat the smell of booze and cigarettes directly into our faces. We sprint across streets in front of cars and leap back onto the curb and we're running flat out to the end of each street, then stop short where Market and Turk meet. The mall across Market is a mass of bright lights. Cars stream down the street and a little green trolley screeches by.

Right across from us it's like the end of the earth, a big drop into a concrete courtyard at the foot of a giant marble building, four floors of Forever 21 and I think that's the cable car across from us. I've always wanted to ride the cable car, but it's so far away, across this cavern. Steps lead down into it and across from us the escalators are filled with people hopping down the stairs or trying to balance shopping carts and giant backpacks and a little guy in a suit has a busy-looking sign on a stick and someone is playing bongo drums.

I know where I am. "The BART train," I say, looking down into the pit.

"Actually it would be the BART," Laura says. "The T stands for *train*."

"No, it stands for *transit*," I say. I nudge Jolene. "Do you have any cash?" She always has cash. I am starting down the stairs, dragging my hand down the metal railings, my footsteps clattering hard and loud. "Let's go to Oakland," I say.

"Who the hell wants to go to Oakland?" Laura says but she's right behind me and Jolene is ahead of me. I stop in front of the ticket machine.

"This is a bad idea," Jolene says.

"Come on, Ashley," Laura says, grabbing my elbow but I shake her off.

"Adventure, okay? I can do this. I can have an adventure. I don't want to sit in a coffee shop. I don't want to be here anymore."

Laura sighs and Jolene is frowning.

"Please," I say.

Jolene digs in her pockets and hands dollar bills to Laura. Laura looks at them, and then sighs again and feeds them into the ticket machine. She punches numbers while the white guy in dreads strums loudly and badly on his guitar.

"I have no idea how much money I paid," Laura says when she hands over our tickets.

"Which way is Oakland?" Jolene says as the narrow escalator carries us down to the train platform.

"Let's just take the first one," I say. "Random chance. No planning." No cords are attached to me, pulling me back. They've all snapped, or they're stretched so thin they could break and we could all go hurtling forward, all of us together. I skip down the last three steps. A train is waiting for us with its doors open and I'm on it without waiting to see if they're behind me. I know they are.

"It's *carpeted*," Jolene says. She's a little out of breath. "Who would carpet a train?"

"Don't touch anything," Laura says, balancing in the middle

of the car, but I am already crawling onto a seat and putting my head on my knees. They slide in across from me. I know they're talking but I can't hear any of it. I concentrate on the noise of the train and the announcements of every stop and the doors chiming open and chiming closed and everything is swimming, spinning, then gone.

I think I sleep for a while. When I lift my head, it feels lighter. Everything is more focused. Laura and Jolene are asleep curled up on the seat across from me, Laura's head tucked into Jolene's shoulder, Jolene's arm draped around her back. Jolene frowns and the blond wings of her eyebrows draw together and she shifts. She isn't even still in her sleep.

I wake her when I laugh. Her eyelids flutter and she looks at me sleepily. I say quietly, "Land cow."

She furrows her brow.

"That guy at the show. He called me a *land cow*. Did he moo at me? I think he mooed at me." I start laughing again, covering my mouth, realizing exactly how stupid that was. "At least I'm not a sea whale," I say. "Or a sky blimp."

She snorts, and then she looks sad. "I don't even know why you were talking to him," I go on before she can say anything. "I mean, land cow? Seriously. I saved you from that."

She says, "Don't do that."

"Save you?"

"Save me," she says.

"I didn't mean—" I say, but she's still talking.

"Do you remember what you said?"

I did. *Next steps,* I had said. *Transitioning,* I had implied.

"Don't tell me what to do. Don't do it. Don't tell me what I need to do." Every word is deliberate and careful.

"Jolene," I say, but I stop before I can say any of the other words in my head, all of which are wrong and unhelpful. She sighs and puts her head down and we're quiet again. Soon she falls back asleep and I lean my head against the black window and look through my reflection. My head aches. I watch the pitted tunnel walls fly by, the stations speed into view, pause, and then recede, listen to the hum of the tracks and let my eyes close and let us be carried forward to wherever it is we're going, just for tonight.

CHAPTER 14

My head hits the window hard and I snap up.

"Hey!" the cop says. "Hey, there's no camping out on the train. All of you get up." He is a giant white guy, just big all over. His hands are balled on his hips primly.

"We're not camping out," Laura says as Jolene pushes herself up. "We fell asleep and that's not a crime."

"It sure as hell is," he says. "How old are you kids? This is the end of the line. You have to get off here."

"Where are we?" I say, and I'm peering out the window but I only see trees, and then the yellow lights of a parking lot below. We're way above ground and I think we're not in San Francisco any more.

"Pittsburgh Bay Point," the police officer says. "Where are you from?"

"Santa Ansia," Jolene says.

He looks at all of us. "What the hell are you doing here?

Someone needs to call your parents."

Laura looks superior and Jolene looks terrified and the look on my face must be similar because he smirks at us. "I'm going to radio you in," he says. "Get off the train. Follow me."

"No," I say. "We're just going to go home, okay?" The ache in my head has turned into a pounding. I pull out my phone but he snatches it. "Hey! You—hey! Give that back."

He's swiped it on and he's expertly flipping through my contacts until he finds my recent calls. "Grandmother," he says. "She's called a few times. Should I call her back right now? I think I'll call her back right now."

"Hey!" Laura says. "I do not consent to this!"

"This is Officer Richard Bryan Smith of the Pittsburg City Police," the cop says. "I'm calling about your granddaughter, who is embroiled in immoral, delinquent behavior and will be taken into detention at the Pittsburg City Po—"

I fling myself at him, trying to snatch the phone out of his hand, and he turns abruptly, his elbow catching me in my breastbone. I stumble against the side of the train, which is still standing there hissing with the doors open. My chest hurts. The lights are blinking inside. Jolene and Laura are crowding the officer but he's at least six-five and his shoulders make him twice as wide as me and he is telling my grandmother how he found us drunk and passed out on the train, hundreds of miles from home, did she know that? He pulls the phone away from his face and looks at the screen.

"Too bad. Your phone is dead," he says. "You're in pretty big trouble at home." He reaches out for my wrist but Jolene snatches my phone away from him and Laura is shoving me from behind and we're sprinting down the train platform toward the exit and down the stairs so fast I lose a shoe like I'm Cinderella but the cop's footsteps are heavy and he's shouting something and I keep running, my bare foot slapping against the tile and metal of the stairs. Laura is chanting "bad idea, bad idea, bad idea." She launches herself over the turnstile and Jolene scrambles under it and I hop up and swing my legs and we're sprinting for the parking lot, dodging the cars that are pulling out of spots as people head out back to their homes, tired and satisfied after a good night or maybe a bad one. I'm limping, my right foot bruised and smarting from the gravel and I'm going too slow and I cannot believe this is happening. I can't remember if he has a gun. A cab with its brights on pulls around the corner and shrieks to a stop in front of us.

"What the fuck?" the guy yells out the driver's window, but Laura is already pulling open the door and pushing Jolene and me into the ripped vinyl of the backseat. The car smells like cigarette butts and take-out Chinese food. Laura slams the door with one hand as she's opening the front door with the other and diving into the front seat.

"Go," she says. "Go, go."

"The fuck I will," the driver says to her. He twists around in his seat to glare at us. "What the fuck are you kids playing here?"

"Just go and we'll explain," Laura snaps.

"Please," Jolene says, and he sighs and I'm looking back through the rear window to see if the cop saw us dodge into a cab. My heart is thrumming so hard I don't even feel the individual beats anymore, and Jolene is wild-eyed, her hair tangled. There's an itch between my shoulder blades where I imagine a bullet going. Just another brown girl shot.

Laura says, "Look." She's fishing around in her giant purse and she sounds so calm and unhurried. "How about a hundred bucks cash to take us back to San Francisco?" She snaps her wallet and waves it at him.

He reaches for it but she snatches it back. "Hang on to this for me," she says and passes it over the seat to me. My fingers feel weak and I almost drop it. I stuff it into my bra. He grunts and puts the cab into gear, whipping around the rows of cars and bouncing back out on to the street.

"How about I get to see your tits too," the guys says casually as he veers around another corner and guns it down a residential street.

My throat catches, but I find myself saying, "How about you just drive us and we won't report you for child molestation," meeting his eyes in the rearview mirror and tensing because I think I am larger than him and I think I could stop him if I had to. Jolene is frozen next to me and Laura has her hand on the door latch.

He snorts. He doesn't say anything, but his foot is down hard on the gas pedal and I see signs for the 242.

"How are we going to buy gas?" I say to no one. My voice sounds high and thin.

"I have my credit card," Laura says.

The driver reaches over and turns the radio on loud, a talk station full of men shouting at one another. Jolene reaches over and squeezes my hand, which manages to squeeze tears out of my eyes. I squeeze back and keep my head resolutely turned toward the window, watching towns pass us by. I've never been to the East Bay before, and it looks flat and pleasant interspersed with strip malls, and then flat pleasantness again, all with a backdrop of hills dotted with houses.

Over the Bay Bridge and there is Alcatraz, dark in the water, and the Transamerica Pyramid and Sutro Tower and I wonder what it's like to see this every day, to have chosen this view for yourself. It is imposing. It is beautiful.

We glide through the streets, around the traffic that's still heavy, and then there's another argument when the cabbie wants to just let us out on a corner.

"I'm not driving up there," he says, pointing up the block and into the Tenderloin.

"You're already in the Tenderloin," Laura says.

"Technically this is the Mission," the driver says.

"The Mission is two blocks that way!" Laura says and he mutters *for fuck's sake* under his breath and swings the next right he can off Market, circling the block until I see the lit-up sign for Grand Liquors.

"There," I say, "right there!" I'm pulling my car keys out and ready to jump out of the moving car but he stops in the middle of the street and says, "Give me your money."

I'm pulling it out of my shirt when he grins and says, "Don't forget my tip," and all the doors lock with a click.

Jolene reaches forward to give him two twenties and he grabs her hand. "How about a kiss?" and I stab at his wrist viciously with my car key and he's screaming at me, but we can't hear what he's saying anymore as we scramble at the locks and crowd out and sprint to the car, which doesn't seem to have gone up in flames. We pile in and the cab driver has thrown open his door and is stumbling over to us, clutching his wrist, but a police car is pulling up behind him and I pull out very carefully, putting my blinker on, taking the left slowly, and meandering up the block and away.

"Oh my god," I say.

"Holy shit," Laura says.

"How did that happen?" Jolene asks weakly.

"It's my fault—" I start to say, but Laura interrupts me.

"We're okay," she says. "We're fine."

"Well, Grandmother knows. Is that fine? That doesn't feel like the definition of *fine*."

Laura laughs, but I can't stop gripping the steering wheel.

"I'm never going to leave my house again," I say.

Laura reaches around the seat to squeeze my shoulder, and then we're silent until we're passing the exit to Carmel.

Jolene turns to me. "Did you give him the hundred?" she says.

"No," I say.

"Good."

"My grandmother—" I start again but then I stop.

We're quiet the rest of the way home.

Laura falls asleep in the backseat and Jolene is curled up in a ball on the seat next to me. I pull off my left shoe and drop it onto the floor behind my seat. My right foot is throbbing, but it's still an ordinary ride home, a straight shot down five lanes of highway through a corridor of scrubby trees. We are alone for a long time but as it gets lighter and lighter other cars appear, pacing us and pulling ahead. I'm not driving very fast. I am driving under the speed limit sometimes, I realize, and put my foot back down on the gas before I start just drifting aimlessly down the highway and off some random exit and park among the trees on a dirt side road and live forever somewhere in Big Sur, eating nuts and berries and telling the squirrels about all the plans I used to have, once, long ago.

I still haven't plugged my phone into the car charger. I focus on aiming us straight down the highway and nothing else, with the sky starting to get lighter and brighter and my headlights weaker in the gray light.

We drop Laura off first. She glides up the walk and slips into her dark house. No one home, or no one waiting up for her, I think with a rubber band–snap of jealousy.

When we swing into the driveway behind Grandmother's Mercury, the sun is just about to rise and all the lights in the house are on. I think for a second and then back out and park on the side of the road. I've forgotten that I'm not wearing shoes. I feel perfectly calm, the way I imagine a circus performer does with her foot about to come down on the wire strung a hundred feet in the air. Jolene seems sleepy. I edge the front door shut behind me, but it screams and creaks at me just the way it always does. When I pause at the bottom of the stairs, Jolene stops.

"Do you want me to come talk to your grandmother with you?" she whispers but I shake my head. She pats my arm and whispers, "It'll be okay," and I nod at her and let her go up first. I follow before I can change my mind. She smiles at me when she slips into her room at the top of the stairs and closes the door behind her. I take the next flight of stairs up and stop when I hear Grandmother's voice.

"Ashley," she says.

It's not a question, of course. I head down the hall to her

rooms. She's sitting in her study, upright in her armchair, wearing her long dark robe and with her hair loose on her shoulders. I can't say anything to her. She looks at me, all of me, and I realize I am grubby, my hair is a tangled mess, I stink like beer and pot and pee, and my feet are filthy and my tank top and skirt are just wrinkles hanging off me.

"I was expecting a return phone call from the police department, not for you to actually arrive home."

"I'm okay," I say.

"You're a disgrace," she says. Her expression hasn't changed. "You will explain what happened."

I lift my chin and look at the picture behind her head, a nondescript landscape in muddy browns and scratches of green. I wonder if it's a picture my father has painted, because why else would it be hanging on the wall? My grandmother has good taste. But my grandmother is not sentimental. I squint to see if there's a signature, but her voice is a crack across my face.

"Ashley."

I try to meet her eyes but each time I am unbalanced by the way she is looking at me. I am hovering for a horrible instant over the idea, the tiniest sliver of an idea, of lying. I could lie to her. How could she ever prove I was lying? Why not just—

"Don't lie to me," she says, and I sigh, the quietest sigh, which she raises an eyebrow at.

"Laura's boyfriend had an art show," I say.

"Omar," she says. "That small boy from . . . San Francisco." No one could have delivered the words "San Francisco" with more derisiveness.

"So we drove up there. And later we took the train but got lost."

"Yes. That's what the police officer seemed to have thought. Though *lost* wasn't the word he used."

"We weren't passed out," I say, but I realize that isn't true even as I say it. That overwhelming tiredness and the feeling that time had stretched so far and wide that I couldn't find the edges of it anymore. "I didn't think we had passed out," I say lamely, miserably.

"Well, you found your way home," she says. She glances at me, up and down, her eyes dragging over every stain and wrinkle and bulge. "It looks like you crawled home from whatever filthy hole you were in. And now," she says, "you're standing there with that foolish look on your face like you've no idea how *ashamed* you should be of yourself. You have spit in the face of every single thing I have ever done for you. You make me regret everything I have ever given you."

I jerk back like she has just slapped me hard. She has never, never thrown her generosity in my face this way.

"I've never asked you for anything," I whisper.

"Ah, but that isn't true," my grandmother says. "I have had to work every day since you were born to ensure that you turn out nothing like that mother of yours."

"You told me to follow in her footsteps. Go to Harvard. That if she could do it—" I'm losing my fight to keep my voice even and I have to stop talking.

"She couldn't do it," my grandmother says flatly. "She wasn't good enough to get in."

"She dropped out," I say hesitantly. "I mean, she had to drop out—" But Grandmother keeps going.

"Do shut up, Ashley. You sound quite stupid when you don't listen. Your mother *did not go to Harvard*. She barely finished high school with a GED. She lied to your father about that for years."

"That's not true," I say, lurching forward, and Grandmother snorts, an undignified sound that she somehow makes elegant.

"Enough, Ashley. Loyalty is lovely," she says, waving her hand dismissively. "And fairy tales are useful for children but it's the truth that's more important now. I have taught you to value the truth."

"Are you saying that—you've been lying to me. For all this time." I am up on my feet and my entire head feels like it is burning. Nothing is right anymore. My mother is a stranger and I am an idiot and my grandmother is suddenly in my face and her voice is deadly.

"Sit. Down. Now."

I drop. I could not stay standing if I wanted to. I have never heard her say these things and I want to make her stop.

None of it is true. I have the proof. I have the photo of my mother—young, smiling—sitting on the lawn in front of Harvard Law School. A student. I want to make fists and shout, to push my grandmother back and make her just stop talking but I only sit there, and she keeps going.

"I let your mother live in my house. I gave her a home despite the fact that I had forbidden your father to marry her. A home. For your brothers. For *you*. Do you understand that?" She raises a dark eyebrow at me. She looks young and almost soft in this light and with her hair down. She looks nothing like her voice.

She leans forward, catching my eyes. She won't let me look away. "But oh, she was ungrateful. She continually defied me. She continually turned her back on the values I raised your father with," she says. "And then she turned her back on *you*. Because you were too much effort to actually raise properly." Her words are bladed and rusty and dripping blood while they're carving through to their point.

I don't say anything. I am staring at her and I can't look away. She takes the saucer sitting on the table at her elbow and she lifts her teacup to her lips.

"She wanted to name you Mariposa," she says conversationally. She shakes her head slightly.

"What?" I flinch at that. More things I don't want to hear.

She frowns and tilts her head. "I never liked 'Mateo' and 'Lucas,' of course, but I didn't have the opportunity to say so. For you, she wanted Mariposa." That slight head shake again. "I put my foot down. Ridiculous name."

"I—I didn't know," I say numbly.

"Imagine, her naming you *butterfly*, and then you growing up to—this." She gestures at my body, and I flinch again. "I have been looking out for you since *before you were born*, my darling."

I look down at myself, the rumpled tank and my boobs spilling out the top and the strap stretched out and falling down my arm and the width of my lap and the broadness of my knuckles and I see what she's saying. I'm living inside what she's saying. My gift from my mother.

"And now you're acting like you've been raised by her." She sighs. "Pretty girls like that Laura can get away with it, darling. Not you."

I drop my head. I don't know when I started crying, but there are tears sliding off my chin and my cheeks are wet with them.

She says, "I see you have my point."

I'm dizzy. I don't answer.

She sets her teacup and saucer back down. "Your mother could not, as they say, get her act together." She clasps her hands on her knee. "Can you? Or are you as bad as she was?"

I don't answer.

"You are not like her, Ashley. You are better. You are stronger. You have me in you." She looks at me again, a more kindly survey of my body that doesn't feel less painful. "Shower," she says. "Sleep. We are going out to select your interview clothes this afternoon."

I lift my head. "My interview," I say.

"Your Harvard interview," she says. She gestures at her desk, and I stare at her. "Get up and get the envelope," she says.

The envelope is addressed to me, torn open. The letter says, *following up on our email earlier this week, we'd like to invite you to meet with a Harvard alumnus as the next step in your application* and then it blurs and washes out and I drop the note.

"Okay," I say. The only thing I can think is, *I thought my mother had an interview at Harvard. My mother never had an interview at Harvard.*

"Do you see why I was so worried about you? Do you see why I was so angry? You can't jeopardize your future. You're so close."

I'm staring at the letter on the floor.

"Go," she says, and I turn and walk down the hall and down the stairs and into the bathroom and I sit on the closed toilet and realize that the last thing I can do right now is strip down naked. I leave the bathroom. My bedroom is already bright, and the scarves draped over the curtain rod are stirring in the breeze coming through the window, tinting the light pink. I climb into bed fully clothed, burrowing under all the blankets and dragging the pillow over my head and doing my damnedest to not think of anything at all until it gets so easy because everything goes dark.

*　　*　　*

Everyone has the same anxiety dreams. You've missed a test, or you suddenly realize you've forgotten to go to class all year and the final is right now and you're late because it's in an entirely different wing of the building you've never been to and it's filled with monkeys and you can't graduate unless you take this test and get it one hundred percent correct, every question, and all of them are written in hieroglyphics. Or you've lost the dogs, all of them, they've all gotten out the front door because you left it open and they've scattered across the neighborhood and it's getting dark and they are lost and alone and it is your fault. Or that your grandmother is a zombie and she is faster than you and smarter and her basic instinctual drive is pushing her forward relentlessly and you are in an endless hallway of wooden doors and every door is locked and she's right behind you with the floorboards shrieking your name under every one of her heavy footfalls.

Classic.

I fling the covers off and drag myself up and look at the window, still bright. I can't tell what time it is. My phone is in the car, right. *And I am filthy,* I think, looking at the trails of greasy dirt streaking down my arms. I drag all the sheets and pillows and blankets off the bed with me, because they will need to be washed at least twice, and sneak across the hall into the bathroom and run the water hot. The water stings my foot and I scrub it clean, wincing but not caring. I am fast and quick and I put my hair in a wet ponytail, even though I know grandmother hates that but she'd hate that I was late even more, and I wish I had pants that weren't jeans or a top that wasn't a T-shirt or something low cut, but I settle on something plain and black and closed-toe flats because haven't my feet suffered enough.

Grandmother doesn't say anything when I come downstairs and she's silent in the car. She is all straight angles, elegantly geometrical, and she is hard to look at directly. We pull into the parking spot in front of Lane Bryant and she sighs. She hates this store. I hate this store. Laura thinks this store is an abomination. But my grandmother is ruthlessly efficient. She walks past all the hangers and the mannequins wearing clothes that are floaty, printed, sporting an empire waist, contrasting trim, embellished with lace or sequins or sparkling threads or strange buttons or—any of the thousands of things that fat-clothes designers want fat girls to wear because maybe enough shiny, sparkly, ruffly bits will fool the eye into thinking you're not actually fat.

My grandmother knows how to strike at the heart of things. She finds slacks that don't have a tuxedo stripe down the side or Lurex pinstripes or an attached brass belt studded with jewels. She glances at me and takes the 16s, the 18s, and the 20s off the rack and I hold my breath but she takes the 22s as well and something about that feels like betrayal. Like the problem isn't my weight or her worry about me and my future or my potential. The problem is that she doesn't see me. She doesn't see my body as more than a problem and I am there lost in it, standing next to her in a hushed, dimly lit carpeted cavern that seems huge but I remember the Forever 21 in San Francisco, the marble mansion full of clothes for girls who have single digits in their size numbers and nothing holding them back.

She holds out her stack of pants and I take them all and wrap them up in my arms and follow behind her, letting her flip through all the blouses that become indistinguishable from one another. They all look like shirts to me in sizes that might fit me, which is strange because I have never felt quite so small.

A woman peeks around the side of a clothes rack and says, "Hi there! My name is Flora! Can I help you find anything?"

My grandmother looks her up and down and seems very discouraged. Flora is a fat girl as brown as me, dressed in the floatiest pink-and-yellow watercolor top with a keyhole neck tied at the top in a bow and the beaded ends disappearing into her amazing cleavage. Her skirt swirls around her ankles in burgundies and greens when she steps around the rack and clasps her hands in front of her and smiles at us. *Pink toenails,* I think numbly for no reason. Her sandals are bronze.

"I am not convinced," my grandmother says.

"I'm sorry?" Flora says, dipping her head down a bit like she's tryng to get close enough to hear.

"My granddaughter has an interview at Harvard," Grandmother

says. "We need a suit. Something that isn't frivolous."

Flora says to me, "Well congratulations!" and I almost say thank you but my grandmother interrupts with, "She hasn't gotten in yet."

"It's just an interview," I mumble.

"Well that's still just great," she says. "We have a ton of suiting separates right back here." She turns and waves us along behind. My grandmother runs her eyes across the few racks and nods, but Flora doesn't recognize being dismissed. "Well, see, here there are a ton of options and if you can't find your size I'll be happy to help you figure something out. I'll just set up a fitting room for you right now and then you can get to work."

"Thank you," I say to her. Grandmother is flipping through the racks already, ignoring both of us. Soon I'm loaded up with one of every size of every piece in this section. I duck into the room but my grandmother is right behind me, and she places herself on the padded stool in the corner.

"I can try on things myself," I say to her. "I'll come out and show you."

"This is more efficient," she says. "Go on."

I turn my back when I lift my shirt and it feels like I am peeling off my skin, leaving behind raw red hamburger that hurts in the open air. I start at the smaller sizes and go up and I don't look in the mirror, I look at my grandmother who does not say a word to me, just shakes her head or nods and in the end, we have two pairs of pants, two jackets, four button-down shirts.

I bang open the door of the dressing room. "Ashley," my grandmother says sharply but I keep going, pushing through the front doors and breathing the hot afternoon air. It doesn't feel as hot as the skin all over my body. Or the tears streaming out of the corners of my eyes. I try rubbing them away with the heels of my hands before my grandmother can see but I can't keep up.

When she comes out I don't know how many minutes later she smiles at me. She doesn't say anything about my red wet face. She just hands me the bag and goes around the side and unlocks the car. All the way home I sit with the bag in my lap and she talks about how we can salvage this and I don't ask "salvage what," but I nod and say *yes* and make noises similar to *yes* but I can't really hear her.

When we pull into the driveway, she turns the key and the car gets immediately too hot with the sun beating down on the windshield. She turns to me and says, "That reminds me! For when shall I schedule the pre-operative appointment?"

All of me wants to pretend that I have no idea what she's talking about but I am not stupid or twelve.

"I don't know," I say. "I don't want to—"

She pats my hand. "I know, darling," she says. "It is hard to let go of old, wrong ideas. Especially for someone as stubborn as you." She smiles at me. "You get that from me." She checks her lipstick in the rearview mirror, and then smiles at me again.

"You finally know how important this is. You're better than your mother ever was, and I am determined to give you every possible advantage." She opens her door and slips out, taps up the stone path in her kitten heels.

I haven't promised anything, I think. *I haven't promised anything.* I follow behind her with the bag in my arms, tripping up the stairs and into the dark coolness of the house.

CHAPTER 15

'm surprised at how glad I am to see Hector's face peering around the giant potted palms that separate the foyer from the rest of the restaurant. Relieved. We've never gone so long without talking. I have wanted badly to call him, to confess to him, tell him about San Francisco, about this new version of my mother I've had to carry around in my head, that I've been shying away from—that she didn't leave because she was too good for us. She left because she wasn't good enough.

But I have been fighting the urge to call because I need to know that I am enough on my own. I can't let him be my center support. I have never noticed before how much I had relied on him to see all of me and still love me and ratify who I am. It scares me.

It's the busiest time of the Sunday rush though, the four-o'clock early-dinner crowd full of seniors and parents with kids they want to get into bed in a couple of hours. I lift my pitcher of water in a salute to him, and he smiles when he sees me. Dimples.

Water runs down my arm and on to Mr. Monroe's bread plate, but he doesn't notice because he's focused on buttering another piece of sourdough. I am tired and my feet hurt and I'm trying to let the orders I need to remember crowd out everything else but that never works the way you want it to.

"Amy," I say to the server at the next table over. "Amy," I say again, and she startles and swings around.

"Hi. What," she says. She looks like a mushroom to me, with a triangle of hair and a soft square face that never changes expression.

"I'll be right back, okay?" I say. I try to hand her the water pitcher, but she just looks at it. "Can you take this?" I say. "I'm just going to be a second."

"No," she says, and turns back to her table full of sunburned tourists, all peeling and dressed like they've been standing on a boat letting the sea air blow through their clothes.

I know if I look at any of my tables someone is going to try and catch my eye so I keep my head down and sidle among all of them, dripping water all the way across the carpet. Hector is examining the leaves of the palm tree, pinching the ends as if he is trying to determine whether they're real, and looking like he's going to pull off one entirely.

"Don't mess with the palm tree," I say to him, but he doesn't laugh at me. He is not even smiling anymore. His face is so still and serious that he looks like a bad photograph of himself. "What is it," I say. I don't think I've ever seen him look sad. That's what this expression is, and it catches me off guard.

"I was going to text you," he says. "I'm sorry." He swallows and his throat bobs. I want to touch the side of his neck where it meets his shoulder, that cord of muscle, but I am still holding a water pitcher.

"You mean what happened at lunch on Thursday? It's fine. I haven't been thinking about it."

"Yeah," he says. "Sort of."

I glance over my shoulder and I see Amy staring at me as she deals out the bread bowls for one of my tables. "Do you want to talk after work?" I say. I should be walking the dogs and cleaning the kitchen and finishing a paper for Literature, not wandering off again, but I shove that thought away.

"No," he says. "I can't wait that long. I went to your house but your grandmother said you were working and I had to talk to you." He still hasn't smiled and he's not looking at me and he is the most transparent person I've ever known.

"Are you breaking up with me?" I say.

Relief like the dawning of the sun across his face, then sadness chasing after it. "You're not happy," he says, and I am silent. "You know, I just want you to be happy. But you aren't and I don't want to hang around making you more unhappy."

I am still holding the water pitcher. He is looking at me very earnestly. He says, "Say something."

"Okay," I say. My grandmother's voice in my head: *Why are you surprised? He's finally woken up. Isn't this what I've been telling you all along?* "What did I do?"

"You didn't do anything," he says. "It wasn't anything you did."

"Okay," I say. I am standing there in my apron and there is sweat in my cleavage and Hector is breaking up with me. It's nothing I said. It was nothing I did. It's me.

He's shifting from foot to foot now, anxious.

"Are you going to get mad?" he says. "I've been thinking about this a ton, Ashley."

"For how long?" I say.

"Well, you've been unhappy for a while," he says. "But I didn't realize it was me until Friday."

"Thursday," I correct him.

"No, when you weren't in school on Friday and you didn't text me at all to tell me where you were and I was going to text you and then—it was like an epiphany."

"Okay," I say.

He puts his hands on my shoulders and peers into my face. "Don't you think this is a good idea?" he says.

Did I think it was a good idea that he was breaking up with me, instead of me breaking up with him? Because that's how it's supposed to go. He'd laugh like a monkey or say something stupid or just be *Hector* and not a person in the world would have faulted me for it. Everyone would have understood.

But now everyone will just assume they understand why he broke up with me. They'll look at me and nod and say yes, of course. How could he look at her every day? And I am weak with this idea, the horrific exposed feeling of it, and all the words have blown out of my head.

"I don't know," I tell him. I can't figure out anything else to say, so I say, "I'm going to go back to work." I lift the pitcher, dripping with condensation, to show him that I was working. My hand is shaking and the ice is clinking against the sides.

"Okay," he says. He reaches out, and then pulls his hand back, and then pats me on the shoulder.

He broke up with me, I think. I turn and hop back through the maze of tables with the pitcher dribbling down into the crook of my arm, and keep going, right into the dark pass-through so I don't have to look at all the tables I'm supposed to be handling, and all those faces. Amy stomps over and says, "Done?" and I say, "Yes," and surprise myself when I burst into tears.

She sighs disgustedly and grabs one of the rolled-up napkins from the top of the stack. It's still got silverware in it when she hands it to me, and it all clatters to the rubber mat when I unroll it. She leaves me there to sniffle, but it was only a short burst. A summer thunderstorm, rattling the windows and making the house creak.

I don't need him to remind me that I am fine the way I am, just fine. I don't.

I should tell someone, I think, and pull my phone out of my pocket. But before I unlock it I realize I can't. I can't tell anyone that he broke up with me, left me behind feeling like I was floating in the middle of the ocean on an inner tube, my legs disappearing into the dark water below me.

CHAPTER 16

I haven't seen Laura in a week—since our trip to San Francisco. She hasn't been in school at all, as far as I know. I've texted her. **WHAT'S UP WITH OMAR?** She never texts back. I've backspaced so many texts to her after just one letter because I have no idea what the next letter is.

Jolene is still staying with us. And she keeps telling me to call Laura and I nod but never do and when Laura shows up at the front door I have to assume that Jolene went ahead and did it for me.

"Interview for Harvard," Laura said, standing on the top step now. "Full speed ahead."

"Oh yeah I'm on the fast track now!" I say brightly, and she frowns. I'm making jokes. She doesn't say anything about it though. We sit in my bedroom the way we always do, a pile of dogs and all of us talking about the easiest subject—when I'm leaving for the interview and how long I'm staying and where I'll be sleeping.

"*And with who,* ha ha," I say, nudging Jolene in the side.

"I'm sorry about Hector," Laura says.

I shrug. I can't explain the hole he has left, how desperately I'm trying to backfill it. I touch the DNA charm dangling at my chest.

"Do you want me to go with you?" Laura says. She's sitting on the floor with Annabelle Lee in her lap, flapping her tiny ears up and down in rhythm. Annabelle Lee is content to be mauled.

"No," I say. "I'll be okay."

"You could stay with my aunt maybe," Laura offers. "On my mom's side, so that could be awkward, but still."

"Maybe," I say. I have been looking forward to the idea of a hotel room and a giant bed and a tub with water pressure and where the water isn't kind of orange.

Laura stands up with Annabelle Lee under her arm. Annabelle Lee hangs there in a very dignified way. "What are you going to wear?" Laura says. She goes to my closet and starts pulling out blouses, T-shirts, dresses, with her other hand, throwing them on the bed.

"I have a suit," I say, but Laura doesn't stop going through my clothes.

She says, "Where's your suitcase?" and I dig it up and she says, "This is so small." She's tossing a pile of stuff in it. I stop myself from trying to catch the things that flap through the air, put my closet back together.

"There," she says, satisfied. "I wonder if it closes." She sets Annabelle Lee down and swings the lid closed. It doesn't close. She yanks on the zipper but it catches in one of the sweaters she packed. Toby pads over to sniff at the zipper and I shoo him away. I hadn't even realized I had sweaters but I suppose Boston might be a cold place in November. "Oh for fuck's sake," Laura says, and punches the side of the suitcase.

I snort. "I think you overpacked."

She throws herself across the suitcase and makes irritated grunting noises while she tugs hard on the zipper again. She looks very artistic in the motes of dust that sweep through the sunbeam illuminating her skin to dark copper and her hair shining black-gold.

"A little help here," she says.

"You have to take some things out."

"No," she says. "You need options."

"It's just a carry-on," I say, but she is still tugging. "I have enough options," I say. "I have plenty of options now." I try not to think of the Lane Bryant dressing room and the dressing-room mirror and the feeling of not being able to breathe.

"Now you do," she says. "You're welcome. Jolene, please come sit on this suitcase. No, stand on it. Stand on it and jump."

Jolene sits up on the bed but I jump up first. "Don't break my suitcase!" I say. It's my mother's ancient plaid hard-sided one. The satiny green-gold lining inside is fraying and a little loose and it smells like mothballs and thrift-store clothing and everything I wear will smell like that too, but it doesn't seem like there's any other appropriate bag to bring for my interview trip. And here is my stomach again, a clenched fist, a helpful reminder from deep inside my body that I am not just a brain in a jar.

I sit down hard. "I don't want to go," I say.

"We know," Jolene says, swinging her legs against the side of the mattress. She has not been sleeping again, and it is like I'm watching her slowly sink every day. I had told her, "I got the Harvard interview," when I came home with the big Lane Bryant bag and she had said, "Congratulations," and then drifted back upstairs with her mug of tea.

"It's important to be honest," I say.

"We know," Jolene says, and her heel bangs against the bedframe. "Ow," she says.

Laura is still grunting at the suitcase and I stand up again.

"I have an idea," I say. I poke Laura in the side with my toe. "Move it, move it." I push with the ball of my foot until she rolls off and lies sprawled on the rug, panting.

"You're not smarter than me," she says.

I drag the suitcase to the middle of the floor and dump it on its side. I pick up the curated list from my desk. "One pair of black slacks," I say, and Laura sighs dramatically, flops onto her back spread-eagle.

"Hooray for gratitude," she says.

"Did you put underwear on your list?" Jolene says. "I think Laura forgot to pack underwear." She's standing up and reaching for the dresser but I swing around.

"No, I got it, I'm good," I say. The idea of someone looking at my drawer full of tucked and rolled underwear in a rainbow of colors makes me nervous, somehow.

"Do you have your laptop?" Laura asks.

"Of course I have my laptop."

"I meant on your packing list. Something to read?"

"I have my laptop," I say. "Things to read are on it."

"Can you even use a laptop on a plane?" Jolene says to Laura.

"I have my calculus book," I say.

Laura rolls her eyes.

"Did you submit your application essay yet?" Jolene says.

I stop in the middle of tucking a pile of underwear into a dark recess of the carry-on. "No," I say. Because I have this terrible feeling that if I sit down and write, I'll do something stupid like pour out my heart. Birthday coupons and my body and this growing, aching fear that I'm not the person I think I am.

"Oh, hell. Give me her laptop," Laura says. "I'll do it."

"I just—haven't finished it yet," I say with my head inside the suitcase.

There's a long silence.

I pull my head out. "I haven't started the essay yet," I say.

"Don't you need to have the application finished—don't they

need to have you as a candidate, on the rolls, ready to go, to actually conduct the interview?" Laura asks.

I interrupt her. "Back off. Like you give a shit if I get into Harvard—"

"I *don't* give a shit about where you go," she says. "End up in community college if you want. Fuck up your fancy life plan."

And that is about all I can take.

"And how's *your* life plan?" I say. "Shouldn't you be up in San Francisco fucking Omar in his crack house?"

"Oh, Omar!" she says. "Yes, Omar. My *ex*-boyfriend who was really excited you burned down his fucking art show."

"I didn't burn it down," I say, and then I kick my suitcase. "It wasn't even an art show! It was a bunch of underemployed date rapists pretending to know shit-all about photography, and Omar being useless."

"Luckily for you, *you* didn't have to date him."

"Lucky for you he dumped you. Hey maybe you can actually do something with your life now."

Laura laughs. "I love how you spend your whole existence telling everyone else what to do, when you have no idea what the hell *you're* doing."

"What are you even talking about?" I snap.

"You are so lost right now you're off the map. You totally pushed Hector away because you couldn't deal with the fact that he sees through you and still gave a shit anyway, and you've finally bought into your grandma's insane ideas, and for someone who thinks she's completely together and knows exactly who she is and what she wants? You are a big fucking mess." She's breathing heavily and her fists are clenched at her sides now.

There is a scream in me, a roar, a gaping hollow full of storming sound in my gut and I am shaking.

"Get out," I say. "Just get out." But I'm the one who walks out of the room, gets in the car, and lurches it out of the driveway, hitting the gas and letting the sound of the engine and the wind fill up my entire head, drown out that noise that is whirling inside me, that is pacing the long path between my stomach and my throat, that is trying to crawl out. I find myself skidding into my usual spot next to Cap'n Bill's and sit there for a minute, wondering how the hell I got there and why. When I slam the door behind me, the whole car shakes.

"Oh my gosh hiiyee!" fluffy pink Jessica says, walking hand in hand with her new idiot boyfriend from the next town over. I grimace at her. She's finally given up on Brandon at least. I raise my hand at the three freshman yearbook kids who swerve to grab my arm and I zoom past them, walking fast to the end of the pier, the fake lighthouse, the hazy horizon, and the water looking like molten silver. There is no one drowning out there, no head or hand or movement at all, just wisps of clouds pulled thin and translucent across the backdrop of sky that makes you feel like you're falling forever. I pretend that everything behind me has toppled into the sea, and I'm just here balancing on the horizon as best as I can. I kick off my flip-flops hard, and one of them splashes into the water, floats briefly, dips, and then starts washing down the side of the pier and away and I catch a sob in my throat. It's too much. A stupid little thing is finally too much.

"No," I say, scrambling after it. It snags on a post, in a haze of seaweed and muck, and I fish it out. The water is so cold. I can't imagine how my grandmother could have plunged into it, swam so far and for so long, there and back again. My hand feels stiff. I throw the flip-flop back onto the dock and just lie there with my fingers wrapped hard around the slat of splintery, rotten wood, my forehead pressed against a gap between the boards. It smells like seaweed and fish and salt. Another spasm in my chest.

I push myself up and stumble to my feet and spin around because I don't know what I'm doing or why I'm here or what this is.

And then—Brandon is coming down the back stairs of the restaurant with his hands in his pockets. I stumble back like I have been pushed on the shoulder. I don't look around for Morgan, who is probably sitting on the hood of his car in her hockey shorts and posting windblown Snapchats. When he hesitates at the bottom of the stairs, lifts his hand to me in a wave, I shudder. A picture of myself as an enormous creeping shadow silhouetted against the bright sky flashes behind my eyes. He recognizes me from this distance because of the space I take up. The enormous cutout against the clouds.

He is standing there and he's waiting for me. I am flailing around snatching up my flip-flops and walking toward him because hunching at the end of the dock and pretending I am just a seagull isn't going to be any less awkward.

"Your hair is a mess!" he says, grinning. "It's a good look for you."

He reaches out to pull a curl away from my cheek but I jerk back, patting my tangles self-consciously. "Great," I say.

He winks and I say, "Oh god, Brandon, *don't wink*. It's skeevy."

"Laura tells me that all the time."

"She's usually right," I say automatically. "Or, sometimes. She's been right before." A pause. "I have to go," I say. "I'm going." I start shuffling over to my car, and he turns to walk with me.

"Have you seen her?" he asks. "I thought she was working today."

"Laura? No," I say. "I mean, not working. She was at my house helping me pack. I'm going to Harvard," I say stupidly.

He stops and pokes me in the arm. "Wait, really? That's great! That's so great!" he says. "Come here!" He slides his arms around my waist and pulls me up against him in a tight hug. He's stroking my back and saying, "Congratulations! Why didn't Laura tell me? The last she told me was that you were still working on—"

"No," I interrupt, pushing back from him, taking a couple of stumbling steps away. "Just the interview."

He reaches out to catch me but I bat his hand away. "Oh. Okay," he says. "Okay. That's still pretty great."

"I don't want to go," I say. I cross my arms. "I don't think I can go, even if I get in."

He frowns.

"Harvard. No one can get in," I explain. "Did you know that they only admitted one thousand, six hundred and sixty-two students last year?"

"Out of how many?"

"Over thirty-five thousand!" I shout. I have flung my hands up dramatically but I cannot stop myself. "Does that seem reasonable to you? Does any of this seem reasonable to you?" It did seem reasonable, when I thought my mother was once one of those just-over-one-thousand students.

But not now. Not anymore.

Seagulls squawk and flap away and my voice echoes off the pier and neighbors are all looking at me. I stop and lean against the railing of the dock. I can't look at him. I drag my fingers through my tangled hair and they catch on the knots, hurt when they pull.

"Where else did you apply?" His voice is soft.

"Nowhere," I say. "I didn't apply anywhere else."

"Oh," he says. "It's not too late."

"I don't want to go anywhere else," I say.

"Well, you could. Your grades are good enough." He sounds so reasonable.

"I don't want to go anywhere else," I say again. "I won't. I can't."

I am almost spilling over with tears and still not looking at him, but I can feel his concern radiating over me. But maybe I shouldn't assign compassion to people whose minds I can't read. "I have to go," I say again, and the truth of that is all around me, in the faces of all the people I know passing us and waving, me feeling so outsized in a town so small. The place my mother had to run away from. The feeling that nothing but the best can make up for all the rest of me. The flaws that everyone knows so well, no matter what I do. They have opinions about how I look, no matter what I accomplish.

Like a cramp in my belly, an echo of Laura. Like my grandmother sitting next to me in the car, saying, "You know I'm right, darling."

"Are you okay?" Brandon says. He cups my neck with his big warm hand and he's peering into my face.

I open my mouth but there she is, Morgan leaning against the side of her little Audi. She's staring at us. "No," I say. "No. I'm going."

He reaches out and runs his other hand up my arm, clasps my shoulder. He's got me surrounded. His thumb brushes the side of my neck and I am frozen. "You're brave," he tells me with a so serious, so sincere look on his face.

I am overcome with the urge to laugh at him.

"I mean it," he says. "I've always thought so."

I push his hand off, swerve around him and around the front of my car. "Great!" I say. "That's great!"

He doesn't mean it. He's making fun of me. What is wrong with him? What is wrong with me? I yank the door open and fall into the car. My hand shakes, trying to fit the keys into the ignition. He's watching me with his hands in his pockets and I give him a thumbs-up that means *fuck off*. He nods but doesn't move and I clench my teeth. Morgan has straightened up, is still watching us with her arms crossed, but he is watching me instead. I pull out fast, swerve away. I can't drive. I am shaking and now I am sobbing, my whole body caught in the storm, all of me hurting, all of it. I pull over and rest my head on the steering wheel.

A knock on the window makes me jump.

"Are you okay, honey?" Mrs. Tam says. Mr. Tam stands stoically next to her, gazing off into the distance.

I look at her.

"Do you need me to call someone?" she says.

I swallow, and I feel the tears still running down my face. I look at my wet hands, short fingers, calluses from volleyball, tanned darker, my hands.

"I'll be fine," I say.

"You don't look fine," she says dubiously, and I'm afraid if I start laughing I'll never stop.

CHAPTER 17

All week: Laura's chair is still empty in every class, in the cafeteria. Jolene draws wobbly overlapping circles in her notebooks, covering entire pages in black lines. Hector and I catch each other's eyes and he smiles tentatively and I look at him, willing him to come say hello but he just looks away. I smile a lot at other people. They keep laughing at my jokes even though I'm not making any. I'm not eating. And every night I get home and lock myself in my bedroom, lock everyone out and write a draft of an essay. At four in the morning I delete it again.

Then, the interview is tomorrow. The application deadline is tomorrow. There can't be any more missing pieces. So I fill it in.

When I write the last word, put the period at the end of the sentence, briefly consider the urge I have to write THE END in all caps at the bottom of the page, I realize my head is pounding.

It's four in the morning again and all the lights in my room are on, and all down the hallway and down the stairs and in the kitchen. I have turned on the few lights my father hadn't, so that the whole house except for the guest room and my grandmother's room is glowing while Dad drools on a pillow on the parlor couch and Grandmother is off in Palo Alto at a conference. The windows rattle in the wind once, and then again, and I hear my father snoring, a sound that has been drifting in and out of my consciousness all night.

I stand up and pace around the bed as Soto watches me with half-closed eyes. I shut the laptop and tuck it under my arm and head downstairs and into the kitchen with her at my heels. Jolene is sitting at the counter eating a bowl of raisin bran. She's wearing my robe, which looks more like a queen-size blanket wrapped around her. She smiles at me tiredly when I'm at the door. Even when she's exhausted she has perfect posture, her spine like the straight stitching on a hem.

"I finished it," I say. "Did you get any sleep?"

"Not really," Jolene says. "Do you want cereal?"

"No," I say. "I have to hit the submit button." I sit at the counter.

"Do you want to submit it?"

"No," I say. "I have to." She picks up the empty bowl to drink the milk, but stops when I say, "I wrote about getting weight-loss surgery. I can't think of anything else to write about. And I have an interview."

"Those aren't good reasons," she says, setting down the bowl.

"It's a lie. I wrote that my weight has been holding me back all this time," I say. "It was a lie." Then I look at her. "What if it's not a lie?"

"Are you trying to talk yourself into it?"

"I don't know!" I say. "I don't know. What if my body really is just broken?"

"You're not broken," she says.

"Neither are you," I say. She smiles at me crookedly, tiredly. Soto stands and nudges her head against Jolene's knee. She drops her hand on Soto's head, who sighs.

Jolene says, "We will be okay. Whatever we decide to do." Her eyes are drifting shut as she scratches Soto's head. Soto is drifting off too. "We don't"—she yawns—"we don't have to decide right now."

"Go to bed," I tell her softly. "Maybe you can get some sleep."

She shakes her head but she slides off the stool. Soto pads after her, up the stairs. They creak all the way up, and the door clicks, and there is silence. Even the wind has stopped outside and it has gotten warm.

I open the laptop. Just a few clicks and my mouse is hovering over the submit button. I read the first sentence involuntarily. "Weight-loss surgery: It is my only choice, and my only chance to make a difference for both myself and the world." This isn't making a decision. It's just presenting a possibility, I think. And before I can call myself on my own bullshit, my finger twitches on the mouse and I've sent it and my application is complete and I am done.

CHAPTER 18

There are biscotti crumbs all over the table, and four crumpled napkins and an empty plastic cup coated with the tannish slime whipped cream leaves behind after you've sucked your drink dry and scooped out the rest of the good stuff with your straw. The interview has been over for ten minutes, but I am still sitting here with my hands in my lap, staring at my empty cup. There's lipstick on the straw. I never wear lipstick. At the end of the interview we both stood up and she looked at her watch and said, "Wow, we've been talking for ages!" and smiled at me widely and warmly. She shook my hand, firm and warm, and looked into my eyes and said, "Good luck, Ashley. I mean it. You're an incredible candidate and deserve all the success in the world."

I said, "Thank you, Dr. McGillicuddy."

She said, "I wish you all the best with your surgery, too. You're a brave girl. Smart, ambitious, and brave."

And I said, "Thank you, Dr. McGillicuddy."

"I'll be looking forward to watching your career!" she said, and then she was out the door into the brittle cold of Cambridge and I sat down hard again on the wooden chair.

I am supposed to text Laura when I'm done, but my phone is still in the bag Grandmother lent me, a sleek black thing with many buckles and a blue satin interior and too many pockets. I have a wallet, and gum, and my phone, and every time I have to check two or three pockets before I can locate what I need.

The night I submitted the essay I had hit send and then picked up the phone and texted Laura: I'VE DROPPED OUT OF SCHOOL AND I'M MOVING TO MEXICO TOMORROW, and she called me because she knew.

I said, "Come with me to Boston," and she said, "Okay," and was getting out her gold credit card and finding a seat on my flight while I held the phone to my ear and listened to her type.

She'll be expecting me to call her now and tell her how charming I was, how animated and lively and forthright and compelling in my enthusiasm.

Five more minutes go by. I'm watching them on the clock behind the counter, next to the chalkboard sign that says BABY IT'S COLD OUTSIDE and then lists eight hot drinks, half of them with peppermint. The iced drinks looked lonely off to the side. I had gotten to the coffee shop an hour early and ordered an iced peppermint one and drank it even though it was so cold outside. I was not prepared for how much the cold outside would hurt, that kind of wind that slices right through you and leaves you shaking in its wake and more vulnerable for the next gust and then even more for the next. Even with my father's ancient cashmere trench coat and a scarf and a knit Red Sox hat I bought at Logan Airport, I have not been able to get warm.

"Hot bath," Laura had said when we finally got into our room. She disappeared into the bathroom for an hour while I lay on the bed in a cocoon I had made of all of our blankets and shook. The heat on the giant wall-length furnace was turned all the way up. It made a keening, howling noise that disrupted sleep but I wasn't going to sleep anyway.

I know I should reach down now and pull my phone out of this strange bag and call Grandmother and say, "She thinks I am a good candidate. She believes that I can do this." I am trying to decide if Grandmother would reply, "Well certainly," in that infuriatingly condescending voice or, "I'm glad you didn't screw it up," or give me a skeptical *hmm* noise. I can't decide which would be worse. I wonder if all of those things are the exact same thing.

I get up from my wobbly café chair because baby, it's cold outside, and I order a peppermint thing, hot this time because I am shaking a bit in the café, where it is a little bit chilly and the bell over the door keeps chiming, chiming as people hustle in looking like they are wrapped in down comforters, all of them with red noses and hats pulled down over their eyebrows. No one in Boston seems to have eyebrows when it snows.

It's snowing and I should go, but the hem of my dress pants is still damp and sticking to my ankles and my feet are still cold. I packed flats. I packed for a whole city I didn't know anything about. I should go out and find the law school, find the spot where my mother sat on the lawn in front of the entrance, the huge white columns and glinting swathes of glass behind her, but I can't move. I need to stand up and figure out how to take the red line to the blue line, where the airport hotel is where everything is beige and other brown colors. And then I will have to tell someone about the interview.

Dr. McGillicuddy had come through the door and I knew immediately it was her because she looked like a Dr. McGillicuddy, like she should be too small for a name like that but she could handle it easily. She had narrow shoulders and an angled bob and horn-rimmed glasses and she smiled at me like she was very pleased to be out in the cold to meet a stranger who was sweating in the unbreathable, unnatural stretchy fabric of her new pantsuit but still couldn't get warm.

She said, "Ashley!" and looked me straight in the eyes and pulled off her gloves to shake my hand. I said, "Hello," and sat back down. I watched her tuck her gloves in her pocket and shrug out of her coat and drape it over the back of her chair with neat, efficient movements.

"Can I get you anything?" she said to me as if she didn't notice the whipped cream melting on the top of the giant iced drink sitting in front of me, and then, "Give me just a sec," when I shook my head no. She returned with hot tea in a ceramic mug and set it in front of her, wrapping her long elegant fingers around it, leaning forward closer to the steam. "Ah," she said. "Finally warm. You must not be used to this kind of cold."

"I didn't pack very well," I blurted out, and she laughed.

"I can't imagine you have winter clothes lying around anyway! Though you're certainly going to have to invest in some for the next four years."

I nodded, and she regarded me over the rim of her cup as she took a sip.

"So," she said. "Let's say I am starting here with a clean slate. I know what you want to study, and I know that you want to do it at Harvard." When she tilts her head her bob swings against her cheek. "Tell me about yourself, Ashley."

"Okay," I said, and there was nothing. Nothing in my head, nothing in my throat, nothing on the tip of my tongue. I opened my mouth as if something might come tumbling out but we both sat there for a full minute, looking at each other. She took another sip of tea and set the mug down, folding her hands on the table.

"You must be nervous," she said kindly.

"I'm cold," I said, and she laughed.

"That too. Well, why don't we start with an easy one. How

long have you wanted to go to Harvard?"

"Always," I said.

"That long, eh?" she said, and smiled.

"As long as I can remember," I said. "My mother—" I thought of the Harvard T-shirt in my suitcase. It was supposed to be for sleeping in but I couldn't make myself dig it out last night.

"Yes, Harvard tends to become a family tradition. I hope my daughter will attend, though she's not particularly interested in medicine," she said wryly. Her lipstick was a perfect dark red that matched her blouse, and she had a double strand of pearls around her neck.

I nodded.

She said, "What made you decide to choose the medical field, Ashley?"

"My grandmother," I said. "She's a surgeon. Was a surgeon. She pioneered laparoscopic surgery at her hospital. She retired. She was the first woman in her class at Stanford. She volunteered for Doctors without Borders. She volunteered for the Red Cross. She volunteers at clinics in L.A." I'm ratatat-chattering but I can't make myself stop.

"And that's what you want to do?" Dr. McGillicuddy said.

"Yes," I said. The train hadn't pulled into the station yet. "I want to change the world. I want to be an agent of change. I want to be the change I wish to see in the world," I said. "I think health care is a universal human right. I think physical well-being is the essential foundation of a healthy world and the first step toward actually making a difference."

"A personal responsibility to design and continually perfect ourselves and our institutions as tools for social development and justice," Dr. McGillicuddy summed up.

"Exactly," I said, sitting stiffly, speaking quickly. "It starts at home, it starts here, it starts with my own body. I'm scheduled for weight-loss surgery when I return home."

She looked surprised. "Gastric bypass? Which procedure?"

"The one that makes you lose the weight!" I said, and laughed, and she laughed with me. I gestured to myself. "I need to be a role model. I need to demonstrate that I understand my responsibility and take my own personal, physical health seriously."

"Aren't you on the volleyball team?" she said.

"Oh," I said. "Yes. I was. I wasn't really a great player? But I am a superior strategist as well as able to influence, encourage, and motivate as a team player." In my head I heard Coach saying, *You think you might want to let someone else score a point?*

"Leadership qualities," she said.

"I like to think so!" I said, and we both laughed. I kept opening my mouth, and the words kept spilling out, piling up on the table between us, face up. Nothing I could take back. Emptying out my brain of everything I ever heard come out of Grandmother's mouth and watching Dr. McGillicuddy nod along with the up and down of my jaw as I talked, and then she was gone and I am sitting at the table alone, wondering why it wasn't buried under a pile of bullshit.

There is dread in my chest, expectation smothering me. Weight-loss surgery suddenly seems real and unavoidable. A feeling like I've just buckled myself into the first car of a roller coaster and it's too late to scramble back out.

I sit there until the bell over the door rings again and a whole army of students comes pouring in, all of them wearing red and yellow scarves, pink-cheeked and shouting at one another. All of them so bundled up, bodies obscured, wrapped in layers and layers of insulation, I don't know how they could tell each other apart or even remember what their own selves look like. The whole place is filled with their noise and the zipping whisper of waterproof fabric as they move and my peppermint thing is getting cold. I stand up and shuffle back into my coat, try to sidle my way around the edges.

"Nice hat!" a person says, nodding at me. They are a perfectly spherical column of tiered down. They push back their hood and I see they're wearing a hat too. Their face is broad-boned and appealing and I like it.

"I got it at the airport," I say stupidly, and they laugh.

"Good deal," they say, and turn away, pulling off their mittens.

It is too cold outside to be alive and it's only early November. I shuffle down the street in my flats and wonder how I will survive this. I think about all the clothes I'll need to buy. I realize I'm planning for the future again, that it includes Harvard, that everything is going the way I planned, but my stomach is too full of liquid and I can taste the peppermint creeping back up my throat. I squint my eyes against the flurries and I keep hurrying, though I don't know where the T stop is and I don't know where I'm going.

When Laura gets back to the hotel, I want to pretend to be asleep. I put my pillow over my head instead and feel her leap onto the bed, bouncing it.

"You didn't answer your phone," she says, shaking my shoulder. She smells like cold and wind and I can feel how icy her hands are even through the covers.

"Oh my god don't touch me you are so cold," I say.

"By which you mean gloriously alive and totally wide awake! I love snow, Ashley. It is beautiful and mesmerizing and hypnotic." Her enthusiasm is as lovely as ever, and I am smiling.

"Mesmerizing and hypnotic are the same thing," I say.

She ignores me. "It glows when it's dark out, did you know that? It covers everything and then it reflects the light so that everything seems brighter and more lucid. *Lucid* is a really good word for it I think. It's a clarity that is just overwhelming, Ashley, I can't even stand it."

I sit up. "Where have you been? What time is it?" I feel

around in the covers for my phone.

She shrugs. "I took the train into town and I've been just walking around and thinking about art and things and life. Kind of my own interview, except with myself and the world."

I snort. "We have been at George Love Academy too long."

She says, "Don't laugh! I was digging down deep to figure out what I really want. What I really need as an artist, you know? But I don't want to know where I'm going. I want that to be the end result, not the goal. I want to have now, and not be worried about later."

"That sounds terrible," I say without thinking. But she laughs.

"It is awesome, Ashley," she says. She's still wearing her coat, a pink designer duffel with fur on the hood that her stepmother had left over from ski bunny days. Laura's eyes are shining and water droplets are sparkling in her halo of hair and she bounces on the bed once, twice, and then hops up. "I haven't ever really thought about the future before. Not like you. I understand why it's important to you now," she says. "And that's why I need to take my time, you know?" She shrugs out of her jacket and tosses it on the chair.

"Hang it up so it dries," I say to her.

She spins around. "Your interview! How did it go? Do they love you?"

"It was fine," I say.

"Just fine?" she says. "I am going to guess it was actually

totally spectacular and you are sitting there thinking too hard about all the things that are the most likely to go wrong and how they're going to go wrong and how terrible everything will be when they do."

"No," I say. "You know I never think crazy, irrational crazy things like that."

She sits down on the bed and grabs my hand. "Okay, what happened?"

She looks so serious that I want to tell her. I have wanted to tell her that the idea of weight-loss surgery won't go away. That the more it sits with me, the more it seems almost possible. Every moment of this trip, all the way from when she and her brother picked me up on the way to the airport, when I opened the back door of Brandon's car and she twisted around in the passenger seat and said, "Boston! We're going to Boston!" I have wanted to tell her. How terrifying it is, the way bullshit can suddenly sound plausible if you keep turning it over in your head.

But then I'd watch her eyes get huge when she realizes what I'm saying and then watch them narrow as her mouth twists into a knot and then she unleashes all the things I should be saying to myself, every word I should be shouting at myself.

I say, "I don't want to talk about it," and she huffs at me, kind of the way Soto does when I won't sit down and let her climb into my lap and fall asleep. Laura stands up. I burrow into the blankets and drag them up to my chin.

She says, "I'm going to take a really long hot bath that I might never ever emerge from, and when it is checkout time you will have to come fish a raisin out of the bottom of the tub."

"I thought you loved the glorious cold, full of clarity and marshmallow candy drops," I say.

"For a little while," she says, pulling her sweater over her head and dropping it on the floor. "Everything in moderation, you know. Everything parceled out in neat packages."

My laugh sounds a little like a shotgun blast and she grins at me and disappears into the bathroom with an armful of pajamas. I feel like I've given up moderation, which is ironic because isn't that what weight-loss surgery is supposed to force you into? Your body scalpeled into pure and perfect medically verifiable control.

Weight-loss surgery.

It's like I've stepped off the top of a cliff and I'm trapped now in the longest empty space between seconds, hanging between immobility and a fall. I don't fall asleep for a long time. The water in the bathroom keeps running, and it's the last thing I hear.

She's up long before me this morning, banging around in the bathroom and leaving the lights on in the closet, and I peer at my phone from under my pillow. It is just seven in the morning and we don't have to check out for five more hours and I am good at math so I put the pillow back on my head and don't realize she's gone until I sit up fast when the alarm on my phone goes off, a blaring air-raid siren that wakes me up angry every time.

WHERE R U, I text but she doesn't answer.

LAURA.

WE R LATE WE HAVE 2 GO

My fingers pounding against the screen with audible thumps.
WHERE R U.

AIRPORT, she texts back. She doesn't answer the phone when I call as I'm stomping through the lobby to the airport shuttle parked outside, my suitcase banging against my knees.

R U KIDDING WHAT IS WRONG W U

She doesn't reply. She's not at security, or the other side of security or the gate, and I keep calling. I go find the security desk to have her paged. I ask the surly woman behind the gate counter if Laura's checked in but they can't give me information about other passengers.

"It's an emergency," I say.

"I doubt that," she says, and turns to another passenger, who is yelling about gluten-free food on the plane.

I run back to the security line with no plans in my head—I have to find her, and I'll wander all of Boston and Cambridge and whatever the hell else is in this place until I stumble across her. I have my suitcase wrapped in my arms and I'm dodging slow walkers who pause in front of places called Dunkin Donuts and I'm getting a stitch in my side and my hair is sticking to my forehead and when my phone rings I stumble and drop my suitcase which explodes open and I trip over it and land on my face on the airport carpet. I'm scrambling for my phone, which has tumbled out of my pocket and the suitcase is broken and my clothes are everywhere, all over the concourse. People stop to help me gather my things but I say, "My phone, I need my phone." It isn't ringing anymore. I dig through the clothes that people are dropping back into the broken bottom of the suitcase and then it starts ringing again. It's all the way across the hallway and under a chair in a Chili's To Go. I dive for it, stab at the button, and I can hear the shriek in my voice. "Where the hell are you what is going on," and she says, "Ashley, I'm sorry, I'm sorry, calm down you're going to miss the plane."

I sit down hard. A Chili's Too patron is sipping his giant margarita through a tiny straw and staring at me through the railing. There is a beer suspended above his glass with a metal contraption and I think about how many things are wrong in the world.

Laura says, "Ashley? Are you there?"

I say, "Where are you?"

She says, "I'm sorry."

I say, "Where are you?"

"Boston," she says. "I'm not going home. I'm going to take a bus down to New York and stay with my mom. I'm going to figure out my future. Like I was talking about."

There is an endless silence while I try to understand what I'm supposed to feel about that. What I'm supposed to say.

I close my eyes. "Okay," I finally mumble.

"You're not going to yell at me?" she says.

"You're going to do what you want," I say. "You don't listen to anyone. You don't have to listen to anyone."

She's silent for a moment, and I can hear traffic behind her.

"You're not going to tell me *I* don't have to listen to anyone either?" I ask.

"No," she says. "You know what I think."

We're quiet again, and I know I am angry, or probably angry, but I'm having trouble feeling it. I'm not sure what this is. I'm picturing her in front of the bus station with her roller bag and her hood pulled up, squinting at the sky with the phone to her ear, and I wish, I wish I were standing there next to her and I can't catch my breath.

This feeling that I have. It feels like good-bye.

That guy's straw makes that bottom-of-the-barrel slurping noise and I stand up.

"Your dad might actually freak out this time," I say.

Another long silence. "Maybe," she says. "I kind of hope he will."

"Laura," I say.

"Really, though, no one will care." Now she's cheery. I know it's not real. But then a group of people all wearing the same red T-shirt come barreling down the hallway and my suitcase is spinning in circles in their wake. It smashes into the wall in front of the restroom.

"Shit!" I yelp.

"What?" Laura says.

"Nothing. Listen, they care," I say, scrambling through the crowd, snatching my clothes off the carpet. My underwear has scattered in rainbow colors and people are stepping on them. I am hot and breathless and my face is burning red.

"When did you become a liar?" Laura says. Her voice is teasing, but my stomach lurches. And I'm dropping everything as I try to hold the phone to my ear, scoop all my things into the crook of my arm.

"I'm sorry!" I say. "I'm so sorry, I have to go."

"Fine," she says. "And hey. Figure out your shit, Ashley, okay? Don't make stupid mistakes. Nothing will get easier. And nothing will be better. Don't change your mind. Don't take your grandmother up on this."

Her words are fierce but her voice is even. Kind. That must be why it feels like a dam has broken and I am being flooded. Crying. She knows. And then she's gone. I push my phone into the pocket of my coat and rub the tears off my cheeks and gather armfuls of clothes and stuff them back into the suitcase. I'm sure I'm missing half my things but I don't care because my flight is boarding. I scoop up the broken pieces of my suitcase, turn and trip over my suit jacket, kick it out of my way, and start running.

CHAPTER 19

know Laura hasn't called her family because Brandon is calling me as soon as I turn my phone back on when I'm finally outside in the smothering hot and humid air.

"Hey, Laura isn't picking up," he says easily. "Sorry. I'm in the cell-phone lot. Tell me where to come get you."

"Sure, okay," I say, and tell him the gate number and hang up before I have to say anything else. There are no messages from anyone and I don't bother to call or text Laura. She wouldn't have thought to tell her family before I got home. She is probably wandering barefoot through the snow and making friends with jackrabbits or homeless people on the bus.

Brandon pulls up smoothly behind an SUV that's crawling with screaming children in cargo shorts and light-up flip-flops and two moms who are bickering about who spilled the orange juice, and who would give orange juice at this time of the day to a kid, do you know how much sugar is in it, and why don't we have any more napkins. I jump into Brandon's front seat with my suitcase in my lap and he peers past me.

"Where's Laura?" he says, and his brow furrows are so cute a whole family of bunnies should live in them. His eyes are bright, puzzled.

"She—she went to stay with your mom," I say, instead of all the sarcastic things I want to say. Brandon sometimes struggles with sarcasm.

"Whoa," he says. "Seriously?"

"When do I lie, Brandon?" I snap.

He lifts his hands from the steering wheel. "Sure, okay," he says. He shifts and we pull out into the traffic circling the passenger pickup. "Is she okay?" he asks.

It takes me a minute to answer. "I think so," I say. "Is your dad going to lose his mind?"

He glances over at me as he takes the right turn out on to the main strip. "He trusts us," he says.

"That's not what Laura says."

He shrugs. "It doesn't matter what my father does. Laura will do what she wants anyway."

I stare out the window with my phone in my hand, wondering again if I should text Laura, as we turn onto the 101. Everything is green and recognizable, unobscured and snow free, which I realize is a relief. Watching the trees pass on either side is like taking a long drink of cool water. We're quiet for a long time.

At Lancaster Brandon says, "So is she running away?" He glances over at me and I meet his eyes. He looks miserable and I want to reach out and put my hand on his shoulder, on his knee. I keep my hands folded on top of the suitcase.

"No," I say. "I don't think so. She seemed excited."

"Yeah," he says. Then, "She didn't tell me. She didn't even warn me. I wish she had told me. She tells me everything." He's chewing on his bottom lip.

"I know," I say. "I think she just kind of came up with the plan at the last minute."

"She's not a long-term planner," he says.

"I like that about her," I say.

He glances over, surprised.

"I mean, it drives me crazy sometimes." I run my hands over the embossed surface of my broken luggage. "I worry about her," I say.

"She thinks you're the only one who does." He's drumming his fingers on the steering wheel, his face serious.

"She—I don't know if she knows exactly what she's doing. But I think she knows what she wants." And then, something clicks into place in my brain. "She feels like she has to pretend to be brave. Except she really is. Brave."

I can't look at him to see how he's reacting.

"You're pretty brave too," he says.

"I'm really not," I say. I know that's not a lie. I know I always thought I was, though.

It is strange to be sitting there in the car with him, so close. Knowing each other our whole lives. Knowing he doesn't actually know me at all.

"I'm sorry I found out accidentally about—"

"I don't want to talk about it," I interrupt him.

A long uncomfortable silence as the trees flash past. I flip my phone in my hands.

"So," he says, bobbing his head like he's listening to music. "How are you?"

How have I never noticed how twitchy he is? I think of all the things I could tell him. "I think my interview went well," I say.

"Oh great," he says, glancing over at me again. "High five!" He lifts his hand up off the steering wheel.

"Don't high-five, Brandon," I say, and he laughs.

"How are *you*?" I ask, and brace myself for anecdotes of dating bliss with—

"I broke up with Morgan," he says, and that is not what I had been braced for.

"What?" I say. I study the profile I'm so familiar with, the cheekbones and the slope of his nose and the square chin that I've so often thought I want to gently bite.

He doesn't look over at me. "She was pissed I wouldn't tell her what was going on with you," he says.

"What's going on with me?" I say stupidly.

"The note. I, uh, mentioned that I found it, and she wanted to know what was in it, and I wouldn't tell her, and she told me I was always choosing you over her and *blah blah blah*, and we broke up." He pauses. "I wasn't going to satisfy her curiosity because it wasn't her business."

I say, "Okay."

"Yeah," he says. He sneaks a peek at my face.

"I'm not going to thank you for doing a basic decent thing," I say.

"That's not why I did it!"

"Then why would you tell me?"

He sighs. "Listen, I know you're going through a lot of—" he says, and pauses. I can see him thinking *big* and *heavy* and discarding each of them in turn. He settles on saying, "Stuff, you know? And I thought you could stand to know that you have a friend. Who's known you forever. And has your back. I've been thinking about you a lot. I'm proud of you."

"Oh," I say. "Well. Okay."

He shrugs, the one-shoulder shrug that reminds me so much of Laura I have to look away and stare at the trees racing by until I can talk again.

"I hope you're okay with the breakup," I say.

"It was a long time coming," he said. "She says stuff. You know. Sometimes I think she's not a great person."

"Usually I think that," I blurt without meaning to, and he laughs.

"She's not as good as you are," he says with a whole lot of gravity, and I cringe.

I say, "She's still pissed she's just salutatorian. And I have better hair."

He laughs again. "You're funny," he says.

"Sometimes," I say.

"Do you want to stop and get food or something?" he says. "I'm starving."

I nod, and then say yes when I realize he's not looking at me. "Sure," I say. I should eat. And I am wondering what he'll look like when he looks at me directly.

"Okay, sure. There's a place right here, actually. This is good."

We pull off at the next exit and bump along side roads until we find a shack called Burgers, with benches set up in front. No one else is here and the kid behind the counter has his chin in his hand, swiping idly at his phone.

I look around at the rotted wood and the scrub brush and the size of the kitchen.

"We are going to die of E. coli poisoning," I say, and he laughs at that too.

He's out the car door and ordering before I have my seat belt off, and then he sits on one of the long benches.

"Why aren't there any tables?" I ask him.

"I think you're supposed to eat in your car," he says.

"Tables are probably also expensive," I say. He laughs and I say, "No, seriously."

"Oh," he says. "Okay."

The road is empty and we are surrounded by trees and the tick of Brandon's engine cooling and the sizzling of the burgers in the shack. He reaches over after a few minutes and takes my hand. I look at him, and then his hand is wrapped around mine. My skin is almost as dark as his.

"What?" I say.

"You're pretty great," he says, and glances at me. I wish he'd just keep looking at me so I could figure out what he really meant. He says, "I've always known that. But lately, like I said, I've just been thinking about you. Not just about you—but about *you*."

"What?"

"You know. Who you are. How beautiful you really are. How beautiful you can be."

Oh, I think.

"I thought we didn't have any chemistry," I say.

"We have tons. Don't you think so?"

"That's not what you said."

"When?" he says. "I can't believe I'd say that." He runs his thumb across the side of my wrist and it feels nice but it should be thrilling me and it isn't. "It's so clear."

"I don't know anymore," I say, and he leans over and kisses

me. His mouth is soft and he smells like saltwater taffy. He puts his hand on my waist, and I stiffen. He runs it down my side and leaves it on my thigh. I don't close my eyes. I have both hands clenched around the bench and I hear the sound of a spatula clanking against the fryer inside. I'm waiting for the fireworks.

He pulls back and looks at me with half-closed eyes. His thumb rubs along the side of my thigh. And it's just a hand on my thigh, not a burning, tingling, maddening sensation like poison ivy of the loins, the way I expected it to be.

I look at him, and it's not the way I expected it to be at all.

I say, "Do you think my weight has been holding me back?" He looks startled, straightens up like he's been poked between the shoulder blades. His hand drops from my thigh.

"Uh," he says. "Well, no. You're so smart—"

I interrupt him. "Has it been holding you back? From dating me, I mean."

Now he's scrambling, his eyes wide. "What? No! I mean, not exactly. Of course not. I mean, you have such a pretty face. Beautiful," he amends, his voice softening. He leans forward like he's going to kiss me again.

I start to laugh. I say, "I'm glad you think so." Suddenly I am giddy.

He jerks back. "What's funny?" Now he's confused. He is still so beautiful, perfect round face and olive eyes and that mouth that was just on mine. But I'm seeing so much more than that.

There's just a tiny bit of clarity, the sun through the clouds. I know what I want for the first time in a long time.

Not him. Not an imaginary future. Not weight-loss surgery.

"I'm going to check on our burgers," I say. I can feel myself grinning like a maniac. I pat his knee.

He jumps up. "I'll check on them," he says. "I'll pay." He is nervous, uncertain. I've never seen him so off balance.

I pull a five out of my jeans pocket. "No, here. Take it." I tuck it into his hand and stand up. "I'm going to go look at—" I gesture over at a pile of rusting farm equipment with hand-lettered signs propped up against it, sitting in the middle of the weeds and scrub grass and gravel. "That." I can't stop smiling.

"Okay," he says. He still looks confused and seems lost and I am sorry, just a little bit sorry, that I can't take him seriously. That I can't explain what he's just given me, because he'd never understand.

Brandon hands me a paper bag a few minutes later. Back in the car, I am warm from the sun on my neck, and a little sleepy. He makes small talk, and I murmur agreement in return. I pull french fries out of my bag one by one slowly. He leaves his bag on the console between us. Finally he stops trying to make any more conversation. He plugs in his phone and tunes in an ambient station and the synthesizers carry us all the way back home.

CHAPTER 20

When I walk through the front door I drop my suitcase on the foyer bench and run upstairs like I am being chased. Jolene's door is closed and I'm glad. I round the corner and head up the second set of stairs. I can see my grandmother sitting at her desk, a pen in her hand and her calendar open. I stand at the door but she doesn't look up. I say, "My interviewer said I'm an incredible candidate and deserve all the success in the world."

She finally glances up from her planner. She's wearing her reading glasses, which I've never liked. They make her look like a stranger. "That reminds me," she says, "I've spoken to the head of the bariatric surgery department at Stanford. They just need your blood work. They're confident they can get you on the schedule within a few weeks. Though I thought perhaps we should arrange for the holiday break so that you don't miss quite so much school." She makes a note on a scrap of paper at her elbow, and she's smiling. "Good news all around, don't you think?"

I open my mouth, but I don't have any air to talk with. It feels like the real world has come crashing back into place. I can't remember why I was so happy.

She pulls off her glasses and puts her arm out. "Come here, darling. I'm pleased to see you. I'm so glad it went well."

She stands, putting her arms around me and patting my back, once, twice. She's warm and she smells like my grandmother. I sag against her, in the circle of her arms and her smile and the cadence of her hands. She squeezes me, and then detaches herself and seats herself again, looking me over. "You don't look worse for the wear," she says to me.

"I talked to the interviewer about weight-loss surgery," I say.

She looks pleased. "Ah, good! I'm sure they were interested to hear that." She turns back to her desk.

"I decided I'm not going to get it," I say.

"I'm sorry, darling?" she says, not looking up. She's gone back to her calendar.

I can't say it again. Not yet. I have time. I just have to figure out what to say. "I'm going to go unpack," I say. "And take a shower."

"We'll order something tonight," she says. "Whatever you'd like."

"I'll make empanadas," I say, and she glances back at me sharply.

"If you'd like," she says, and when she flicks the page sharply I know I'm dismissed.

Instead I say, "Laura stayed," and she looks up, annoyed.

"Stayed where?" my grandmother says.

"On the East Coast," I say. "She didn't fly back with me."

"Why on earth would she do that?" she says, turning around in her chair.

"She wasn't ready to come home," I say.

My grandmother shakes her head. "That girl is going to come to a bad end. She is smart, savvy, and has a great deal of potential. But she just runs wild. She's lucky she's attractive."

"She's good at being herself," I say.

She smiles at me. "I'm glad she's having her adventures rather farther away than will get you in trouble." She sighs. "She's a bad example."

"She's not—" I start to stay, but Grandmother interrupts.

"Go find Jolene and tell her everything. She could use good news."

I find Jolene in the backyard, lying in the grass spread-eagle with her hair fanned out around her. She's floating in a sea of green.

"You look like a mermaid," I call from the deck, and she cranes her head around.

"I feel like one," she says. She sits up as I shuffle through the too-long grass and sit next to her. I bump my arm into hers.

"So how was Harvard?" she says.

"I didn't even go look at it," I say, plucking a blade of grass and tearing it down the center. "I sat in a Starbucks."

"That doesn't seem very logical," she says.

I shrug. "I didn't want to look at it. I was afraid I'd—if all this doesn't work I don't want to have anything to miss." I pause and correct myself. "Anything more to miss." I add, "Also it was really cold."

Jolene laughs at that. I've torn the blades into tiny pieces. I drop them in my lap.

"Laura is going to go stay with her mom," I say. "And Brandon kissed me."

"Oh," she says, startled. She examines my face.

"Why would he do that?" I say.

"Maybe he wishes he were more like you. Or Laura."

"Laura doesn't want to kiss me," I say.

"I mean that he wishes he could do what he wants. Without worrying what other people think. So are you going to—"

"No," I say. I squeeze my eyes shut.

"I'm glad," she says.

A sandpiper hoots. "What about you?"

"My parents are coming to get me," she says. She puts her chin on her knee.

"Do you want them to?"

She shakes her head. "They were screaming on the phone at

Clara for ten minutes and finally she hung up on them. And they called me to tell me they were coming to get me before I could make an irretrievable mistake."

"What mistake?"

She gives me a sidelong glance. "They think that your grandmother is scheduling surgery for everyone in the house."

"Where did they get that idea?" I say, and I can hear the cords of tension twanging in my voice.

Jolene sighs. "I have no idea."

"This small fucking town," I say, and I find myself standing and pacing.

She looks up at me with a small smile on her face, her chin on her knees and her arms wrapped around her legs.

"I'm safe here," she says. "In a small town where we know how people will react. Where we can handle what anyone says. We're safe."

"Except from our parents," I say.

"Except from them," she says. She pauses. "I think they could understand. If I could figure out a way to explain it to them."

"That's not your job," I say.

"I would like to be able to do what they want," she says suddenly. "A part of me wishes that. It would be so easy to just give in."

"It would be a lie," I say to her. I ignore the flashback to my grandmother's office. My hesitation.

"Yes," she says. "I know." She reclines back on the grass with her arms above her head. She is glowing pale in the light that's fading, brighter than everything around her. "I'm not going with them," she says. "I may be here for a long time." Her voice is as quiet as ever, that same gentle cadence, and her face is calm. She knows such a different Clara than I do—my grandmother has taken her in, smoothed her anxieties away, held her hand, and accepted her wholly. The thought is a stone lodged in my throat.

There's banging in the house, and voices. "I think they've arrived," I say.

She pulls herself to her feet and squeezes my hand.

"Do you need me to go with you?" I say.

"I'm okay," she says. "It'll be fine."

I believe her when she says that, and watch her pick her way through the grass, back to the house where lights are starting to come on in every room, which means my father is home too. The lights switch on in the kitchen just as Jolene reaches the patio door, and my father opens it for her. I can hear them talking in low voices, and Jolene shakes her head, slips by him. He looks up and spots me standing in the grass.

"Ashley!" he calls. "Ashley, what the hell is going on?" He leaps down the steps with a couple of jumps and is striding through the grass to me. He looks grim and confused all at once, like he is not sure what is happening and he really isn't digging it.

"Jolene's parents want her to go home," I say.

"I got that part," he says. "Jolene's parents are saying something about surgery. That you're getting surgery. What the hell do they mean that you're getting surgery?" His voice is getting louder with every word. I don't think I've ever seen him this emotional.

"I'm—" I pause. I had never even considered telling my father about any of this. He would have laughed and made a joke about how he'll be leaving me in stitches and he would go back to his romance novel, his feet propped up on the arm of the couch.

But instead he's here glaring at me now.

"What are they talking about?" he says. "Are you sick? Are you hurt? Are you doing— Is there something you need to tell me? Why do *they* know about this and *your father* is just now finding out, Ashley?" His words make me think, for the briefest moment, of Hector. My father has my shoulders in his hands now and I don't think he realizes he's shaking me gently with every word.

I push him off. "They're talking about weight-loss surgery," I say, with my arms crossed over my chest. He looks confused. "To lose weight. Gastric bypass. Like celebrities do."

"Weight-loss surgery," he says. "You're getting weight-loss surgery?"

I just look at him. I am not interested in offering him relief.

He runs his hand through his hair, looks at the house. "You

weren't going to tell me. You were just never going to mention you were going to get this surgery to lose weight."

I shrug, look over at the house. There is no yelling yet. I wonder if they are letting Jolene talk.

He turns and walks away from me, stomping across the lawn, leaving a trail of flattened grass behind him. "Goddammit," he says, lifting his foot and examining it. He's stepped on one of Soto's toys.

"You forgot to mow the lawn again," I say, and he turns with the toy in his hand. "I always remind you and you never remember."

"Not now, Ashley," he says, and tosses the toy away, turns back to the house.

"They're still talking," I call. "Let them talk."

"They can talk for as long as they want," he says. "I'm going to speak to your grandmother."

He's off across the lawn. "My interview went well, thanks for asking," I say, but he's already gone.

All the lamps in the house cast rectangles of light scattered across the overgrown lawn. Jolene comes to find me, the dogs following behind her in an orderly fashion. Toby flings himself into my lap, his nails scratching at my shirt, jumping up and squirming and bouncing back onto the grass and running laps around me like he can't believe his luck, just finding me out here. Annabelle Lee has wandered off, but Soto sits calmly, her tongue hanging out. Soto is always relaxed.

"What happened?" I say. I can't see her face very well, but I see her shake her head.

"Everyone is gone," she says. "They all left."

"Together?" I say. "Are they forming a bowling team?"

She laughs. "No," she says. She sits down next to my other side, and Toby swarms into her lap. "Shh," she says to him, but he doesn't like to hear that. He wiggles out of her arms and races off barking into the dark, his little yap echoing under the trees.

"Are you staying?" I ask.

"Yes," she says. She exhales. She looks just like she did when she was seven. Soft cheeks and sad eyes. Shattered heart.

"Let's go swimming," I say, and stand up, hold out my hand to her. Her face is a soft blur in the dark. I can tell she's staring at me, deciding how serious I am. The air smells like salt and wind and pine and I close my eyes for a moment so I can smell it better.

"Yes," she says. I open my eyes. She lets me pull her up.

We wind down along the narrow path through the trees, the ground changing from soft dirt littered with dead leaves to shifting sand. We stop at the edge and kick our shoes off the way we always do, the way we always will. There is no moon. It looks like the ocean is a stretch of black glass that goes on forever and we are racing toward it, our feet digging into the sand but it can't slow us down until we're splashing into the water, splashing and then wading and then throwing ourselves headlong, letting the water catch us and lift us up off our feet and carry us away.

CHAPTER 21

The main office is dark because Principle Simons does not approve of overhead lights anywhere near her personal space. On the front counter there's a desk lamp that looks like the kind my grandmother collects, with a floral stained-glass shade that is pretty but blocks out most of the light. A slightly brighter lamp sits on Quincy's desk, but he is still hunching over to look at the papers he's shuffling through. I feel like I should pull out a flare to signal my entrance, but he looks up when I come in, the light glinting off the lenses of his enormous black-rimmed glasses.

"Absence slip," he says as he pushes his chair out from his desk. He prides himself on being able to tell what every student is coming in for with just a glance. "Legit," he says, looking me over. "Ponytail, tired eyes, skin color is off—"

"Quincy, how can you even tell in this light?" I say, putting my hand on my cheek.

He shrugs. "I know what you look like. And you've been

sick." He holds his hand out, palm up, for me to slap my weird old-fashioned slip on it like we're high-fiving.

"No," I say. "Just tired." I dig it out of my bag and hand it over.

"Oh sure, sure. Stress is the worst," he says. He squints at the slip. "Oh, right, you were scheduled to be out. For your interview! I heard that went well."

I sigh. "She said she looks forward to watching my career," I say, holding on to the strap of my bag. I want to lean on the counter but I stay upright.

"That's good, right? There's no implied 'crash and burn' at the end of the sentence. Of course there isn't. You're a rock star. And your *thing*, when is that going to happen?"

I shrug. "I don't know. I haven't been accepted yet." I think I'm too tired to feel anxious about that.

His eyes get big, and he leans forward. "Accepted? You have to apply for permission? You're kidding me!"

I pause and look at him. I say, "I don't think we're talking about the same thing here."

He waves his hand. "The gastric thing," he says.

"Oh," I say. "Right. That. Who told you?" I try to sound casual but my voice is lifting up a bit at the end. I reach out my hand and carefully place it flat down on the counter. It is cool marble and I concentrate on the feeling against my palm.

"Hmm, Principle Simons, probably?" He lifts his shoulders,

tilts his head to the side, hands palm up. "Who knows? But," he continues. "It's pretty exciting, isn't it? You're going to want to do it before college starts in the fall."

"That's my grandmother's plan," I say. The bells for first period chime and I back away from the desk. "Okay, I have to go," I say.

"Have a good day!" he says, waving the permission slip at me. "Get some sleep!"

And when I'm back in the hall and my classmates are streaming around me I realize I'm not imagining it. They are actually looking at me as they talk and their voices get lower when I come close and then the bright cheerfulness of an ordinary day snaps back into place with *hello Ashley, hi Ashley, hey Ashley!*, and the question that lingers at the back of their throats is jostled aside by all the other small talk I wave off.

It's out. In the days since I left, it burst and started to spread like poison and this time Laura's not here to menace the chatter into silence. It's an intravenous overdose of humiliation coursing through me and I am shaking. I start walking faster, pull out my phone and frown at it like I'm looking at something important. The screen is blurry because my hands are trembling. I weave through the crowd and pretend I don't hear anyone calling my name and that I don't know that they're talking about me, all of them. Everyone has eyes. Everyone knows I'm fat. I have spent so long making sure that it mattered as little to them as it did to me, playing by the rules, and it still wasn't good enough.

I should have told my grandmother. I should have shut this down before all hell broke loose and went rampaging through school. I should have known this town was too small to let anyone really keep a secret. I should have known.

There are the double doors to the parking lot and I see my car pulled up under the shade of the sunflower bush because I got here early. But there is a surge of *fuck that*. I'm not running. I turn left and start heading to Calculus instead. Then Brandon is rushing toward me, his hand outstretched.

"Hey," he says. He pulls his arm back before he touches me, and he's looking at me so seriously again, I think it's actual worry. "Hey," he says. "It wasn't me."

People are eyeing us while they pass in the hallway.

I say, "Are you still expecting me to thank you?"

"Look, I'm just saying—"

"I know it wasn't you," I say abruptly. "I think you probably wouldn't lie."

"Only probably?" he says, with a weak little grin.

"I'm not going to talk about it right now," I say.

"Okay," he says. "But I hope that—"

"I'm late," I say, and push around him.

A text comes up on my phone ten minutes later.

I HOPE EVERYTHING IS OKAY. Brandon.

I leave it unread. I lift my phone a few times to reply, but

I keep setting it back down until finally I shove it under my textbook.

In third period my phone goes off with the text chime again.

WHAT THE HELL R U THINKING?? from Laura. Brandon must have related the news.

NOT TRUE, I text back. She replies with a line of question marks and I turn my phone off.

In fourth period, I turn my phone back on to text Jolene.

> **DON'T WANT TO GO TO LUNCH**
>
> **NOT HUNGRY?**
>
> **PEOPLE**
>
> **NOT HUNGRY FOR PEOPLE??**
>
> **YES**
>
> **COME TO LUNCH I AM HERE**

Jolene has a table in the corner near a window. She's unpacking her lunch bag, pulling out hummus and crackers and pretzels and cheese and an apple. I sit with my back to the tall glass walls, facing the rest of the room, but I keep my eyes on Jolene as she keeps pulling food out of the bag.

"I was hungry this morning," she says, when she sees I'm watching her.

"Everyone has heard that I'm so fat I need weight-loss surgery," I say. "How did this happen?"

She shakes her head. "Don't know. No one has asked me directly. But . . ." She nods at Morgan, who's sitting on a table at the other side of the room, laughing at something Oliver from the swim team is saying to her. He's got his hand on her bare thigh and she's not breaking his fingers off so I guess she's okay about breaking up with Brandon.

"How would *she* know?" I say, watching them. Then I remember Morgan in Guidance last week, digging for info. She must be so delighted she turned out to be right.

I see Hector weaving between seats, holding his full tray up over his head with one hand. When he sees me, he smiles big, and then looks away fast like he didn't mean to. When he glances back, I smile back at him. I pull out the chair next to me. He cocks his head and smiles again, then turns toward our table.

"I wanted to call you," he says. His hair has gotten way too long in just a couple of weeks, and he is tanned dark. His mom is probably mad about that. He must be skateboarding again. He's looking at me like he's trying to catalog that all my parts are present, intact, and accounted for. "But I deleted your number off my phone because I was afraid I'd call you."

I laugh at that. I want to reach out and touch his wrist. I want to say, *Thank you for all the good things you thought about me. Thank you for believing I really was the person I wanted to be.*

"You don't have it memorized?" Jolene says.

"Why would I memorize a phone number?" Hector says. He picks up his vegetarian sloppy joe and demolishes half of it in one bite.

"Don't talk with your mouth full," I say automatically, because I know him.

He pretends to be wounded, clutching his chest but keeps chewing. When he swallows he says abruptly, "Is it true?" He looks genuinely upset. He's watching me with wrinkles in his forehead as I work out a way to explain it all, and then his face goes suddenly sad and resigned. "It *is* true."

"No!" I say. "It's just complicated."

He nods and swallows, draws a line with his finger in the sauce on his plate. "Well. I know you've had a crush on him forever so I guess it's not surprising."

It takes me a moment to realize what he's saying. And then I laugh and I can't stop. I cover my mouth with both hands. Hector seems bewildered. I try to talk but all I can do is just shake my head and giggle.

Jolene is smiling at me and leans over to correct Hector, I think, but then her smile drops. She says, "Did you want to talk to Morgan? Because she's coming over here."

Hector stands up. I say, "Sit down, Hector. Please."

Her mother probably loves her, I remind myself as Morgan stops short at our table.

"So you're going to be all skinny for Harvard," she says. "Weight-loss surgery. Aren't you so embarrassed?"

But now I can't imagine why her mother would love her.

"Why should she be embarrassed?" Hector says. He has a

smear of sloppy joe grease on his chin. I hand him a napkin but he just holds it.

"Uh, because she's so fat she needs to get surgery," Morgan says. She says the word *fat* like a whip crack, and I wait for it to lash against me. But it misses. It sounds ridiculous outside my head. She says it again. "Sad, fat people—so desperate to be normal."

"Ashley isn't sad," Jolene says.

"Maybe when you're a normal girl Brandon will actually like you instead of feeling sorry for you."

A click of a puzzle piece. My giggles bubble up again. "Are you—*threatened* by me, Morgan?"

She tosses her head like she's in a soap opera. "Hardly. I'm embarrassed for you."

And that means nothing at all to me. It is absolutely unimportant, what she thinks.

"You know, it's a little uncomfortable the way you're obsessed with my weight. And whether I get weight-loss surgery. And whether I care if anyone else knows my grandmother wants me to get weight-loss surgery."

"Oh, it's your grandmother's idea!" she says triumphantly, her hands on her hips.

"Yes." I sigh. "Yes, it's my grandmother's idea." My voice is getting louder. I stand up. "My grandmother decided I needed it." I put my foot up on the chair and pull myself up. Jolene pops up to hold me steady. I'm yelling now. "My grandmother thinks it would be a great idea for me to have weight-loss surgery, everybody!" I spread my arms wide. Kids I've known my whole life almost are turning around in their seats. "Do you want me to have weight-loss surgery, everybody?" They're glancing at each other. "I don't care! Do you care? No? I don't blame you! Thank you for your time!"

"You're going to break the chair if you're not careful," Morgan says.

"Oh my god, Morgan, just go away," I say. I jump down, plop down in my seat, and take one of Jolene's carrots and I don't watch Morgan walk away and I don't look at the rest of the room. I don't want to know who is staring, or talking.

"Are you going to do it?" Hector finally says. He's still got the grease on his chin.

"Napkin," I say.

He dabs at his face.

"No," I say finally. "I'm not going to do it. But my grandmother is still scheduling it."

"You haven't told Clara?" Jolene says.

I look at him, and glance over at Jolene. They're both looking at me very seriously.

"I will," I say finally.

CHAPTER 22

They were excellent, perfectly logical, and reasonable reasons. Of course I couldn't play volleyball anymore—I was studying for the SATs. I was running for student government. I was working. My knee was acting up after one too many midair collisions where everyone landed ungracefully.

They were sincere reasons, real and true reasons that had nothing to do with my weight, or feeling so wide next to tall, wiry Amy, and lanky and muscular Justin, tiny Emily always gunning for captain. Or because I had to play harder, because everyone was skinnier than me. Play better, because they were skinnier than me. Be fierce because I had to be brave. Force myself on the court every single practice.

I threw up before every single game, my stomach heaving at the sound of the crowd outside the locker room. A hundred strangers with their eyes all on me, everyone wondering, how is that fat girl supposed to play volleyball?

Having to prove myself, over and over.

I have never allowed myself to acknowledge this, not really. More important, no one was ever supposed to know. Somehow, I really believed no one ever suspected I had this frantic, terrified center, a churning, overheating engine constantly propelling me forward. The energy behind everything I do. Everything I am.

The thought tears through me, leaving me feeling bloody and ragged. My head is down and my fists are in my pockets and I'm walking fast. I'm not skipping my last class, because I'm not running away. I don't run away. But relief slams me in the chest and stops me short when I see the classroom door is open and the light is off and no one is inside. I don't care why no one is there. I spin and I march through the emptying halls and right out the back door, flinching at the brightness of the sun after the dimmed lights of the hallways. I'm ducking my head and moving more and more quickly, the farther I get away.

When I pass my car I drop my bag and kick it underneath and keep going. I don't want to stop moving. If I stop, all these thoughts will catch up and swallow me. The faster I move, the louder the silence that fills my head. When I'm in motion, I'm just long breaths and bunching muscles and moving limbs. When I'm not thinking about my body, just using it, everything makes more sense.

I dodge through the gravel divider and over the sidewalk, across the road to the bike path that winds down to Main Street and the beach. When I cross from the bright sun to the shade of the trees I break into a run, my flip-flops slapping the dirt and branches dragging across my bare arms, leaving white scratches behind. I don't stop at the end of the trail. I hit the cobblestones of Main Street, veer toward the boardwalk, leap off the boards onto the sand. I'm breathing heavily, too hot in the sun. But I feel light and invisible. I don't notice anyone, and they won't notice me if I keep moving. I kick off my flip-flops and I pound through the sand, chasing the gulls down the beach.

I run through the stitch in my side.

I run through the burn in my lungs.

I run through the image of my mother, laughing on the lawn of Harvard like she had some right to be there.

I run through my grandmother's promises.

I run through the idea, the seductive, twining, choking-vine idea that everything could be *easier*. Everything could be *simpler*. That I never have to feel like this again. *That skinny is so much easier than fat.*

I run through the idea that I am not strong enough to do this anymore.

The beach ends abruptly at a sheer rock wall that stretches so high overhead it can block out the sun. I am running flat out now, straight for it, my legs pumping and on fire. My whole body burning. The sand drags at my feet but I am stronger, and faster. I run hard at the wall and throw myself at it, gasping, clinging to it, sliding down until I'm sitting on the rocky sand, pressing my face against the rough, warm stone and gulping air.

I feel empty. The space behind my eyes feels like it should be filled up with tears, but it's gone dry. I'm miles from home and it feels like no one but me has ever been here. It's an unfound beach, the sand littered with broken branches and drifts of seaweed. The smell of salt and sulfur and sand is almost as big as the sky, and the sun is turning everything gold. I feel like I am the first person in a while—in maybe ever—to churn up the sand, disrupt the tide, startle the gulls.

I sit and let my breath calm and wait for a revelation. A sense that everything is going to be okay, that I've found an answer, the key to everything, the end-game solution. I spread my hands out in the sand and close my eyes against the slowly dipping sun. *Invisible gamma rays, help me,* I think.

No answers, I know. Just me.

I am the sum of my parts. Everything I've ever done and everything I've ever achieved and everything I have ever been. Fat and smart and afraid and fierce and angry and brave all together right here, and every piece of the puzzle fits the way it's supposed to and I can't pretend anymore. It's always been true, no matter what I've told myself or hoped or tried to believe.

I wobble a bit when I drag myself standing, wait for a moment to get steady and sturdy on my feet, and head home.

CHAPTER 23

The entire house is filled with smoke. It's pouring out the windows and through the screen door. Mateo and I are standing on the lawn, but we can hear our father inside shouting at Lucas to find wet towels, and about whose idiot idea was it to not own a fire extinguisher, and *goddammit*. He tried to deep-fry the Thanksgiving turkey and no one is surprised that it's gone as badly as it has.

Laura is still in New York. Grandmother is in Toronto, and then Hawaii, and then Germany and Italy, her yearly round of talks. But Lucas and Mateo came home, and Jolene might go over to her parents' for dessert, and Hector stopped by with some of his mother's tortilla soup because we are friends again, I think.

Jolene volunteered to go to the co-op and find something not burned to eat, and Hector ran back home to see if his mother could spare some of the second turkey she always cooked for just-in-case. And I'm outside with the grass tickling my calves, a little chilly in the darkening light, feeling a little bit useless and incredibly irritated. "Not *now*, Ashley," my father had said, pushing me back from the flames pouring out of the oven, and I had stormed out the door. Let him burn down the house. I didn't care.

I stomped down the back stairs to where Mateo was lounging in the grass. Mateo never bothered to try and help.

"I'm hungry," Mateo says, squinting up at me and taking a swig of his Corona.

"Nice to meet you," I say absently. "I'm Ashley." I cross my arms over my chest and tap my foot. "If he had just listened to me for once he would have known—"

"Forget it," Mateo interrupts. "He's never going to listen. He has to learn from his own mistakes."

"That would be *great* if he ever *learned* anything."

Mateo knocks his knee into mine, hard. "Hey. He tries, you know. He really does."

"Tries to screw everything up?"

"That's not fair," Mateo starts, but I'm not finished.

"Don't try to defend him. You don't live with him anymore. You don't know what he's like. He's just—he's exhausting." We've barely made eye contact since our argument on the lawn.

Mateo shrugs, swigs his beer again. "He's gone through a lot of shit," he says, glancing up at the deck. The smoke has gone white instead of dark, but it's still pouring through the windows and door.

"He just tried to set us all on fire."

"Mom used to take care of him," he said. "And Clara just kind of ignores him. She's always focused on you."

I look at him sharply. "Well, he's an adult," I say.

"Mom still calls me to check in on him," he says, and I suck in a breath.

"You talk to Mom?" I want to ask questions, but I smash all those words right back down. I'm sorry I said anything at all.

"Yeah," Mateo says. He looks at me. "You look just like her. It's weird."

"You've seen *her?"* I can't stop myself from saying it.

"She's on Facebook," he says.

"Of course she is," I say. I've never been tempted to search for her.

"She's doing good," he says.

"Okay," I say. "I wonder if Jolene is back yet." I start across the yard toward the driveway, but he grabs the sleeve of my sweater.

"Hey," he says. "She worries about you."

"Yeah, it's too late for that," I say.

"She knows that," he says.

"Good for her."

"I'm just saying don't believe everything Clara tells you."

"I *don't,*" I say. I want to brag about turning down the coupons, but Mateo and I don't have heart-to-heart talks. It would be ridiculous to start now, but he seems determined.

"You're more like Mom than you are like Clara." He won't stop talking. I yank the beer out of his hand.

"You're drunk, right? That's the only reason you could possibly be saying these things. Mateo, I don't care."

He hesitates, and I freeze, then close my eyes. I remind myself that I *don't* care what people think anymore. These are easier words to say than to live every day. Every time I flinch in a spark of humiliation, I get furious with myself and crush it out.

"I'm not getting weight-loss surgery," I say. "Dad knows I'm not." And then I realize I haven't actually let my father off the hook yet. "I'll tell him I'm not. Because I'm not."

"Mom is furious about it," he says, and I shove the beer back into his hand and stalk away.

"I don't give a shit," I call over my shoulder, and then spin around, my hands on my hips. "Do you know she never really went to Harvard? I bet she couldn't even get in. All these years I thought she had maybe done something worthwhile in her life but it was a lie. And I'm nothing like her."

"And you're pissed at Mom for not having gone to Harvard instead of at Clara for lying to you."

"I'm pissed that—" and I stop. I shake my head and everything is rattling loose. I tuck my arms around myself again because it's starting to get cold.

Mateo doesn't say anything. He's just standing there, looking at me kindly, almost like he isn't my jerk older brother.

"I'm not getting weight-loss surgery," I say finally.

Mateo shakes his head. "She'll bully you into it."

The wind sends a gust of smoke whirling around our heads.

He doesn't follow me when I turn and walk away without a word.

CHAPTER 24

rehearse.

Grandmother, I am rejecting your proposition. Grandmother, I cannot accept your offer. Grandmother, cancel my appointments. Grandmother, all bets are off.

I never see it coming.

December 15. I know she's back from Venice because there's a letter on my pillow when I get home from school. There's the red Harvard crest, and there's my name typed out neatly on the front and the envelope slit cleanly on the top.

I shake the letter out and unfold it and I read, I am delighted to say that the Admissions Committee has asked me to inform you that you will be admitted to the Harvard College Class of 2019. And—no scholarship.

I drop the letter on my pillow. Roaring white noise in my head.

Also on my pillow, a small white card, creased and torn and with a thumbprint right in the middle over my name.

Ashley Maria Perkins. Weight-loss Surgery in Exchange for Four Years of Tuition.

I can hear footsteps overhead and I freeze. I close my eyes as if it will hide me. Jolene calls my name and I can't move. When she appears at my door, I still can't move.

"What is it?" she says. She looks at the bed where I point, picks up the letter. "Ashley," she breathes. "Ashley, you got in. Of course you got in! You got into Harvard! This is such good news!"

I shake my head. "No."

"Are you kidding? You must be kidding."

"I have to go," I say.

"Well, of course you have to go. You have gotten into Harvard!" Her face is shining. "I am very proud of you." She leaps forward to hug me. I must feel like a statue.

"If I go to Harvard, I have to get weight-loss surgery," I say into her shoulder, and then push back. I put my hands over my stomach, which is churning.

Jolene looks worried. "I don't understand. Is it the tuition?"

My laugh is closer to a sob. "Oh god, the tuition. Yes. That too." I can't afford college without a scholarship. I can't afford it without my grandmother. It is all piling on, collapsing the fragile structure I had built inside me.

"What is it?" Jolene says. She grabs my hand. "What's going on?"

I can feel my hand shaking in her grip. "If I don't get weight-loss surgery, I'm a liar. I lied to get into Harvard. I said I was getting weight-loss surgery to change the world. My interview. My essay."

"Oh, Ashley," Jolene says softly.

"I can't do that," I say. I know I sound hysterical. I can hear how shrill my voice is. "I can't do that, Jolene."

"I know," she says. She pulls me down to sit on the bed next to her.

All of this—this *bravery*. This *conviction*. It's been useless.

She looks at the letter in her hand. She picks up the card. We're both quiet for a moment. Her mouth quirks up on the side. "Laura would say, 'At least you'll get free tuition.'" She looks at me anxiously. She's got tears in her eyes.

"I'm going to Harvard," I say. I hear the tears in my voice.

"Congratulations, my darling," my grandmother says, coming into the room, enveloping me in her arms. "I am so proud of you. This is such good timing. When I was in London I spoke to Stanford again."

"I have a surgery appointment," I say.

"You have a surgery appointment," she says, holding me by the shoulders and beaming at me. "Right after Christmas."

"That's so soon," Jolene says. She's still holding the little white card. She looks back and forth between us.

"Merry Christmas to me," I say, and it does not come out sounding jolly.

Grandmother frowns, then briskly says, "I'm proud of you." She kisses me, a warm dry peck on the temple. "Your mother would be proud of you," she says, and I stiffen.

"I don't know about that," I say.

She shrugs. "True. How could we know? But I'd like to think she would at least be smart enough to recognize how well her daughter is turning out, despite everything. What an amazing woman she's becoming."

"I don't feel amazing," I say.

"We'll have a party to celebrate," Grandmother says.

"No!" I say.

"Your acceptance, darling. I know you're sensitive about the surgery thing." She pats my shoulder.

"I don't care about the surgery thing. I just don't want a party." I can't look up at her.

"You'll change your mind," my grandmother says. "Get ready for work now." She sweeps out of the room.

"I'm not a liar," I say softly. And I can't lie to myself anymore.

The tiniest, pinprick bright spark of relief, and it burns.

CHAPTER 25

At work I am not an incoming Harvard student or a weight-loss surgery patient. I am a server and I am not thinking, I am filling up bread baskets and spending a lot of time explaining the special, which is Manhattan clam chowder and seems to worry quite a lot of people because it doesn't sound like clam chowder to them and they're not sure they can trust us anymore after all these years, since we seem to have gone off the rails in unpredictable ways and the world isn't a safe place for anyone, anymore.

"I just don't understand how anyone can call that chowder with a clear conscience," Mrs. Monroe is saying as she loads the last of her sourdough into her giant black purse.

"Well, I think chowder is a blanket term that covers a basic kind of fish soup," I say, "which offers lots of opportunity for experimentation—"

"That's exactly right," she says to me. "It's the experimental stuff that gets you in trouble. You have to stick with the classics."

Mrs. Monroe's new girlfriend Sadie says, "I don't know. I'm always up for adventure." She winks at me and I tamp down the urge to ask her not to do that. I smile at her instead. I hope it's a real enough smile.

"Well, maybe you can try it next time," I say.

"Sadie, don't you dare," Mrs. Monroe says, taking her arm.

"It'll be good for us, Martha," Sadie says as they slide their chairs back. "I'm going to be dead soon enough. I can't keep always doing the safe things."

I hope we're still talking about soup, I think.

Mrs. Monroe shakes her head and Sadie says, "You have a good night now," to me, and I look up to see my father standing outside on the deck, staring out at the lighthouse. My phone says I still have another hour of my shift, so I go to the pass-through instead, out the back way, and make my way around my tables, making sure every one is covered.

"How's Laura, honey?" one of Laura's regulars asks me. "I haven't seen her in a while. Her dad and mom either."

"Stepmom," I say automatically, just like Laura would. I miss her. I have spent my whole shift expecting to look up and see her standing at a customer's elbow, making them laugh as she points something out on the menu and offers sage and serious advice about the difference between various types of whitefish. I've spent the whole shift waiting for her to text me. About Harvard. About weight-loss surgery. But my phone stays dark.

"Right," he says. He is a deeply tanned and deeply wrinkled white guy and very blond. "She doing okay?"

"I think so," I say. "I'm going to talk to her later. I'll tell her you were asking about her." I glance up. My father isn't on the deck anymore.

In the pass-through, Nancy peers out of the kitchen. "How are they liking the chowder?" she says. She wipes her forehead with the back of her wrist.

"They are very confused by it," I say, pulling my phone out.

"Good, good," she says. "I'll have the next order up in a jiff. Wait right there."

I pull my phone out and text Laura. I type, **MISS YOU**, and send it and put the phone away when another two bowls are up.

When I come back onto the floor, my father is lingering by the hostess stand. For a minute I forget where I'm supposed to drop the soup, until I see the Tams' expectant faces.

"It's red," Mrs. Tam says when I set it down.

"This isn't chowder!" Mr. Tam says. He seems to regret venturing out of the house more than usual.

"It's Manhattan clam chowder," I say. "It's a variety. Like chardonnay is a variety of wine."

"Oh, I see," Mrs. Tam says, and picks up her spoon. "Pick up your spoon, Frank."

My father is looking at the giant fiberglass swordfish on the wall like he's never noticed it before, and I suppose that's possible.

He says, "I thought Moby Dick was a whale," when I hurry up to him.

"Why are you here?" I say. Then it occurs to me in a rush. "Is everything okay? Is Grandmother okay?"

"I wanted to talk to you," he says. He pulls me into a hug, levers me up off my feet. "You got into Harvard!"

"I'm still working," I say when I land with a huff. "I have another forty-five minutes." I glance back at the dining room to make sure that no one is trying to get my attention.

"Can I sit down?" he says.

"Where are the dogs?" I say. "They're not tied up outside, are they?"

"No," he says. "I brought them back home."

I grab a menu from the rack next to the hostess stand and say, "Follow me." I lead him over to the table by the window. "Can I get you anything to drink besides water?" I say.

"So professional!" he says.

"I'm working," I say. "The specials are on the inside cover. I'll be back in a couple of minutes to take your order."

There's only so long I can hide in the pass-through rolling silverware into napkins. When I poke my head out, my father is staring out the window with his chin in his hand.

"Have you decided?" I say.

"I'm going to live a little," he says.

"Don't you always live at least a little? I mean, if not, we'll have to fit you for a coffin."

"Ha ha! Touché!" he says.

"What do you want?" I ask.

"Pick something for me," he says. "I trust your judgment. You're a Harvard girl." He shoves the menu over to me and is trying to make really significant eye contact.

"Great," I say. I check my phone when I'm in the back. Laura has written, I MISS U 2. B BACK SOON. I want to tell her that I'm getting surgery after all, despite all my pronouncements. But I don't know what to say. I stand in the pass-through just staring at my phone until Amy hip-checks me as she stomps by.

"Wake up," she says, and I shove my phone back into my pocket.

When I come back to my father's table with Manhattan clam chowder and a basket of bread, I see he's shredded his coaster into bits of confetti. He doesn't look at the bowl when I set it down. I say, "Can I get you anything else?" and he says, "I'm worried about you, Ashley."

"What happened to 'Hooray for Harvard'?"

"You know what I want to talk about."

"This is a really bad time, Dad," I say, and turn to go.

"I do trust your judgment," he says. "But I don't trust your grandmother."

I swing back around. "She's taken care of us since Mom left. She's done everything for us! We wouldn't have a place to live.

The twins wouldn't be able to go to college. You'd have to get a real job."

"I have a real job," he snaps.

"When was the last time you sold a house?" I hiss.

"Recently," he says. "It's not really what I meant to do."

"Real estate, or being a grown-up?" I ask.

He looks down at the mess of confetti in front of him and sweeps it up into a pile.

"Is that why Mom left? Because I can see why she wouldn't want to spend her whole life taking care of you."

"Your mother left because I didn't stand up for her," he says. "She left because your grandmother—"

"Tried to help her. How terrible."

"Tried to do to your mother what she's doing to my daughter right now."

This stops me. I feel the tears in my eyes and I stomp away, taking deep breaths.

"Are you okay?" Mrs. Tam says, reaching her hand out to me as I pass their table.

"The soup is really good after all," Mr. Tam says soothingly.

That is not as comforting as they mean it to be.

My father sits at his table for the rest of my shift, looking out the window and ignoring his chowder. I close out all my tabs and I fill Amy in on everything that's left to do. I go sit at my father's table. It's gotten dark out, so the lighthouse is lit up with red and green bulbs, because Christmas comes sooner every year.

"Are you ready?" I say.

"I thought you'd leave without me," he says.

"I'm not vindictive," I say. "That's not the sort of thing I would do to you."

He nods. "I know," he says.

We don't stand, and I'm glad. My back aches and my feet hurt and I am tired.

"You're right. Your grandmother gave you everything," he says, looking at his hands.

"Yes," I say. I rest my chin on my hand. I feel my eyes closing.

"You don't have to give her everything in return," he says. His words echo around behind my closed lids, in the dark of my head.

"I'm leaving when you leave for college," he says.

I sit up. "What? Why would you do that?"

"I don't want to owe her anything more," he says. "I don't want *you* to owe her anything for supporting me."

"I don't . . . It's just . . ." I stutter and stumble over my words. In the end, I give up trying to get them out.

"Let's go home," he says, pushing his chair back.

We walk in silence down the pier and onto our back roads,

where the streetlights are spaced far apart. It's not a long walk, but this is the longest it has ever felt.

"I'm sorry," he says, when we get to the start of our street.

"For what?" I say. I stop, but he keeps walking ahead of me.

"I would have done anything for you when your mother left," he says when I catch up. "But I couldn't."

The familiar exasperation wells up in me. "You mean like the way you *can't* mow the lawn."

A silence stretches out between us, and then my father speaks. "Your grandmother found me on the floor in the bathroom. I couldn't live without your mother. And I thought you kids didn't deserve to have a father like me. A father who didn't stand up for her."

It's a moment before I realize what he is saying, but then—

"Oh god, Dad," I whisper, but he keeps walking slowly ahead. I lunge forward to clutch at his sleeve to make him stop. "Dad." He looks at me, and I fumble for something to say. "I didn't know."

He smiles. "Stop feeling sorry for *me*, Ashley," he says. "You took care of your older brothers and you took care of me and now you're taking care of your grandmother. You're the one who works to make her happy. You're the one who takes on everything she gives you."

"No. She—she gave us everything," I say again stubbornly.

"That shouldn't have been your job," he finishes. He hugs me then, and I realize I'm almost as tall as he is. I let him hug me as long as he wants and I hug him back.

"Don't do it," he says. He's hugging me tighter. "Don't get weight-loss surgery. Don't do it, Ashley, you don't need to do it."

I pull back. "You don't understand at all," I say.

"You don't have to do anything," he says. "Well, except die eventually."

"Oh, that's comforting."

"Why do you need to be different from how you are now?"

I try to call up all of my grandmother's reasoning—the words that sound so sure, so logical. I reach for them, but they fade away. The sound of waves crashes behind us, churning up the sand.

"It's more complicated than you think," I say. I can hear the pleading in my voice. "I have to do this."

"You can do anything, baby. I've seen it. Anything you want. Just make sure it's what you want to do."

I am pleased when my voice comes out sounding casual. Worry free. "You sound like an inspirational Facebook post," I say. "I don't like it when you're sincere."

"I'm not Sincere," he says. "I'm Dad, nice to meet you." He holds out his hand to me.

"No," I say.

"That's my girl." He smiles.

"What do you want to do about dinner?" I ask.

"Eat it," my father says, and I punch him in the arm.

We walk the rest of the way home in silence.

CHAPTER 26

have spent so much of my life pretending that it is easy to act as if everything is going to plan. That I am excited about Harvard, my inevitably bright and fantastically successful future, that I had a real, deep change of heart and know that weight-loss surgery is the right choice for me.

But the pre-surgical appointment does not go well. "I don't want to take a laxative," I tell the doctor. I'm sitting at the edge of the exam table and my back is cold because this gown is too small. You'd think they'd have larger gowns for all their bariatric surgery patients.

She doesn't look up from her checklist. "Well, you have to."

"Are there any alternatives?"

"No, there are not. Laxatives. Nothing but ice water for twenty-four hours. You are going to have to cooperate or this surgery will be dangerous." She looks at me now. "Frankly I'm concerned about your compliance."

"I signed the papers," I say. I initialed over and over again in the waiting room while my grandmother watched. Scrawling AMP next to words like *pulmonary embolism* and *gastrointestinal tract leak* and *death*. "My grandmother says it's safe."

"Yes," Dr. Alvarez says. "But are you ready for this?"

"No," I say. "Of course I'm not."

Her face changes—she's less annoyed at me now. She's feeling sorry for me. She pats my knee, and her hand is cold. "It'll be okay," she says, instead of the medical jargon I'm expecting about *.05 error and complication rates.*

"Everyone keeps telling me that," I say.

She flips through the papers on her checklist. "We're going to take good care of you. You just have to take good care of yourself." She hands me the clipboard and a pen. "Sign here at the bottom."

I'm promising to do everything she tells me. Give myself diarrhea and drink only water and shower in the morning but don't put on any lotion, or deodorant, or perfume, or jewelry. Show up at the hospital at six in the morning and let them stick me with needles.

"This is serious," I had told my grandmother, looking up from the sheaf of papers I was initialing.

"Of course it is, darling," she said, not looking up from her book.

*   *   *

If I don't open my mouth, I won't say anything I regret. I nod when my grandmother talks to me. We are staying at a hotel in town because my grandmother does not want to drive two hours before dawn. I go to bed early, but I am up often, sitting in the bathroom in the dark with my head on my knees.

She wakes me up at four, and I stand in the shower for a long time, until she knocks on the door. I look down at my body, which feels hollowed out and empty. But it still belongs to me. I haven't turned it over yet.

I know every part of it. The scars on my knee from crashing into the net frame during practice, the muscles in my thighs that jump and twitch when I've run too far, my belly, which is soft and curved, and the width of my hips and the size of my breasts and the strength in my arms. I wipe the steam from the mirror and rub the towel over my face, squeeze the water out of my hair. My DNA pendant is glinting at my throat and I remember my pre-surgery instructions. I reach behind my neck, unclasp it, and let it fall into a puddle in my hand. I put it on the shelf above the sink, touch my chest. It feels empty without my necklace. It looks naked and blank. I breathe in, breathe out. Watch my bare chest rise and fall.

"Ashley," grandmother calls, and I come out in my towel. She's bought me comfortable clothes to wear, a pair of soft jersey pajamas in a ruby red that makes my skin glow dark and gold. She hands me a cup of ice water and points at my slippers.

At the hospital, she knows what to do. She ushers us through check-in, to the waiting room, through the doors with the beds separated by curtains. A young orderly with his hair covered hands me two gowns, one for my front and one for my back. He looks like some white kid playing dress-up. "You'll stay warm that way," he says. He can see that I am shivering. "I'll be right back," he says.

My grandmother takes a seat next to the bed in a small plastic chair. Her hair is pulled back and I realize she's not wearing any makeup, not even lip gloss. She takes my hand. "Don't be nervous, darling." She pats my hand with her other. "It'll all be over quickly."

I reach up to touch my pendant, but it's gone. I place my hand flat against that empty space on my chest, where I can feel my heart beating behind my breastbone, a little too quickly. A little too hard.

The orderly comes back with a warm blanket and a rolling pole with an IV bag hanging from it. He tucks the blanket around my legs and pats my ankle. "Now which hand is your dominant one?" he says.

"My left," I say.

"Hold out your right arm for me then," he says. "Let's see what kind of veins you've got here."

"No," I say. I keep my hand against my chest. Heart thumping.

"The left one then," he says. "But it'll be less comfortable once you're up and moving around."

"No!" I say louder.

My grandmother stands up. "Could you excuse us for a moment, please?" She smiles at him as she herds him out of the room and whips the curtain shut behind him. "Stop being unreasonable, Ashley," Grandmother says. "I know you're nervous but I've told you a thousand times you're going to be just fine." Her voice switches to soothing tones. "You know what this means. You are going to Harvard, darling. You told them yourself. You're going to change the world, isn't that right?"

"I told them that," I say. "But I lied."

"It wasn't a lie," she says, her voice sharpening again.

"It was," I say. "The surgery part was. I'll change the world some other way."

Grandmother laughs. "So, then, you're just going to give up Harvard?"

I think of the photo of my mother sitting on the lawn, those huge columns and that smile on her face. I wonder what her dreams were—what she gave up for us, to move to California, to live in my grandmother's house.

"Yes," I say. "I give that up."

"You're joking," Grandmother says.

I stand up from the bed. The orderly says, "Knock knock!" and I pull the curtain aside. "Excuse me," I say, and shoulder my way around him.

Grandmother snatches up her purse and storms after me. "Ashley! My offer will not stand if you do not get this procedure done. You will be giving up your future," she hisses. She is walking next to me while I pad down the hallway barefoot, push through the double doors and through the waiting room. People are turning to look at us pass.

"No," I say. "Not the whole future. Just this version of it."

"You are brilliant!" she grits out. "And beautiful! And I will not see you throw away your potential, Ashley." Her voice is rising. She is almost—shouting. "I can't change—this is the only thing you can fix. I will not see you suffer and struggle and be overlooked. I can't protect you once you leave," she says. "Do you hear me? I won't be able to protect you!"

I stop there in the hallway and see her. Her eyes are wild. Her plain face shows what she's been hiding so well. She's frightened. She is . . . panicked.

My indefatigable grandmother.

Is *scared*.

Of the world, and its judgments.

I could laugh and never stop. I could cry.

I say, "That's okay." I pat her shoulder the way she has patted mine a thousand times. I say, "I can protect myself."

I say it and I know I can. After all, I'm so much like my mother.

My feet are slapping against the linoleum floor, and the

automatic doors yawn open. I march out onto the sidewalk. It's gotten bright since we drove over here, the sun still that early-morning gold.

"You are out here in your hospital gown. Come inside. We'll talk about this rationally." She takes my elbow but I shake her off.

"I have never liked saying no to you," I say, struggling with the tie at my neck. "I've always been grateful to you." It's knotted and I start to tug at it, pulling hard, shrugging out of the gown.

"Ashley, for god's sake." She snatches the gown up from the ground, but I'm shrugging out of the other one.

I am light-headed from lack of food, from feeling so empty. I laugh. I drop the other gown on the sidewalk and she picks that up too. I back away from her.

"I'm not going to do this. I'm never going to do this. This is my body right here. This is what I have to work with. Are you listening to me?"

She stops. She can hear the tears in my voice. She can hear that I am telling the truth. She looks at me. I am standing there with my hands at my sides and I am naked and tired and dizzy.

She looks at the gowns in her hand, and back at me.

And she nods.

She nods, and I sag against the wall. Relief. Finally, relief.

She holds out the gowns to me. When I don't take them, she says, "Your clothes are upstairs. I will go fetch them."

I gather the gowns into my arms and let my cheek roll

against the bricks behind me.

She touches my forehead. "You are burning up. Put those on, Ashley. Please."

I shrug into both gowns, but can't figure out how to tie them. She gently moves my hands aside and ties neat, clean knots. She looks at me for a moment. "Wait here," she says. "I'll be right back."

When she's gone, I slide down the wall, sit on the concrete walkway. I put my head down on my scarred-up knees, and laughter is filling me up. Bubbling over and floating free.

CHAPTER 27

aura licks the spoon clean and drops it into the sink. She is back for the second half of the year. We've finished filling the empanada dough, and I'm brushing the tops with egg. "So, no plans. None plans. No, none plans at all?"

"None plans," I say, shifting over a row of dough balls to fit the next on to the pan.

She high-fives me. "That's a good plan," she says.

"You should do Peace Corps," Jolene says. She's sitting on one of the stools, watching us work. She's cut her hair short, a spiky pixie that makes her eyes look huge. "Not that I want to give you advice," she says.

"Maybe," I say.

"What does your grandmother say?" Laura says.

"Nothing," I say. She has not spoken to me since we checked out of the hospital. She brought me home and fed me broth and put me to bed. I slept for three days. When I woke up, there was porridge and tea and more soup in the cabinet and she stayed in her office all day, and I couldn't bring myself to go up that extra flight of stairs.

"She'll be proud of whatever you do," Laura says. "She just won't say anything."

I don't answer her.

"You could move to New York with me," Laura says brightly. She narrows her eyes at Jolene. "Are *you* still going to Sarah Lawrence?" Jolene grins, happy like a kid, and nods.

"I would like to maybe go to New York," I say. I open up the oven when the preheat timer goes off, and slide the trays in. "I don't know what I want." It is a feeling that is awful and wonderful at the same time.

Laura starts talking about the apartment we can share in Queens, which is the new hip place because Brooklyn has been priced out and Manhattan is where all the rich people live now, and then the empanadas are ready and we eat them with our fingers in the parlor with the television turned on, but muted. Laura falls asleep facedown on the rug with Toby tucked under her arm and Jolene is curled up in the armchair and Annabelle Lee is snoring in the crook of her knees.

I pull myself up and take our plates to the kitchen. Soto pads behind me, nudges her head under my hand.

"Hello, beautiful puppy," I say to her. I lean down to kiss her head. She follows me up the stairs, climbs onto the bed, and watches me as I rummage through my drawers. I pull out my box of stationery, a pen. I set a card in the middle of the desk. I write,

Clara Ruby Elizabeth Rumsen Perkins
Good for one talk about the future

Her light is on when I reach the top of the stairs. She's sitting in the corner armchair with an afghan over her legs. She is as beautiful as ever, her hair glowing silver in the lamplight. I knock. She looks up at me, puts her book down. I extend the card to her, and she looks at it for a long moment before she looks back at me, reaches out, and takes it from my hand.

ACKNOWLEDGMENTS

I would like to first of all acknowledge that I am among the luckiest of humans and I am so grateful.

This book wouldn't exist without my amazing agent, Cheryl Pientka, who said, *You should be writing YA*.

This book also wouldn't exist without the lovely Claire Zulkey, who asked me over the course of an interview about my first book, "What are you working on next?" I responded, chirpily, "A young adult novel!"

This book certainly would not exist without my brilliant editor, Kristen Pettit, who made me burst into tears on the California Zephyr train somewhere between Salt Lake City and San Francisco, as I read her first email to me. She wanted that YA book, and then helped make it far better than I could have hoped.

This book couldn't exist without beautiful Monique van den Cullen, who has always been my model for body confidence and self-esteem, and who has been bitching with me about the need for awesome fat protagonists in books for, like, 20 years. Hers is next, you guys.

This book shouldn't exist because I went through an infinitely long existential crisis trying to write it, trying to make it *right*, but the so-astonishing Karen Meisner put her arms around me literally and figuratively and helped me keep all my pieces together.

This book almost didn't exist because still I froze and stared wildly around me, startling at bright noises and loud lights, but my gorgeous Kelsey Van Tassel, of the greatest name and the loveliest heart, showed me the past, the present, and the future. Her love and support and belief in me are some of the greatest gifts I've ever been given.

This book went on to exist because the beautiful and gifted Sage Romano kept kicking my ass and taking my name and providing me with an extraordinary, inspiring example of an incredibly hardworking, dedicated, talented writer.

This book, now in existence, would not be nearly so beautiful without the amazing talent of Sarah Kaufman, whose patience was endless and whose design just glows, and Ellice M. Lee, the immensely talented layout design artist who made it just as pretty on the inside.

This book would not be so cohesive, smart, grammatically correct (will I ever, ever be able to figure out *lay* and *lie* or will I die ashamed?), and error free without genius copyeditor, Claire Caterer; razor-sharp proofreader, Tania Bissell; and production editor, Alexandra Alexo, who orchestrated the whole thing. You are completely the best.

The whole process of publishing a book, from submitting

a manuscript to answering dumb author questions like "What? An author questionnaire?" to shifting around covers and flaps and copyedits and page proofs and all the endless important bits, wouldn't have gone so smoothly and happily and well without the basic awesomeness of Elizabeth Lynch.

I wouldn't exist without my very cute mom, from whom all the things I am have sprung. She has always tried to protect me and has always loved me fiercely.

So much love and many thanks for above-and-beyond kindnesses, support, giggle-snorts, and general wonderfulness to: my aunt, Elizabeth Fitzgerald; my brother, Ken Larsen, sister-in-law, Carrie Ellman, and perfect nephew, Oliver; the astonishing Alex Duke; oldest friend, Rodrigo Trujillo; quietly and enduringly supportive Justin Pierce; ridiculously beautiful-faced and -hearted Jenny Shaw, Kristin Guthrie Brandt, Brooke Duncan, Brittany Woods, and Heather Haskett; immortal beloved Amy Hawkins; and the very attractive Jeff Dillon, who has many excellent qualities.

If I have forgotten anyone, it is because I have a mind like a steel sieve, and I am sorry and I love you because you are a perfect you, inside and out.

JOIN THE

Epic Reads
COMMUNITY

THE ULTIMATE YA DESTINATION ///////////////

◀ **DISCOVER** ▶
your next favorite read

◀ **MEET** ▶
new authors to love

◀ **WIN** ▶
free books

◀ **SHARE** ▶
infographics, playlists, quizzes, and more

◀ **WATCH** ▶
the latest videos

◀ **TUNE IN** ▶
to Tea Time with Team Epic Reads